I0523506

Katy More is an enchanting storyteller whose passion for creating vivid worlds and complex characters draws readers into unforgettable adventures. A dedicated mother, wife, and retired co-founder of *The Local Times* newspaper and *Feature Magazine*, her life is as rich and varied as her stories. Author of The World According to Kate and Consistently Inconsistent, Katy has a gift for blending intense emotion with gripping, high-stakes narratives.

Honed through her executive media background, Katy's unique perspective breathes life into her work. When she's not crafting her latest saga, she enjoys the quiet moments spent with her border collie, Keisha, and cherishing time with her family.

In her latest novel, The Nxyara Chronicles: Echoes of Treason, Katy demonstrates her ability to weave character-driven, thought-provoking stories. Her years of experience and love for imaginative storytelling make her a rising star in speculative fiction, captivating readers with every page.

THE NXYARA CHRONICLES

ECHOES OF TREASON

KATY MORE

BookTree
Publishing

First published in Australia in 2025 by Booktree Publishing.

Copyright © 2025 by Katy More

The moral right of the author has been asserted.

All characters and events in this publication, other than those clearly in the public domain, are fictitious, and any resemblance to actual persons, living or dead, is purely coincidental.

All rights reserved.
No part of this publication may be reproduced, stored in a retrieval system, or transmitted in any form or by any means electronic, mechanical, photocopying, recording, or otherwise, without the prior permission in writing of the publisher, nor be otherwise circulated in any form of binding or cover other than that in which it is published and without a similar condition including this condition being imposed on the subsequent purchaser.

ISBN: 978-0-6455003-9-4

Cover Designed in Canva.com
Images created by Canva.com AI

Printed and bound in Australia by
BookTree Publishing.

PO Box 105
Narangba Qld 4504
Australia

www.booktreepublishing.com.au

To Darren.
My loving husband.
For the endless coffee and unwavering
support that kept me going.

and

To Richard.
My mentor, harshest critic, and driving force.
For pushing me to reach new heights.

This book is for you both.

The Nxyara Chronicles unfolds in a cutthroat and unforgiving, all-female world. It delves into themes of rebellion, genetic experimentation, civil unrest, loyalty shifts, and the struggle for survival.

The narrative features explicit depictions of physical and psychological conflict, intense violence, assassination, warfare, bloodshed, severe injuries, emotional strain, and manipulation.

If you're sensitive to these themes, take caution as you journey to Nxyara…

ONE

Renewal Day is always joyous. Nestled into the cliffs of jagged rock formations, our city, Kael'thar, buzzed with anticipation and celebration. Occurring once every three centuries, when the twin suns hung low in the Nxyaran sky, this event was not to be missed.

"I'm absolutely thrilled! This is going to be incredible!" Nova exclaimed, a wide grin illuminating her strong, angular face.

Standing at her side, I couldn't help but admire my best friend. Her piercing blue eyes sparkled with excitement as she imagined the festivities ahead. Festivities which neither of us had attended, until now.

Nova's long dark hair was tied back in a neat bun. Her practical yet stylish deep-blue outfit reflected her commitment to functionality and a touch of personal flair as she exuded a quiet strength and resilience that had always defined her.

"Do you think the High Council will approve a regeneration increase this time?" I asked as I glanced at the military tattoo on her forearm.

Nova's eyes brightened with curiosity. "Possibly. They can't afford to let the population dwindle. Boosting our numbers could profoundly impact Nxyara's strength and longevity."

"That would benefit everyone."

I exploded with happiness as Elana approached us, arms outstretched and beckoning for our embrace. We wrapped ourselves around our trusted advisor, warmth and familiarity enveloping us. There was a sense of security and understanding beyond words. In her presence, we were not just Nxyarans. We were... family.

Now, there is a word that isn't used often. I considered quietly, reminding myself that we are a species entirely composed of females reproducing through self-replication; therefore, the word or concept of family isn't relevant to our reproductive and social structure.

Subtle hints of fresh nxyflowers mingling with the comforting aroma of aged Nxyaran wood drew me back into the moment, evoking memories of conversations filled with guidance and reassurance.

"I can't believe Renewal Day is almost upon us again," Elana remarked, her voice carrying a mix of nostalgia and hope as our trio started off toward the Emporium. "It feels like each one gets more significant, especially this year, with everything that's been happening."

I nodded, feeling a mix of excitement and nervousness twisting in my stomach as Nova casually plucked a nyxflower from a nearby bed and tucked it into my hair.

"I have been told that this Renewal Day could set the tone for Nxyara's future. That the High Council's decisions will shape our society for generations."

"You will find it a very traditional ceremony," Elana reassured us. "Renewal Day is a time for unity and reflection; whatever it brings, we'll navigate it with strength and resilience."

Nova flashed a determined smile, her eyes reflecting her resolve. "I'm just curious to see what all the fuss is about now that I'm no longer a Neophyte!"

We chuckled at Nova's disdain for the title. Whilst I was relieved to be leaving behind the label of Neophyte, I didn't share in Nova's strong aversion towards it. After all, it had been two hundred and thirty-six years since I was created, and two hundred and fifty-two for Nova. We were no longer inexperienced or naive; we were no longer considered the youngsters of our species and we were filled with excitement for our first Renewal Day.

As we discussed our plans for the celebration, I felt a surge of gratitude for my companions. In Elana's wisdom and Nova's unwavering loyalty, I found the strength to face the uncertainties of whatever trials awaited us beyond renewal.

Elana placed a comforting hand on my shoulder as if she knew what I was thinking. Her long fingers almost reached the top of my breast, and I noticed the deep wrinkles that marked her age. Elana generated nearly 1,467 years ago, making her part of the Elder class, whilst Nova and I were on the cusp of entering the Primevex class. This class included individuals who excelled in their capabilities, were optimal in condition, and highly functional.

"I have to run some errands and get ready for my duties tonight," Elana said, her voice tinged with disappointment amidst the excitement. She departed as quickly as she had arrived, leaving Nova and I on our journey towards the Emporium.

We strolled through the bustling streets of Kael'thar. The vibrant cityscape engulfed us. The twin suns – Solara and Lunara - loomed with deep blue and fiery orange hues, casting shifting shadows across the towering rock formations, defining the city skyline.

"I love how the suns create a surreal twilight," Nova remarked as we passed under the warm glow of Solara, the larger sun. "It's like walking through a painting."

I nodded in agreement, taking in the play of light and shadow on the basalt structures that flanked the street. With deep grooves and shimmering minerals, each formation seemed to tell a story of ancient cataclysms and cultural reverence.

"The Emporium should be just around this corner," I said, pointing ahead where the street widened into a bustling square. "I heard they've imported some new crystals. Maybe we'll find something truly unique to wear at the ceremony."

As we approached the Emporium's entrance, the aroma of freshly brewed cosmic tea wafted towards us from a nearby vendor. Nxyaran chatter filled the air, interspersed with the occasional hum of hovercrafts navigating the city's intricate pathways. Floating sculptures and holographic advertisements were strategically placed for optimal exposure. Inside, the atmosphere shifted to one of hushed awe.

Glowing crystal displays refracted Solara and Lunara's light, casting prismatic patterns across polished floors.

"Zarya? Nova?"

We turned towards the direction of a warm voice carrying a subtle hint of scientific precision. With identical high-tech outfits the twins, Astra and Lyra, glided towards us. Their hazel eyes, always sparkling with curiosity and sharpness, grew even brighter as they smiled in our direction.

"It's good to see you both," they chimed in unison.

"The latest shipment of crystalline formations is quite impressive. We're hoping to find some new insights for our research," Lyra shared, her expression reflecting genuine interest.

Nova chuckled softly as I smiled, appreciating their enthusiasm for the scientific intricacies that defined their work.

"These crystals could potentially reveal secrets about the ancient past of Nxyara, and possibly even connections to the new technology we are researching."

Astra's eyes gleamed with intellectual curiosity. "Indeed. The alignment of the two suns during Renewal Day ceremonies often correlates with significant archaeological findings. It's a prime opportunity for us to gather data."

Lyra nodded thoughtfully, and I felt their camaraderie and shared purpose.

"These crystals are stunning," I murmured, tracing my fingers along the patterns etched into the transparent surfaces.

"They remind me of Elara's shimmering ice formations."

"They do," Nova smiled. "It's like bringing a piece of our moon into the city."

We spent the afternoon exploring, marvelling at technology and purchasing a few artistic creations before going our separate ways to prepare for the eremony.

I looked into the grand mirror. Its polished surface showed me everything I had been through—the struggles, the determination. Tonight wasn't just another event but a turning point for Nxyara. I wanted every part of me to reflect the hope and determination I felt for our future.

I ran my fingers over the intricate braids in my hair. Adorned with silver threads that shimmered in the soft light, they weren't just a hairstyle; they symbolised my role as a future leader. I traced the patterns with a mix of pride, contemplating the heavy responsibility to lead our society into the future.

The mirror reflected my blue eyes, sharp and intense from the triumphs and sacrifices that had brought me here. An old battle scar ran from my left temple to just below my cheekbone. Neophytes were often used for fighting as they were the only class viewed as having to prove their worth to society. Tonight, all that would change.

A flowing ceremonial gown made with fabric woven from glowing threads was draped around my shoulders. Adjusting the gown, I wondered what my first Renewal Day Ceremony would hold.

I nervously played with the bracelet on my wrist, grateful for its intricate design. It was a multifunctional device that hummed against my skin, reminding me of its force field ability at a simple press of a hidden trigger.

"For the future of Nxyara," I murmured, the words echoing through the room. They weren't just a pledge; they were a vow that I would learn to lead with courage, wisdom, and compassion and to guide our people toward a destiny defined not just by tradition but by our collective potential.

Stepping back from the mirror, I stood tall,

drawing strength from my reflection. I prepared to leave for the ceremony. I was considered a potential leader now, part of the Primevex class and determined to be the best Primevex in history.

As I finished adjusting my gown, the door to my chamber opened and Nova entered with a grace that commanded attention. Her presence, always a blend of strength and elegance, filled the room with a quiet power that was impossible to ignore. Not one for traditional gowns, she wore a tailored ceremonial suit symbolising the progressive ideals we championed.

"I bet the Twins had something to do with that," I smiled as I admired the sleek, metallic fabric catching the light. It was a fabric that spoke of innovation, of a future unbound by the constraints of our past.

The suit's design was functional and striking, hugging Nova's athletic form and accentuating her toned physique, a result of rigorous military training. With its high collar and fitted silhouette, the stitching glowed as if imbued with the essence of Nxyara's hopes and dreams.

"Sure did! "She grinned as she opened her jacket, revealing a fitted top made of a softer, iridescent material that glistened, like the surface of a calm, moonlit sea. The top was designed for comfort and movement yet exuded a quiet sophistication that was unmistakably Nova.

Nova's pants were tailored to perfection. The same shimmering fabric as her jacket, catching the light with every step she took. Tapered neatly at her ankles, they met a pair of sleek, ankle-high boots adorned with subtle engravings, harmoniously tying her entire ensemble together.

Nova's hair, a cascade of rich, dark waves, was pulled back into a loose, elegant braid that fell over one shoulder. Tiny, luminescent threads were woven into the braid, catching the light. Her eyes, a deep, penetrating green, glimmered with a determination that matched the fire in my own.

Around her neck hung a simple yet exquisite pendant from the Emporium made of a rare, luminescent crystal that pulsed with an inner light, casting a soft glow that matched the aura of resolve and purpose Nova carried with her.

As she approached, I couldn't help but admire the balance she struck between tradition and the future we envisioned.

"Ready for the Renewal Ceremony?" she asked, her voice a calm, steadying presence amid the whirl of my thoughts.

"Yes," I replied, meeting her gaze with a nod. Together, we would celebrate renewal and face the challenges of Primevex.

As we left the room, the excitement of the impending Renewal Ceremony pressed upon us. The hallway outside was a corridor of ancient stone, lit by flickering sconces casting a warm, amber glow on the intricate carvings lining the walls. We walked side by side, our steps echoing through the stillness, a reminder of the seriousness of the night ahead.

Halfway down the corridor, we turned a corner and nearly collided with Astra and Lyra. Their identical features could easily cause confusion, but we knew them well enough to distinguish their subtle differences.

Astra was on the left, her expression softer and more open. Dressed in a flowing gown of deep emerald, intricate golden embroidery wrapped around her like delicate vines. Her raven black braids were adorned with tiny glowing nxyflowers, adding a touch of ethereal beauty to her striking appearance. Her eyes sparkling with curiosity and gentle understanding.

Lyra's gaze, on the other hand, was piercing and intense, revealing a sharp mind and unrelenting determination. Her stark white gown, almost austere in simplicity, yet elegant in its sharp lines and angular design. Made from fine, shimmering silk, it flowed around her like liquid moonlight, accentuating her more severe and formal demeanour. Her hair was styled in an elaborate updo, interwoven with silver threads that sparkled with each movement, giving her a regal, almost intimidating presence.

"Zarya, Nova," Astra greeted us with a warm smile, her voice a melody of kindness and excitement. "We were just on our way to the ceremony. You both look prepared for the night."

Lyra nodded in agreement, her expression softening as she glanced at me. "Zarya, Nova," she said, her tone more formal, but not unfriendly. "It's good to see you. I trust you are both as excited as we are for the ceremony?"

"Indeed, very excited," I replied, returning her gaze with a measured smile. "The first Renewal Ceremony for our little group of Primevexes-to-be, and we are ready for whatever comes."

We continued down the corridor, our conversation topic changing to the Renewal Ceremony. The ancient tradition marked a new beginning for our people. Only at this ceremony, and with the expressed permission from the High Council, was self-generation allowed. It was impossible, if not illegal, to self-generate outside of it, and the Ceremony was only held once every three hundred years when Solara and Lunara hung low in the sky.

"What are your thoughts on the council's recent decision to increase self-generation numbers this ceremony?" Lyra asked, her eyes narrowing as she probed for my opinion.

"They are necessary steps," I responded, carefully keeping my tone neutral yet firm. "Change is never easy, but it is essential for our survival and growth."

Astra nodded thoughtfully. "I agree. Our people need to see that we are not bound to the past but are looking towards the future."

"The path ahead is fraught with challenges if we think we can continue as a self-generated society of women," Nova, always the voice of pragmatism, added. "Or has no one else noticed that things have become rather boring around here?"

"Sounds like a challenge for Astra and Lyra," I laughed, lightening the mood. "How do you feel about inventing a new way to stop Nxyara from being boring?'

Astra and Lyra exchanged awkward glances at each other, which raised several questions in my mind. Still, before I could voice them, we approached the grand hall where the ceremony would take place, and the sounds of hushed conversations and distant music reached our ears.

The hall, a magnificent space of towering columns and arched ceilings, was draped with banners bearing the symbols of Nxyara—stars, vines, and the ancient crest representing our unity and strength.

We paused, taking a moment to gather ourselves before stepping into the Great Hall. Astra and Lyra exchanged a look, a silent communication that only Twins seemed to share, before looking back at us.

"Shall we?" Astra asked, her smile warm and encouraging.

"Let's," I agreed, taking a deep breath.

Together, we stepped into the hall, ready to face the challenges of the night and embrace the promise of a new dawn for our people.

Standing at the edge of the stadium with the Primevex Class, overlooking the Great Hall, my heart pounded. Nova fidgeted beside me, her fingers tapping against her thigh. We had waited so long for this day. This ceremony. Today, we would be part of it.

The crowd had separated us from the Twins

and my lips formed an amused grin as I wondered what scientific tidbit had intrigued them enough to distract them from such an event.

"Can you believe it?" Nova whispered, her voice barely audible over the growing hum of the crowd. "We're finally here."

I agreed, unable to tear my eyes away from the centre of the plaza where the High Council had assembled. They were a formidable sight, draped in their ceremonial robes, faces obscured by decorated masks. Seraphina Drakonis, Head of the High Council, was at the forefront, her presence commanding and unyielding. Piercing eyes, hidden behind her mask, threatening to expose our deepest thoughts and desires.

The air was electric. Nxyflower arrangements glowed softly around us, a gentle reminder of our planet's beauty. The seas in the distance shimmered, reflecting the light of the twin suns and the neighbouring, uninhabitable planet that loomed large in the sky. It was a breathtaking sight that accentuated the power and majesty of the evening.

The High Council raised their hands in unison, and a hush fell over the crowd. High Councillor Drakonis stepped forward, amplifying her voice.

"Today, we honour the cycle of life and death,

the renewal of our society. Today, we celebrate our strength and unity."

The crowd erupted into a wave of cheers, their voices rising as the resounding, primal thud of drums echoed through the Great Hall. The rhythmic pounding awakened something deep within, a primal call resonating through every part of us.. Dancers, young and old alike, stepped into the hall's centre, encircling the Renewal performers, whose silhouettes cast long shadows against the flickering glow of torches. The atmosphere thrummed with an undeniable energy, heavy with the weight of eager expectation.

The dancers were dressed in elaborate ceremonial attire. Flowing maroon robes adorned the Elders, intricately embroidered with gold symbols that represented their status and past. Their belts, ladened with delicate charms, jingled faintly with every graceful step. Primevex dancers had sleek, fitted outfits of rich indigo and silver, their bodies wrapped in cloth that hugged their athletic frames, allowing for the freedom of movement that their youth demanded. Jewelled armbands sparkled at their wrists, catching the light as they twirled, and long, sheer sashes trailed behind them, fluttering with every spin.

"Let the ceremony begin!" Drakonis announced as the audience returned to their allocated observation areas. We positioned ourselves for a better view. There was no way we were going to miss any of this!

The official dance began slowly, the Elders leading with fluid, deliberate movements that spoke of years of honed skill. Their steps were soft and calculated, their arms moving in graceful arcs that seemed to trace invisible patterns in the air. Each gesture reflected their wisdom, their long fingers extending outward as if offering their knowledge to the universe. Their faces remained serene, expressions calm and distant, embodying the deep sense of ritual that the moment demanded.

The Primevex dancers joined in, their movements a stark contrast to the measured grace of the Elders. Leaping and spinning with boundless energy, their limbs stretched out in powerful, athletic motions that filled the performance with youthful vigour. They executed flips and twirls effortlessly, their sashes whipping through the air like streaks of colour, adding to the visual splendour. Their prehensile feet synced with the heavy drumbeats, creating a rhythmic pounding against the stone floor. Together, the two groups made a perfect balance, an embodiment of both tradition and renewal, their contrasting energies interwoven into a seamless whole.

As the dance progressed, the tempo of the drums quickened, and so too did the intensity of the movements. The Primevex performers spun faster, their sashes now a blur, while the Elders' motions became sharper, more defined, their arms slicing through the air with precision. A low hum began to rise from the crowd, a communal chant that grew louder with every passing moment, merging with the pounding of the drums, creating a sound that vibrated in our very bones. I could feel the excitement building inside me, a rush of adrenaline that seemed to quicken my pulse in time with the ceremony.

I glanced at Nova beside me. Her eyes wide with awe and her composure replaced by wonder. She moved with the rhythm, her body swaying to the beat, casting off the serious demeanour she always wore. The extra digits on her feet seemed to have a mind of their own as they tapped along.

The atmosphere crackled with excitement as the sacred self-generation ritual drew closer. Unique to our female-centric planet, this mysterious reproduction process was always shrouded in an almost mystical reverence.

"Look!" Nova gasped, her voice filled with excitement as she pointed across the hall. "Why didn't Elara tell us she was dancing this year?"

I followed her gaze to Elara, who stood out even among the sea of dancers. She, too, was dressed in ceremonial garb, her gown a deep shade of midnight blue, trimmed with silver thread that glittered in the torchlight. Her attire was more ornate than the others, befitting her role as advisor to Drakonis, with a long cape that flowed behind her like a shadow.

Elana's stern face was softened by a rare smile, her eyes alight with joy as she danced with a grace that belied the weight of her responsibilities. Her movements were smooth and confident, as though the intricacies of Nxyaran politics had fallen away, leaving only the simplicity of the dance. Each spin sent her gown swirling around her, the silver trim catching the light, and for a brief moment, she seemed to float above the stone floor. We watched her with quiet fondness, a shared pride for the Elder who had guided us through so much.

As the tempo peaked, the Primevex dancers shifted into a new formation. Moving in perfect unison, they produced slender, jewelled blades from their garments, the sharp glint of steel catching the light as the crowd erupted in song. The energy in the hall intensified, the atmosphere electric as the dancers raised their daggers high above their heads. The crowd surged, moving and swaying with the rhythm, caught up in the frenzied excitement of the moment.

The dancers began a new sequence with a deadly elegance, spinning and twirling with their daggers flashing in the firelight. Each movement was calculated, every step choreographed with precision, their bodies moving as one. As they spun faster, the air was pierced by the sharp hiss of steel slicing through the space, their steady hands guiding the blades in one swift, seamless motion toward the Elders.

Crimson arcs burst through the air, vivid against the firelit backdrop, as the lifeblood of the Elders spilled from their throats. The crowd's song reached a fever pitch, and the metallic scent of blood, mixed with the cool night air, filled the hall with a heady, sacred aroma. The Elders, their roles fulfilled, crumpled gracefully to the ground, their bodies resting peacefully as the ritual climaxed.

Elara was the last of the Elder dancers to fall. My breath faltered as she stared at me, unflinching, whilst the blade cleaved through her. It was evident that her sacrifice was voluntary.

The once-immaculate floor of the Great Hall was now stained with dark, shimmering pools of blood, each droplet a symbol of the eternal cycle of sacrifice and renewal. The atmosphere was thick with reverence, the weight of the ritual settling over us like a shroud, reminding us of the price that must be paid for the continuation of our people. The drums slowed, their once-frantic beat fading into a soft, steady rhythm. This heartbeat echoed the closing of another chapter in our society's endless cycle.

Time seemed to stretch into eternity. The sight of the blood, the stark finality of the act sent a shiver down my spine. My heart pounded in my chest, a visceral reaction to the horror I was witnessing. Was this really the moment of Renewal? The sacred tradition that had been veiled in mystery for generations?

Elara's lifeblood pooled around her while the crowd joined together in a low, reverent chant, praising the sacrifices. My mind reeled, grappling with the brutal truth laid bare before me. The young eliminate the old to ensure our society's continued strength and vitality.

This was our way, the dark secret at our existence's heart. Elara's serene face was etched into my memory, and I stood there, paralysed by disgust and awe. Nothing would ever be the same. The Renewal ceremony had revealed our society's true nature—a relentless pursuit of perfection, paid for with the blood of the willing.

Nova's hand found mine, her grip tight and trembling.

"Zarya," she whispered, her voice barely audible over the beat of the drums. "This is…"

I couldn't respond, my eyes locked on the scene unfolding before us. We stood frozen. The reality of our society's traditions crashed down on us with a brutal finality as the drums ceased, leaving an eerie silence. The younger dancers stood tall, their faces expressionless, their blades dripping with blood. The High Council, led by Drakonis, stepped forward. The crowd remained silent, a collective breath held in reverence and fear.

Drakonis inspired awe amongst the crowd as she stood tall and imposing, her sharp features and piercing blue eyes commanding attention effortlessly. The battle scar on her right cheek and a discreet tattoo on her left shoulder suggested a hidden depth of knowing.

Her dark grey tailored suit perfectly combined practicality with style. Every detail, from the understated stud earrings to the faction emblem brooch, spoke authority and purpose, exuding an unwavering dedication to Nxyara's traditions even in a crowd.

A reputation for a strategic mind preceded her. A trait that had undoubtedly shaped Nxyara's destiny. Yet, despite her inflexibility and lack of empathy, one couldn't help respecting her commitment to preserving her planet's legacy. Drakonis was not just a leader. She was a guardian. One who fiercely protected whatever she held dear.

With a slight gesture of her hand, the crowd voiced a harmonious chant that filled the air once more.

I squeezed Nova's hand tighter, a knot of anticipation tightening in my gut.

"It's not finished," I whisper, the weight of uncertainty settling in.

TWO

"What the hell?" Astra and Lyra whispered simultaneously.

I turned to see the Twins standing behind me, faces drained of colour, eyes wide with horror. Astra's hands trembled, clutching a railing until her knuckles turned white. Lyra, usually composed, had tears streaming down her cheeks, mouth slightly agape in shock.

As Elana's lifeblood spilled onto the Great Hall's floor, mixing with that of other sacrificed dancers, Astra let out a strangled gasp. "Is this really how it has to be?" Her voice barely carried over the reverent chants of the crowd. Her eyes searched mine, desperate for reassurance I couldn't provide.

Lyra wiped her tears her expression hardening. "We've been deceived," she muttered, voice trembling with anger and sorrow. "All those tales about Renewal being a joyful celebration. They never told us it would be like..... like this."

The chanting swelled, filling the Great Hall with a haunting melody. Astra turned away from the gruesome scene, shoulders shaking as she struggled to hold back sobs. "I can't believe Elana just accepted it. She didn't even flinch," she choked out, voice thick with emotion.

Lyra gripped her sister's hand, her own trembling slightly. "She must have believed it was for the greater good," she said, steadier but still disbelieving. "But that doesn't make it right. This can't be the only way."

Their reactions mirrored the turmoil inside me. We had been raised to view this ceremony as a joyful rite, a celebration of our society's continuation. But witnessing it firsthand, seeing Elana's serene acceptance of her sacrifice, shattered that illusion.

In that moment, amidst the chanting and the blood, an unspoken pact formed between us. The Renewal ceremony had revealed our society's harsh truth, and we couldn't stand idly by. Our first Renewal ceremony had become the catalyst for change—a path that would challenge our world's foundations.

A charged energy crackled in the air, like the calm before a storm, whilst the slain dancers continued to lay motionless, their sacrifice a grim, brutal reality. Scattered among them, the Primevex dancers stood with eerie calm, eyes fixed on Drakonis, whose demeanour was now tempered with resolve.

Our hands still clasped tightly, Nova and I felt a shift as the crowd murmured in hushed tones, eyes fixed on the Primevex dancers who commenced moving with purpose.

As a surge of energy rippled through the Great Hall, the dancers stepped forward in unison, eyes blazing with determination. Raising their hands, they began to replicate as Nxyaran technology and biology intertwined in a dazzling display.

First, a subtle shimmer, like a mirage. Then, with a blinding light, each dancer split into two identical figures, united in fiery intensity and flawless synchrony. Gasps spread through the crowd like wildfire.

"We are Nxyarans," they declared in unison, voices ringing with authority and defiance. "Born of sacrifice, bound by duty."

Their proclamation echoed off the walls, mingling with stunned silence. The clones continued their seamless dance, with High Councillor Drakonis joining in and lending solemnity to the proceedings. Her stare was steady as she matched their harmonious movements as if they were rehearsed.

Nova's grip tightened. "It's... incredible," she murmured, filled with awe and uncertainty.

I nodded silently, transfixed by the clones. The ceremonial dance ended with a final, graceful flourish as applause and murmured conversations erupted.

As the crowd dispersed, their voices lingering in the air, I turned away from the Great Hall, unable to witness the cleanup that felt like erasing the traces of our awakening... and Elana.

"If they're clones, what does that make us?" Lyra's question reverberated in my mind as the four of us moved through the corridors, each step heavy with the burden of contemplation. Her words demanded answers we couldn't give.

Nova's eyes mirrored my turmoil as she searched my face for understanding.

"What are we, Zarya?" Her voice tinged with uncertainty. "Are Nxyarans merely echoes of the past, destined to endlessly repeat the same cycles?"

I sighed heavily as the question loomed over us.

"I don't know, Nova," I confessed. "But today

has raised too many questions for us to ignore. The clones... they challenge everything we've ever believed."

Nova, Astra, and Lyra nodded in quiet agreement, their gazes drawn back to the Great Hall where the ritual of Renewal had unfolded. "It's as if our entire existence is being called into question," Astra murmured in disbelief.

"We must seek answers," Lyra asserted firmly.

I nodded in solemn agreement, feeling my resolve harden despite the uncertainty gnawing at me. "We can no longer accept things blindly. We must uncover the truth, no matter how unsettling."

Nova and I departed from the Great Hall, leaving Astra and Lyra engrossed in their debate about the cloning process and its technology.

The corridors of Kael'thar were dimly lit, shadows dancing along the ancient stone walls as we walked. Nova stayed by my side, providing a sense of comfort as I battled an overwhelming anxiety. Walking past Nxyarans performing their daily tasks, I wondered if they truly were oblivious to the horrors that had just occurred.

As we neared the city's edge, where cliffs framed the serene seas below, I halted, absorbing the familiar view that had always provided me solace.

Tonight, not even the ethereal gleam of Elara, our small moon, could soothe the mounting anxiety within me.

"We need to find out more," Nova said quietly, breaking the silence.

"I know," I replied, my voice steady despite the turmoil. "But where do we start?"

"This secret must have been kept for eons. Finding answers, let alone a solution, won't be easy before the next Renewal ceremony," she mused.

I nodded. We had three hundred years until the twin suns again hung low in the Nxyaran sky. Until the next Renewal Cerem.... Slaughter. "What if there are records, ancient texts that tell us more about our origins?"

"It's worth a try." Nova's expression brightened with hope. "I'll start researching tonight. Meanwhile, you should rest. Elana was closest to you, and you will need space if you are going to find a way around this."

I hesitated, torn between finding answers and the grief threatening to overwhelm me. But Nova's concern was genuine, and I knew she was right.

"Alright," I finally conceded. "But keep me informed of anything you find."

With a nod, Nova left me alone on the cliff's

edge, the gentle breeze carrying the faint scent of the Nxyflowers. I felt a renewed sense of purpose as I watched her disappear into the city's embrace. Today's revelations had shaken our beliefs to the core but had also ignited a determination to uncover the truth, no matter the cost.

I knew one thing: we could never give up. The fate of Nxyara, and perhaps our entire species, hinged on what secrets we could uncover.

"It doesn't make sense," Astra muttered in frustration, her words bouncing off the sterile walls of the Twins laboratory. Her brow furrowed, and she paced back and forth, a bundle of nerves and questions. "How could they have perfected cloning without anyone knowing? It goes against everything we've been taught."

Lyra shook her head, her serene expression marred by conflict. "Maybe it's not cloning at all," she countered, her voice rising with agitation. "Maybe there's something else, something we haven't considered."

Nova and I exchanged wary glances, sensing the storm brewing between the Twins. This wasn't just a scientific puzzle anymore; it now posed a challenge to our deepest convictions.

"Whatever it is, we need to approach this rationally," Nova urged, her gaze shifting between the sisters. "We can't jump to conclusions without evidence."

"But the ethical implications..." Astra's voice faltered, wavering with emotion. "If they're creating life like this, what does it mean for us? Are we even real?"

Lyra's eyes flashed with frustration. "Of course we're real," she retorted sharply. "But what if our entire existence is based on a lie? If we regenerate, why the death?"

I stepped forward, attempting to diffuse the rising tension that threatened our unity. "We need to investigate," I interjected. "We can't let fear or uncertainty divide us."

Astra turned to me, her eyes pleading for answers. "But how do we even begin?" Her voice trembled with desperation.

"We start with what we know," Nova replied, her tone unwavering. "We gather information, ask questions, and don't stop until we find the truth."

Lyra nodded, her features softening with resolve.

As we each contemplated our next move, the

silent divide between Astra and Lyra remained substantial. Never before had our comradeship been tested this way.

"I think we should start by approaching High Councillor Drakonis," I suggested, breaking the tense silence that enveloped us.

"She's been at the heart of Nxyaran traditions for centuries. If anyone knows about the Renewal Ceremony process and origins, it's her."

Uncertainty settled over us like a suffocating blanket. Nova, Astra, and Lyra exchanged uneasy glances, fear and concern etched on their faces.

"Drakonis has made her feelings towards you very clear," Nova pointed out, her brow furrowed with worry. "Approaching her could be dangerous."

"She's not just disapproving," Astra added, stepping closer, her voice tinged with apprehension. She glanced nervously down the corridor as if Drakonis herself would appear any minute. "She's violently opposed to your ideas. Confronting her will put you in serious danger."

Lyra crossed her arms tightly over her chest.

"We can't let fear stop us," she insisted. "If Drakonis holds the answers we need, we must face her, no matter the risk."

I took a deep breath, my mind racing as I strived

to control my conflicting emotions. The prospect of confronting Drakonis filled me with a gnawing dread. She had made her staunch disapproval of my proposals for change clear and unwavering, having already threatened me with charges of heresy, punishable by death. Nova and Astra were right; approaching Drakonis about – anything - would provoke her wrath.

"What if she sees our questions as a threat?" Nova whispered, her concern mirroring mine. "What if she sees us as a danger to Nxyara's traditions?"

I swallowed hard, pushing aside my fears as I met Nova's gaze. "We need answers," I tried to quell my rising apprehension. "I agree with Lyra. If Drakonis has the answers, we must face her, no matter the risk."

Astra's hands shook as she glanced nervously down the corridor again. "Just promise me you'll be careful, Zarya," she pleaded softly, her voice thick with concern. "We can't afford to lose you."

Lyra nodded in silent agreement, her eyes reflecting the same fear that I was having difficulty suppressing.

"Stay vigilant," she cautioned. "And remember, we're in this together."

The decision settled, a heavy silence fell upon

us, thick with unspoken fears and trepidation. Nova stood by my side in an unspoken promise of protection as Astra and Lyra exchanged tense glances.

"Be careful, Zarya," Astra whispered. "And Nova, watch over her. Drakonis cannot be trusted."

Nova nodded solemnly, her eyes never leaving mine. "I won't let anything happen to her," she vowed.

"We'll continue researching the cloning technology and see if we can at least replicate it," Lyra declared. "Hopefully, we'll have some answers when you return."

My head bobbed in a sharp, frantic nod as my nerves coiled like tight springs. Images of the impending showdown with High Councillor Drakonis ran through my mind, each one more terrifying than the last.

"Thank you, all of you," I murmured, trying to mask the tremor in my voice. "We'll reconvene as soon as possible."

With a final nod to the Twins, I turned and walked down the corridor with Nova close behind me.

It had been two weeks since our request for an audience with the High Council. As we ventured deeper into Nxyara's inner sanctum, towards the Council chambers where Drakonis resided, every shadow and sound seemed to be amplified by my heightened senses. Nova's steady presence behind me provided a semblance of comfort, reminding me that I wasn't alone in this perilous quest. Our senses were on high alert, urging us forward.

Suddenly, we were there. A part of me wanted to turn back, but I knew that facing Drakonis and the rest of the Council was inevitable. I gathered my courage for whatever destiny lay behind the towering Council Chamber doors in front of me. Those colossal, menacing doors.

I pushed them open, Nova shadowing me as I held my breath, anticipating High Councillor Drakonis' greeting. I imagined her stern gaze ready to pierce through my resolve, consuming me. We moved forward. Our heads lowered in respect as tradition requires. When I finally lifted my gaze, it wasn't Drakonis I saw, but Elder Miriam - countless years of contemplation and guidance reflected on her weathered face. Her deep and knowing eyes demanded an explanation.

Nova and I stood frozen in momentary shock.

Miriam's tall and graceful presence, commanding a quiet authority, blocked our path. She donned simple yet elegant robes symbolising her connection to Nxyara's spiritual heritage and an ancestral pendant around her neck; a token of wisdom passed down through generations. Her ceremonial staff was an unmistakable mark of her role as a spiritual guide and historian.

"Zarya," she began, her voice a soothing melody laced with controlled anger. "Explain yourself."

I hesitated, glancing at Nova before responding. "We need answers. About the... about everything."

Miriam nodded, her expression thoughtful. "I understand. But this is not the place for such a conversation." She gestured towards the door. "Walk with me."

Reluctantly, we followed Miriam out of the chambers, the tension intense between us. As Miriam led us through the city, the beauty of our surroundings did little to ease my anxiety.

Kael'thar was a marvel of engineering and nature, seamlessly integrated into rocky cliffs. Stone and wood structures rose in terraces filled with lush vegetation that added a touch of green to the otherwise stark landscape. Nxyarans moved about tending to plants and navigating the vertical settlement with practised ease.

Miriam guided us down a quiet path, her gait unhurried despite the gravity of our mission. Agitation flickered subtly in her movements as the suns glowed over the city, the soft light highlighting the unique details of the architecture.

"Kael'thar is a place of harmony," Miriam said, her voice carrying a hint of pride. "Proof of our ability to thrive even in the harshest environments."

I remained silent, my mind racing with questions. How long has Miriam known about the sacrificial process? More importantly, why did she bring us here, away from the safety and security of the High Council chamber?

As we walked, I found my voice. "Why could we not speak in the High Council chambers?"

Miriam paused, turning to face me, eyes filled with what I could only describe as boredom.

"Because some truths are too dangerous to be spoken within those walls," she sighed.

Panic built up inside of me at the thought. Drakonis had never been subtle about her disdain for my radical proposals. I could only imagine the consequences of questioning her directly. Did Miriam get to us just in time? Was this an... intervention?

Miriam continued to lead us deeper into the heart of Kael'thar. Our path wound through the terraces, offering glimpses of the lives of those who called the city home. Neophytes grouped together in the sunlight, their laughter a stark contrast to the heavy burden we carried. Some from the Elder Class tended to gardens, deftly caring for the plants that sustained our community.

"This way," Miriam said, leading us to a secluded garden, a quiet haven away from the bustling activity. "Rhea," she added, gesturing to a Primevex standing beside a large, complex piece of machinery. "Join us."

Rhea turned towards us, her warm brown eyes widening slightly in surprise as she stepped forward. Her round face was framed by auburn hair pulled back into a practical braid, and she wore dark coveralls boasting numerous pockets which she had filled with various tools. It was... practical.

Rhea inclined her head in a humble greeting, a hint of pride flickering in her eyes whilst Miriam's gaze shifted between us.

"Rhea is my understudy in matters of engineering and technology. She has been instrumental in refining our understanding of ancient mechanisms."

The twin suns cast long shadows across the stone

bench where Elder Miriam gestured for us to sit, the cool surface a welcome relief from the day's heat.

"Now," Miriam began, her voice low and steady. "Ask your questions, and I will answer honestly."

Nova and I exchanged wary glances, our concerns deepening over Elder Miriam. She hadn't disclosed how she anticipated our visit to the High Council or the exact timing of our arrival. With no certainty whether she would relay our intentions to Drakonis, mistrust crept in.

"Are we all replicas?" I blurted out, unable to contain my curiosity.

"Clones?" Nova corrected.

"Yes," Miriam's expression softened, understanding the urgency of my question.

Well, that didn't tell me much. I shifted in my seat, feeling slightly embarrassed.

"How does it work?" Nova leaned forward, probing for more detail. "And why the secrecy?"

Miriam sighed.

"The process is a blend of advanced technology and ancestral knowledge," she recounted as if reciting from a textbook. "It involves replicating genetic material with remarkable precision, ensuring each Nxyaran is generated with the knowledge and memories of their predecessors."

"But why keep it hidden?" Nova pressed, her brows furrowed in frustration.

"Because knowledge is power," Miriam explained. "And power, especially in matters of reproduction, can be perilous if misused. The High Council believes safeguarding this method prevents exploitation and maintains our societal order."

Rhea, revealing her logicality, spoke up. "But at what cost? The sacrifices, the ethical implications... Is it worth it?"

Miriam's wise eyes met mine, filled with a melancholy that spoke volumes. "That's a question we all must ponder. Our traditions have preserved us but also blinded us to alternative paths."

Nova nodded thoughtfully, her military mind sensing more profound implications. "Could there be another way, a better way?"

Miriam hesitated, choosing her words carefully. "Perhaps. But change comes slowly to Nxyara, especially concerning such foundational matters."

I frowned, feeling a spark of determination ignite the defender within me. "What about societal stability?"

"A society without genetic diversity may struggle with innovation, limiting our ability to adapt to new challenges," Miriam replied encouragingly, implying we were on the right path.

Rhea absorbed Miriam's insights, her mind racing with technical possibilities and ethical quandaries. "Is there precedent for this in our history?"

"Societies that embraced diversity often thrived," Miriam replied, her gaze turning inward as she recalled ancient texts.

"Those resistant to change risked stagnation. Our challenge is finding a balance between tradition and necessary evolution."

Nova leaned in, her determination clear. "Why hasn't this been brought to the High Council's attention? If we don't address these issues, Nxyara could face extinction."

Miriam fixed her gaze on Nova. "The High Council is deeply rooted in tradition. They fear disrupting the status quo, especially in matters as fundamental as our reproductive methods."

"If they won't listen," I intervened, "how do we change their minds?"

Miriam bursted to life. "Education and persuasion. Gather allies. Present reasoned arguments. Show them that our strength lies in adaptability, not just tradition."

Rhea nodded, and I could almost see her mind already forming strategies. "We need to make them see the risks of continued self-generation and the potential benefits of diversity."

"Change won't be easy, but with unity and perseverance, we can guide the High Council toward a future that ensures our survival and prosperity," Miriam concurred.

Hours later, we walked back through the winding paths of Kael'thar. Elder Mirian had assigned Rhea to assist us, much to her excitement. As Rhea cheerfully followed, Nova and I exchanged thoughtful glances as Miriam's last words replayed in our minds: Remember, change is not just about what we gain but also what we may lose. Approach Drakonis with caution.

THREE

High Councillor Seraphina Drakonis sat in a high-backed chair of ebony and silver on the raised dais at the far end of the Council chamber. Dressed in the colour of blood and power, she was decorated with emblems of her office. With an insatiable grace, her cold blue eyes bore down upon our trio with chilling intensity.

Iron-grey hair, meticulously coiled into a crown-like braid, accentuated her regal bearing. Around her neck hung a heavy, exquisite piece that pulsed with ancient authority. The air grew tense as we stood in uneasy silence, acutely aware of her threatening gaze.

The Council Chambers of Nxyara stood as an imposing structure of authority and tradition, its walls adorned with intricate carvings of the planet's storied history. High arched windows let pale light filter through onto the dark, polished stone floor.

At the centre of the room, a grand circular table dominated the space, flanked by towering statues of Nxyara's revered leaders.

Drakonis rose from her chair, her movements deliberate and menacingly slow. The subtle rustle of her robes was the only sound in the vast chamber, amplifying the tension that crackled in the air. She stopped mere centimetres from us, her icy breath ghosting over my face. Younger and inexperienced, Rhea swallowed hard as Nova's fists clenched, her loyalty a fierce but fragile shield against such an opponent.

I met the eyes of the High Councillor with defiance. Though a flicker of uncertainty betrayed her resolve, she pinned me in place with an almost predatory focus. The other High Council members, each an influential figure in their own right, remained seated in a semi-circle around us. Their expressions ranged from stern disapproval to silent curiosity, but none matched Drakonis' sheer, commanding presence. The room filled with unspoken words and looming judgments.

"Bow your head in respect," Drakonis commanded with a voice like a sharp crack of thunder. Nova and Rhea exchanged a brief, nervous glance, but the High Councillor's glare never wavered. I submitted.

"You stand before this council to question the renewal process," Drakonis continued, her tone as cold and unyielding as the stone beneath our feet. "Do you truly understand the gravity of your insolence, or have you been blinded by ambition?"

My heart pounded in my chest. I could feel Nova's steadying presence beside me and Rhea's quiet resolve at my back. Still, at this moment, Drakonis' unwavering scrutiny consumed me.

"High Councillor and esteemed members of the Nxyaran High Council," I began, trying to hold back my breakfast from rising inside me, "we would like to know more about the reproduction process we witnessed at the Renewal Ceremony. We seek this information for the future of Nxyara."

A murmur rippled through the council members but was silenced with a mere lift of Drakonis' hand. Her eyes narrowed, and a faint, dangerous smile played at the corners of her lips.

"Zarya Elyssan," Her voice was a silken snarl, each word meticulously enunciated to pierce like a dagger. "Your audacity knows no bounds. To question our ancestors' reproduction method... it is heresy, an insult to our society."

Rhea straightened, summoning every ounce of her courage. "It is not heresy, High Councillor," she corrected respectfully. "It is genetics and technology. Methods we must understand, or our species will perish."

A dangerous glint sparked in Drakonis' eyes. "To what end must you learn? Replication? Or destruction?" She glanced sideways at me as she continued. "Your friends' reckless ambition has already sown discord among our people."

She returned her gaze to Nova, her eyes narrowing. "And you," she hissed, "do you stand with her in this madness?"

Nova's voice trembled as she spoke, "We stand for the future of Nxyara. We are trying to—"

"Silence!" The High Councillor roared, stopping Nova instantly. Her gaze bore into Nova and Rhea, stripping away every layer of their resolve. "Your loyalty is misplaced. Loyalty to a heretic is no loyalty at all."

Her gaze settled on Rhea, whose tense face betrayed her pounding heart. The High Councillor's expression brimmed with disdain and curiosity like a predator sizing up its prey. "And you, Rhea Talyon, an engineer. Do you truly believe you can forge a future from Zarya's... fantasies?"

Rhea's mouth went dry. She forced herself to speak, though her voice was barely a whisper. "I believe in the potential for improvement, High Councillor. The technology—"

Drakonis cut her off with a mocking laugh. "Technology. Such faith in cold metal and circuits. But it is not technology that rules Nxyara. It is strength. It is tradition." She leaned in closer, her voice dropping to a venomous whisper. "And it is fear."

Anger and helplessness overcame me as the words reminded me of the High Councillor's power. The oppressive silence was shattered only by the pounding of my heart.

"Mark my words," Drakonis continued, her voice rising once more to fill the chamber as she turned to face the rest of the High Council. "If they persist in this folly, they will ruin us all. And I will not stand idly by as they dismantle everything our ancestors have built."

Drakonis took her seat, her robes settling like a dark cloud around her. The air felt heavy, charged with the weight of decisions yet to be made. For a moment, the only sound was the soft rustle of robes and the faint murmur of voices passing between the High Council members. Their faces remained unreadable, masks of authority and contemplation. Each of them, representatives of the highest order, had the power to shape Nxyara's future.

A sense of dread crept over me. Standing before these imposing figures, the reality of our situation settled in. We weren't merely speaking to Drakonis but addressing the entire High Council. The rumours of Nxyarans being executed for even the slightest misstep, for displeasing just one of the High Council members, echoed in my mind. Our decision to present our concerns about the renewal ceremony suddenly felt like a colossal mistake.

The Elder at the far end of the table, with silver-streaked hair bound behind her head, cleared her throat. The murmurs ceased, and all eyes turned to her as she spoke with measured authority.

"The matter you have presented is of great consequence," she began, her voice steady but charged with the Council's power.

"The renewal ceremony is a sacred tradition, integral to the survival and strength of our people. To question its purpose and origins is no small thing."

She paused, allowing her words to sink in. I could feel my pulse quicken.

"We will deliberate on the concerns you have raised," another High Councillor added, her tone more neutral but no less imposing. Her robes were embroidered with symbols of rank, the golden threads glinting in the soft light.

"However, such decisions cannot be made hastily. The implications of altering or questioning the renewal ceremony are profound."

Drakonis, silent until now, leaned forward. Her piercing gaze locked onto mine, and I could feel her scrutiny.

"You must understand," she said, her voice like silk over steel, "what you ask of us is not simple. You question the very foundation of our society. The High Council does not take this lightly."

I swallowed hard, my mouth dry. Nova stood firm beside me, her shoulders squared, but I could see the tension in her jaw. Ever the optimist, Rhea remained still, though her eyes darted between the High Councillors, calculating, analysing.

"The High Council will convene privately to discuss the matter," the silver-haired Elder declared. "You will be informed of our decision in due course. Until then, you are dismissed."

Dismissed.

The word felt like a reprieve, yet also a sentence. We had done what we came to do, but now the future hung in the balance.

With a nod from Drakonis, the chamber doors

opened. The guards stood at attention, waiting for us to leave. We bowed respectfully and turned to exit, our footsteps echoing in the vast hall as we retreated from the High Council's formidable presence.

As the heavy doors closed behind us, sealing us from the judgement that would soon follow, I exhaled, realising I had been holding my breath.

The waiting had begun.

It had been hours since we presented our questions to the High Council regarding the renewal ceremony. Yet, time felt stretched, as if days had passed. The silence in the chamber thickened, looming like an impending storm about to break. I could sense the weight of every gaze fixed upon us, scrutinising, evaluating. Nova stood steadfast beside me, her resolve unwavering, her jaw firmly set despite the earlier tremor in her voice. Rhea remained resolute; her faith in the potential of technology offered me solace.

"We... we understand the gravity of our questions," I began again, my voice wavering as I steadied myself. "But we believe that knowledge is our greatest asset. To safeguard Nxyara's future, we must understand and explore all avenues, even those that challenge our traditions."

A murmur of disagreement swept through the High Council chambers. Eventually, they passed a small scroll containing their decision. Drakonis lifted her hand again, halting the murmurs with a swift gesture, her gaze fixed firmly on mine.

"Zarya Elyssan," she intoned, her voice cold and cutting, "you have always been headstrong. But this... this is beyond recklessness. It is defiance of everything we hold dear."

I met her gaze, refusing to falter under her scrutiny. "With all due respect, High Councillor," I replied evenly, "we seek not to defy but to understand. The future of Nxyara rests upon our ability to adapt, to evolve."

A tense pause followed, and the chamber filled with an uneasy stillness. The council members exchanged looks, deliberating among themselves. Each passing moment felt like an eternity, the outcome of our bold inquiry hanging in the balance. Drakonis's following words shattered any lingering hope of a peaceful resolution.

"You will not have your answers," she declared with an air of finality that made my blood run cold.

"But you will have a lesson in humility."

Before I could comprehend her intent, strong grips forced my arms behind my back. Guards had moved in undetected. Rhea was similarly restrained, her eyes wide with shock and fear. My heart pounded against my ribs amidst the chaos, and then I saw her.

Nova.

She stood a few feet away, her eyes locked onto mine. There was a look of determination, of defiance, as if she was about to take a stand. But in an instant, her eyes widened, a sharp gasp escaped her lips, and she crumpled to the floor.

"No!" The word tore from my throat, raw and desperate.

Time seemed to stretch and distort. I watched in horror as scarlet liquid soaked into her tunic. The world around me blurred. The only clear image was Nova lying there, her blood pooling around her.

This couldn't be happening. This had to be some twisted nightmare. Nova was strong, invincible. She was the one who always had the answers, the one who always knew what to do. She couldn't be...

"Nova!" I screamed her name, struggling against the iron grip of the guards. "No, no, no!" My voice broke, the words coming out in choked sobs.

Nova looked up at me, her eyes filled with pain and something else, something like an apology. Her lips moved, forming words I couldn't hear over the pounding in my ears. I fought harder, the guards' hold tightening, but it didn't matter. I had to get to her.

My knees buckled, and I sagged in their grip, my vision blurring with tears. This wasn't real. It couldn't be real. But the sight of my best friend lying motionless on the cold, hard floor, her life slowly slipping away, was all too real.

"Please," I whispered, barely able to form the words. "Please, don't leave me."

Drakonis descended from her elevated seat with deliberate steps, her stare unfeeling and resolute as she approached me. In her hand gleamed a heated iron rod, its tip glowing with an ominous crimson hue. My heart sank as the realisation of her intentions dawned upon me.

"This mark," she pronounced, her voice cutting through my hysteria like a blade, "shall brand you as a traitor. A Rebel. A reminder to all who dare defy our traditions."

I fought against the guards' hold, but their strength was relentless. Fear coursed through me, mingling with a bitter sense of betrayal. The symbol of shame, searing into my flesh, would forever stain my reputation all because of what? A few questions?

Rhea's voice rang out, desperate and defiant. "Stop this madness! She has done nothing—"

A guard's firm hand silenced her with a forceful grip. I could see the same anguish and helplessness in her eye that I felt, as injustice unfolded before us.

The iron rod neared my skin, its heat intensity magnified by Drakonis's grim determination. She pressed the burning symbol against my shoulder. Agony exploded through me, a searing pain that consumed my every thought, every breath.

I clenched my teeth against the scream that clawed at my throat, unwilling to give Drakonis the satisfaction of my anguish, the smell of burning flesh filling the air. Through the haze of pain, I caught glimpses of Nova's tear-streaked face whilst Rhea struggled helplessly against the guards. Their silent agony was a shared torment that bound us together in this moment of betrayal.

Remember, change is not just about what we gain but also what we may lose. Approach Drakonis with caution. Miriam's last words echoed in my mind as the branding iron was finally withdrawn, leaving behind its cruel mark. I staggered under the weight of both physical pain and shattered ideals.

"Let this be a lesson to all who challenge our ways," Drakonis's voice boomed through the chamber. She turned to face the rest of the High Council, the accomplices to my fate, the searing iron held high in the air like a trophy.

"Tradition is our strength. Deviation is our downfall." The glint in her eyes and the fierce set of her jaw spoke of victory. Triumph reverberated through every corner of the room as the Councillors applauded.

I refused to meet her gaze again, unable to bear the satisfaction I knew lingered in her eyes. The room spun around me, a blur of accusing faces and stifled murmurs. Nova's whispered words reached my ears like a fragile thread amidst the chaos.

"You will find a way, Zarya," her voice fading. "This isn't over."

The guards led me away. The searing pain from the branding iron felt like fire coursing through my veins. Blistered and raw, the deep welt was cruelly simple—a stylised representation of Nxyara's emblem, twisted into a shape that marked me as a rebel. The edges of the mark glowed faintly, showing that the heat had permanently altered the texture of my skin.

The guards' grip dug into my flesh as they

dragged me from the Council chamber. My legs felt like lead, each step an agonising effort. The corridors blurred past as we descended deeper into the bowels of Kael'thar, the air growing colder and the light dimmer. Every shadow seemed to whisper of forgotten horrors, of souls lost to the dungeons' depths. The clanging of iron gates echoed ominously, each slam resonating with finality.

The scent of damp stone and decay filled my nostrils, mingling with the lingering odour of burnt flesh. My burnt flesh. My mind raced, a frantic whirlwind of thoughts and fears as the guards' grip tightened even more. We stopped before a heavy, reinforced door. They exchanged curt nods before one produced an iron key, its surface worn smooth from use. The key turned with a loud, grating sound, and the door creaked open to reveal a dark, foreboding passage.

My pulse raced as they shoved me forward. The passage was narrow and cold, the stone walls damp. Torches flickered dimly, casting eerie shadows that seemed to dance and mock my plight. Each step echoed through the silence, and I fought to suppress the instant rise of nausea as I thought about the isolation that awaited me.

The guards said nothing as they led me forward,

their faces impassive masks of duty. They were mere instruments of the High Council's will, devoid of empathy or understanding. To them, I was just another prisoner, another soul condemned to the darkness below.

A draft swept through the passage, causing me to shiver. The deeper we went, the more oppressive the atmosphere became. It was as if the dungeon's walls were suffocating any flicker of hope that dared to arise.

The guards stopped before another door, this one even more imposing than the last. My pulse quickened as I realised there was no escape, no way out of this. The sense of helplessness was overwhelming.

The door swung open, revealing a vast emptiness. The guards pushed me inside without a word, the finality of their actions accentuated as the door slammed shut behind me, sealing my fate with a resounding thud.

I stood there, encircled by the darkness. My pulse quickened as I felt the cold, unforgiving stone beneath my feet and the grim reality of what awaited me settled in. I was alone, trapped in Nxyara's dungeons, with no hope of escape. And Nova.... Nova was dead.

Despair washed over me. The deafening silence was broken only by the haunting echoes of my own sobs. As the final remnants of hope began to flicker and fade, I could almost hear the triumphant laughter of Drakonis and the other Councillors, their victory complete.

I could do nothing but succumb to the helplessness that enveloped me. A prisoner of both body and spirit. I dared not look directly at my new mark; its presence reminding me of the price paid for challenging the rigid traditions that governed our world.

The cave was a labyrinth of ancient stalagmites and stalactites. The air was cool and damp, carrying the faint scent of mineral-rich water trickling somewhere in the depths. Fungi clung to the walls and floor, casting an eerie, otherworldly glow, flickering like ghostly fireflies. Aetheris, now fully awake, stood on a ledge, her shimmering fur reflecting the faint light of the Nxaran Moon in a mesmerising dance of colours.

The feline flexed her wings again, this time more deliberately, feeling her transformed body's unfamiliar weight and balance. The once tiny, delicate wings had grown into majestic appendages, their span nearly twice her previous size. She took a tentative leap to a nearby rock, landing awkwardly and unsteady. Her paws slipped on the slick surface, and she barely caught herself before tumbling into the chasm below. She dug her claws into the rock, her tail lashing in irritation.

Smooth, Aetheris, real smooth, she scolded herself, voice dripping with sarcasm. Frustration flared in her chest. As if adjusting to a new body wasn't enough, this cave is a death trap.

She tried again, determined to master her new form. Crouching, wings outstretched, she sprang towards another ledge. This time, her wings caught the air unevenly, and she veered off course, crashing into a cluster of stalactites. Pain shot through her wing as she yanked it free from a jagged edge.

Damn it! she hissed, eyes blazing with anger. Get it together.

The cave seemed to mock her with its vast emptiness. Aertheris closed her eyes, focusing on the steady rhythm of her heartbeat, willing herself to find balance and control.

She launched herself into the air once more. Her wings beat powerfully, propelling her upwards, but her movements were still clumsy and uncoordinated. Frustration gnawed at her as she clipped a stalagmite, spinning out of control before managing to right herself.

Okay, Aetheris, you've got this, she reassured herself. It's just a larger body. You've adapted before; you can do it again.

Slowly, she began to find a rhythm, her flights becoming more fluid, more controlled. As she flew, she focused on each movement, each adjustment of her wings. The cave's twisting passages and jagged obstacles forced her to navigate with precision, honing her instincts and reflexes. A year of sleeping had her muscles burning with the effort, but she embraced the pain, using it to fuel her determination.

Finally, after what felt like an eternity, she reached the cave's entrance. The first rays of dawn filtered through the opening, casting a warm, golden light that seemed to welcome her back to the world. She landed on a rocky outcrop, her body trembling with exertion but her spirit unbroken.

Not bad, she congratulated herself, a note of pride in her voice.

The vast landscape of Nxyara spread out before her, a mesmerising world dominated by tranquil, otherworldly seas and jagged rock formations. Twin suns created a symphony of deep blues and soft purples, casting their dynamic lightscapes across the terrain.

The wind ruffled her fur, filling her with a sense of freedom and possibility as Aetheris took a moment to savour the view. The dark, imposing rocks, with their deep grooves and fissures, varied in height and structure. They ranged from towering monoliths to sprawling outcrops made of basalt and volcanic materials that shimmered with minerals. Their dynamic interaction with the sea created temporary lagoons teeming with iridescent lichens and alien creatures. They seemed much smaller now than when she entered the cave as a cub.

Below, the waters of the tranquil sea glowed, reflecting the sky's colours. Its unique, gummy texture hosted diverse marine life, and each creature was illuminated as they appeared to travel to varying destinations. Rugged shorelines were dotted with glowing Nxyflowers, their mystical qualities believed to hold secrets of the planet's past.

Practising her moves as she made her way to a quiet cove where the rocky shoreline met gentle waves, she paused to admire her reflection.

Each strand of her black fur caught the fading light in a cascade of colours that danced like starlight upon the water. Her wings, radiating grace and power, were folded with precision against her sleek form, displaying hints of silver and azure.

Her purr reverberated softly as she studied herself, not out of vanity but out of quiet satisfaction with the creature she had become. She was no longer just a Nxyaran pet but a protector. Two hundred and thirty-seven years old... or was it two hundred and fifty-seven?

Irrelevant, she hissed as she gazed into her reflection. A sense of peace settled over her. It wasn't just the reflection of her physical beauty that captivated her, but the reflection of her spirit—fierce yet compassionate, mischievous yet steadfast.

Only the top Neophytes were granted the honour of a pet, and Aetheris had been Zarya's loyal companion since a kitten. However, the cruel twist was that one month before joining the Primevex Class, Nxyaran pets were taken away and forced to transform into their adult forms. To be separated from her lifelong companion after two hundred years was nothing short of heart-wrenching. Still, one could not stay a kitten forever.

The giant sun, Solara, emitted warm, golden light, creating an eternal summer atmosphere as the minor sun, Lunara, began to dominate, casting a silver-blue glow that marked the twilight hours. This duality of light and shadow played over the landscape, highlighting its beauty and filling Aetheris with a renewed sense of purpose. The world was hers for the taking, and she was more than ready. She stretched her wings with a soft sigh, feeling the familiar tingle of anticipation for adventure.

As Aetheris took to the air, the breeze carrying her aloft, a sense of unease gripped her. Usually attuned to Zarya's presence, her inability to sense her companion anywhere on Nxyara sent a ripple of confusion through her. Fear clawed at her heart, a cold knot tightening in her chest as she scanned the horizon.

Where are you, Zarya? She whispered with urgency and concern. The absence of their usual connection left her feeling adrift, uncertain of what to do next. Her eyes narrowed with focus. She had no idea how long she had been gone, but it was time to get back.

The world below seemed to blur as she soared higher, her heart pounding with exhilaration and dread. Her wings cut through the air with precision, each powerful beat fueling her determination. Aetheris knew one thing: she would find her

Nxyaran companion, and nothing would stand in her way.

FOUR

One hundred years. I have spent over one hundred years rotting in this dungeon, but it feels like a lifetime. Darkness has seeped into my soul, a constant reminder of the questions that condemned me. Harmless questions, I thought. Harmless until they cost me everything—my freedom, sanity, and most painfully, Nova.

Nova's death shattered me. Losing her was like losing a limb, and the pain of her absence was a constant, throbbing ache. My grief did not take a linear path. I lingered in denial for decades, refusing to accept that she was truly gone. Every time the cell door creaked, I hoped it was her. I hoped she had somehow survived and found a way to rescue me. But it was always just the guards, their faces twisted in cruel amusement.

Anger came next, a fierce, burning rage. I hated everyone—Drakonis for her tyranny, the guards for their sadistic glee, and even the other imprisoned Nxyarans for their resigned acceptance. But most of all, I hated myself. I hated myself for asking those questions, for dragging Nova into my curiosity. If only I had kept my mouth shut. If only I had heeded Elder Miriam's warning. She might still be alive.

I prayed to any god that would listen, offering anything for a chance to see Nova again, bargaining with silent, desperate pleas to the universe. I promised to be good, never question again, and to do anything they wanted if only they would bring her back. But my prayers went unanswered, and the only thing that changed was the growing hum of hopelessness that settled over me like a suffocating blanket.

I stopped speaking, stopped caring. I let the decades blur together, each a monotonous repetition of the last. The other prisoners avoided me, and I welcomed the solitude. It was easier to bear the crushing weight of my grief alone.

Acceptance of my plight finally came like the first rays of dawn after a long, dark night. Nova was gone; nothing I did or felt would bring her back. There was no rescue. She would not want me to waste away in this hellish place. I forced myself to eat, to talk, to endure. I had to survive if only to honour her memory.

The dungeon is a nightmare, a place meticulously crafted to crush spirits. We are dragged from our cells to face the daily torment of constructing a bridge over a bottomless pit. The materials we are given have been crafted to randomly decay and crumble. Each day, we teeter on the edge, knowing the bridge will never be completed and that it is a death-wielding task designed to kill us.

Today was no different from all the others. We work relentlessly under the watchful eyes of sadistic guards who revel in our suffering. The air, thick with the scent of sweat and fear, carries the constant clamour of construction echoes through the cavernous pit. We are pushed beyond exhaustion, our bodies trembling from fatigue and hunger, knowing that punishment awaits any perceived laziness.

Every step on the bridge is a gamble with death. The wood creaks ominously underfoot, threatening to give way at any moment. The weight of my survival rests on each plank, each precarious step. My heart pounds in my ears, a deafening reminder of what's at stake. I glance back at a Neophyte with wide, terrified eyes, diverting my mind by wondering what someone so young could have possibly done to be put here. Then again, I only asked logical questions.

I was torn back to reality by a sickening crack. The plank beneath the Neophyte had snapped, and her eyes widened even more as her scream pierced the air. Reflexes kicked in as I grabbed her hand, but her grip was loose, and she slipped away. "No!" I shouted, lunging to catch her, but she was gone, swallowed by the darkness below. Her scream echoing long after she vanished.

I didn't have time to process. The bridge swayed beneath me, and I saw one of the Elder Class ahead, her confident steps faltering. Elders have always been so surefooted, but she was struggling. Slipping on a loose board, her arms windmilled for balance.

"Stop!" I called out an instant before she fell, disappearing into the abyss. Her face, etched with shock and horror, was the last thing I saw.

I forced myself to move, my steps slow and deliberate. Another Primevex was just ahead, her determination evident in every step. She's strong. She can make it. I looked ahead only to see the rope she's clinging to is... fraying.

"Watch out, the rope!" I shout, as her fingers clawed at the air, her cry a raw, primal sound of fear and despair. Her scream abruptly silenced by the depths below.

Three deaths in under a minute. I clung to the broken rope, using my prehensile feet to help me reach a more secure position. My breath came in shallow gasps, my palms sweaty as I continue. I couldn't afford to stop, couldn't afford to think. I calculated each move. The wind howled around me, and the bridge swayed, adding to the vertigo. My heart skipped. Planks were missing up ahead. Calculating the distance, I bent my knees to jump.

I lept, the chasm yawning beneath me. For a moment, I was weightless, suspended over the void. Then, my feet hit solid wood. I stumbled forward, clutching the rope for support. My vision blurred with sweat and fear.

A creak behind me sends a jolt of terror through my body. I turn just in time to see another Primevex fall, their scream blending with the wind. That makes four today... that I know of. I bowed my head with a deep sigh. I didn't even know their names.

My muscles ached, my mind a whirlwind of fear and determination. I kept moving, using my terror to drive me ever forward. The end of the bridge was in sight but felt miles away. Each step was torture, each creak a reminder of how close I was to death.

Eventually, I reached the end, collapsing onto solid ground, my body shaking with relief and exhaustion. Gasping for breath, I looked back at the rickety structure mocking me, daring me to try again. This time, I survived. But there will always be tomorrow.

Each death was a stark reminder of our insignificance and fragility. The abyss was a hungry beast, always ready to claim another life. Our work a constant battle against the elements and our own dwindling strength. Outside of work, we are treated like animals, beaten by guards for the slightest mistake. We are denied clean water and, at times, much-needed food. Life in the dungeon existed in a state of perpetual exhaustion, bodies and minds pushed to their limits.

And yet, we endure. We cling to the hope of escape, to the dream of freedom. We form bonds, find strength in our shared suffering, and fight to survive another day. The dungeon may be designed to break us, but those of us inside will resist as long as we draw breath.

It was a rare privilege for us to eat together, and although today marked one hundred years of my imprisonment, I still couldn't help but feel on edge.

We had all been put here for various crimes, most often for questioning the regime or being suspected of disloyalty. Each clink of metal on metal, each whispered conversation, made me more aware of the surrounding dangers. I learnt to navigate the treacherous terrain both physically and psychologically, but forged alliances with only one other prisoner. As I picked at the gruel before me, I sensed a presence at my back.

"Guess who," a voice whispered, dripping with playful sarcasm. I turned to see Maren, the closest thing I had to a friend in this forsaken place. Her eyes sparkled with mischief despite the darkness hanging over the dungeons.

"Maren, you know one day you're going to get yourself killed doing that," I said, trying to sound annoyed but unable to hide my relief at seeing her.

She flopped down next to me, her presence a rare comfort in this hellhole. "Ah, Zarya, you worry too much. What's life without a little excitement?"

I raised an eyebrow. "Excitement? In here?"

Maren snorted, eyes scanning our fellow inmates as they divided themselves into groups, ever vigilant for signs of danger."You'd be surprised. Speaking of which, have you figured out who all the lovely folks are in our little social club?"

I shook my head. "Not really. Enlighten me."

Maren leaned in, her voice dropping to a conspiratorial whisper. "Alright, let's start with the Fangs. See those guys over there?" She nodded towards a group huddled in a corner, their eyes darting around like predators. "They're the Fangs. Mostly former mercenaries and assassins. They are a really charming bunch. Their leader likes to collect teeth as souvenirs. Not his own, mind you."

I glanced at the group of Nxyarans she was referring to, a chill running down my spine. "Lovely."

"Oh, it gets better," Maren grinned. "Next, we have the Night Crawlers." She emphasised the name with her best scary voice, pointing to a group sitting almost in the shadows.

"They're a mix of thieves and smugglers. Real sneaky types. They can get you anything—if you're willing to pay the price. Their leader keeps a spider as a pet. She has a thing for arachnids if you can believe it."

"That's... disturbing." I shuddered. Insects on Nxyara, let alone arachnids, wasn't common.

"You don't know the half of it," Maren laughed. "Meet the Chitin Clan." She gestured to a group that moved as a swarm.

"They're all about strength in numbers. Used to

be part of some underground fighting ring. Tough as nails, but not the brightest bulbs in the box. Karak is their leader. She has a scorpion tattoo on her face. Subtle, right?"

"And the last group?" I muttered, dreading the question as I voiced it.

"Ah, the Etherborn," Maren mocked. "The mysterious mystics of the dungeon. They dabble in the arcane and have a thing for all things ethereal. Rumour has it they can actually use magic. Their leader speaks in riddles half the time. They mustn't be very good at magic if they can't get themselves out of here. No one has ever escaped."

I sighed, taking it all in. "So, we're surrounded by killers, thieves, brawlers, and mystics. Great."

Maren patted my shoulder. "Hey, at least it keeps things interesting. Besides, it's not like we have much choice in our company."

"True," I said, poking at my food again. "But it doesn't make me feel any safer."

Maren's expression softened, just for a moment. "We look out for each other, Zarya. That's all we can do. Just keep your head down and stay out of trouble."

I nodded, feeling a strange sense of camaraderie despite the dire circumstances. "Thanks, Maren."

She gave me a crooked smile. "Anytime. Now, finish your gruel before it decides to crawl away."

I couldn't help but laugh. In this place, humour was our only weapon against the darkness. As we ate, I noted a smaller group of prisoners that Maren hadn't covered; their faces, smooth and pale, were a striking canvas of beauty, unlike anything I've seen among the other Nxyarans in the dungeon.

"What about them?" I asked, daring a quick glance in the direction of the close-knit group.

Maren paused mid-bite, following my gaze to the small group I had indicated. Though tattered like ours, their clothes seemed to hold remnants of a forgotten elegance, a hint of sophistication amidst the squalor. Each had high cheekbones and prominent foreheads, giving them an almost statuesque appearance. But their six eyes, symmetrically arranged in pairs, truly captivated me. Eyes that glistened like black obsidian moving independently, scanning the room in a manner that set my nerves on edge. It was as if they could see into every shadow and corner, leaving nowhere to hide. Elongated, pointed ears tilted back slightly, adding an alien-like allure. Their noses almost blended into their face's intricate contours. Their deep black lips parted somewhat into smiles hinting at hidden knowledge and concealed threats.

Their hair, thick and dreadlocked, cascaded around their faces like dark halos, intertwining with the natural patterns on their Nxyaran skin. The ridges and grooves of what one could only describe as wrinkles caught the dim light, creating complex tapestries of textures that added to their eerie beauty.

Protruding from their heads and necks were large black appendages that resembled tusks, giving them a menacing yet regal aura. Collectively, they were perfect blends of beauty and terror, commanding my attention and curiosity. My breath caught in my throat as I realised that I was both observer and prey in this encounter, hopelessly drawn into their multi-eyed surveillance.

Compared to the other Nxyarans who were held prisoner, they were like dark, majestic spectres. Their presence challenged my understanding of our species, and questions swirled in my mind as I remained transfixed.

"Them?" Maren repeated my words, her voice lowering as if speaking of something forbidden. "Those are the Forgotten Elders."

"The Forgotten Elders?" I repeated, my curiosity piqued.

Maren nodded, her expression turning serious for once.

"Yeah. Supposedly, the High Council have forgotten they are down here; otherwise they would have been sacrificed at a Renewal Ceremony before their two thousandth generation day like all the Elder Class are."

Memories of Elana's sacrifice, no, execution, came flooding back and filled me with dread.

Maren shrugged, her usual bravado faltering slightly. "No one knows for sure. All I know is, they give me the creeps."

"We have nicknamed them Hexaryans," Maren advised, her tone sombre. "They're what the Elder Class would evolve to if they were allowed to live."

I nodded slowly, taking in her words as we silently finished our meal. I couldn't bring myself to look away.

"But some of them are... different," I noted in a hushed tone, my attention drawn to a few in the group who stood out, their presence was even more commanding and unnerving.

Similar yet distinct, they possessed an additional pair of eyes—eight in total - arranged in an almost hypnotic pattern that drew me deeper into their perplexing gaze. Their faces were just as smooth and pale as the others, but the added eyes gave them an even more profound air of omniscience. Each eye moved of its own volition as if to consume every detail in the room, making me feel like they could see straight into my soul. Their very existence defied the natural order.

The eight-eyed Nxyarans' ears tilted back even more dramatically than the others. Their noses blended seamlessly into their face and their lips were an abyssal black. Dark lines and delicate tattoos around their mouths seemed to shift and change with the flickering light, as if their very skin told a story, one that I was desperate to understand. Compared to the other Nxyarans in the dungeon, even the Hexaryans, these eight-eyed figures were like dark, majestic demigods.

"Octaryans," Maren's whisper cut through the shadows. "It's said to be the evolution of the Hexaryan. Some of my sources say that those tattoos indicate that they are over ten thousand years old. From what I gather, Nxyarans never die unless someone – or something - kills them. We're designed to... keep living."

Maren dropped her head in memory of the dead, and it hit me like a sledgehammer. It hit me: The idea of facing that endless bridge day after day, for the rest of... well, forever. Watching others fall to their deaths and never knowing when you are going to be next. It felt like the cruellest fate imaginable. The thought of it was so overwhelming that even a death sentence seemed like a mercy in comparison.

Eternity! Immortality! Forever! The words echoed in my mind, reverberating off my cell's cold, stone walls. Six months had passed since the last communal meal, and the gruel pushed under my door, touted as tonight's dinner, lay untouched before me, my stomach rebelling against the sight and smell of it.

My mind had been obsessed with questions. Why were the Elder Class sacrificed before their two thousandth generation day? Were there more classes after the Octaryan? Is our species genuinely immortal, and if so, why do we have the ability to self-generate? It defied all logic—why would we need such a capability if we never die?

Never die. What if I never die? A desperate need to escape gripped my thoughts, and just as despair began to seep in, a tiny movement flickered in my peripheral vision. I spun around, my attention laser-focused on my dinner tray. Was that an... insect?

I learned about insects as a Neophyte. They are practically non-existent on Nxyara due to its unique atmospheric composition and environmental conditions. The planet's atmosphere lacks essential gases for insects to survive. For the few insects that can, Nxyara's climate and terrain lack most of the necessary habitats and resources to thrive. The local flora and fauna also tended to eat insect populations. Yet here seemed to be an insect standing in, no, eating, my dinner!

"I bet you taste better," I muttered, a sudden hunger igniting my determination. With that, I began to stalk the minuscule intruder, every movement calculated with precision.

I crouched low, my eyes fixed on the tiny insect darting across my dimly lit cell. "You're not getting away from me," I muttered under my breath, the pleasurable thought of something to eat other than the crap on my plate driving me forward.

With all the stealth I could muster, I lunged towards it, only for the creature to dart away at the last second, mocking me with its erratic flight. "Oh, you think you're clever, don't you?" I chuckled, trying to keep frustration at bay.

Time and again, I chased after it, my hands swatting through the air like a clumsy dancer. Each attempt failed, the insect slipping through my fingers with infuriating ease. "Just stay still for a second!" I exclaimed, my patience wearing thin.

As if sensing my growing annoyance, the insect seemed to double its efforts to evade me, zigzagging with an almost comical agility. "You're really pushing your luck," I warned, a grin tugging at my lips despite myself.

Finally, I saw my chance—a swift swipe that would surely catch it. I lunged forward, fingers closing in... but it vanished.

I blinked in disbelief, my hand frozen mid-air. "Where did you...?" My voice trailed off as a strange sensation washed over me. Shadows lengthened, and then, with a surreal twist of reality, it reappeared. Except it wasn't tiny anymore and definitely was not an insect.

"Aetheris?" My heart raced. Over two hundred years had passed since Aetheris had been taken from me as a cub. Memories of her playful antics and comforting presence came flooding back, but before me was a creature transformed by time.

Her sleek form glowed with a lustrous coat that shimmered in midnight blue and silver shades, catching the faint light that filtered through the chamber's high windows. Her once tiny frame had grown into a majestic beast, muscles rippling beneath her fur. Now fully developed, the tips of her wings glistened with a subtle iridescence.

"Aetheris," I whispered, hardly daring to believe my eyes. "You've grown so... magnificent."

She turned to regard me with eyes that held a wisdom far beyond her years, a gaze that spoke volumes despite her inability to speak. There was a hint of youthful defiance that I remembered, and a playful arrogance danced in her demeanour as she sat, the crown of my head barely reaching the top of her foreleg.

I reached out to her, unable to contain the flood of emotions welling up inside me. "Do you remember me, Aetheris? It's Zarya ."

Her whiskers twitched, and I saw a flicker of recognition in her eyes. Her posture conveyed a mix of pride and indignation. She tilted her head as if contemplating my question before responding with a disdainful flick of her tail. Her body language spoke volumes: Of course, I do, I'm not an idiot. Why else would I be here?

Her response, though silent, was a reminder that despite her playful arrogance, the bond we shared transcended time and distance. Tears welled in my eyes as I gently stroked her fur, overwhelmed with gratitude to have my faithful companion back by my side once more.

"You've changed," I murmured, wrapping my arms around her foreleg, barely able to make my fingertips touch. "But you're still as beautiful as ever."

Aetheris leaned into my touch, her warmth reassuring against the cold of our surroundings. Her purr rumbled softly, echoing through my cell like a gentle breeze. "We have much to catch up on, Aetheris," tears brimmed in my eyes. "But for now, I'm just grateful to have you here."

She gazed at me, acknowledging my emotion and nuzzled against my chest. Perhaps my prayers had been heard... or was this just another cruel torment. Had Aetheris been locked up in here, too? Can Nxyaran pets be locked up? Worse, did anyone hear or see her come in? Because we sure as hell weren't getting out!

FIVE

My heart raced as I embraced Aetheris, her warm, familiar fur comforting me in the dark, damp fortress. A sigh of relief escaped my lips as I hugged her close, her purrs a soothing balm to my frayed nerves. But that was my mistake. The sound echoed through the stone corridor outside, louder than it should have been. I froze, my breath catching in my throat.

Footsteps.

Terror settled in my chest like a lead weight. The guard was coming. I had learned the hard way that fighting back was futile; the guards were trained, brutal, and relentless. They took perverse pleasure in punishing any form of resistance.

The footsteps grew louder, more distinct. Each step sent a fresh wave of fear crashing over me. What would they do this time? What punishment awaited? And, worst of all, what would they do to

Aetheris?

I could hear the clinking of keys and the heavy thud of boots stopping outside my cell door. My heart pounded in my chest, every beat a count-down to the inevitable as I turned to Aetheris, now grooming herself with deliberate, unbothered strokes, seeming blissfully unaware of the danger. Her nonchalance was maddening, yet I envied her innocence.

The door swung open with a groan. The guard's silhouette loomed large in the doorway, a dark fig-ure against the faint light from the corridor. Her eyes locked onto mine, cold and devoid of any em-pathy.

"Well, well," she sneered, stepping into the room. "What do we have here?"

I stood, placing myself between the guard and Aetheris, though I knew it was a futile gesture. "I don't know how she found her way in," I said, trying to keep my voice steady.

The guard's gaze shifted to Aetheris, who contin-ued grooming herself, indifferent to her presence.

"Looks like she doesn't share your fear," she chuckled, not at all phased by the feline's unusual size.

"Please," I whispered, the word slipping out before I could stop it. "She is harmless."

The guard took another step forward, her eyes narrowing. "Harmless, you say? We'll see about that."

She reached out to touch Aetheris. Her purrs turned into a sharp hiss, but she remained focused on grooming.

"No!" I lunged forward, but the guard's other hand shot out, backhanding me across the face. I staggered back, the metallic taste of blood filling my mouth.

The guard smirked. "Remember this, prisoner. You are nothing here. And neither is your pet."

A low, menacing growl generated within Aetheris as she coiled her muscular tail around the guard's leg with lightning speed. She barely had time to re-act before Aetheris whipped her into the air, pro-pelling her through the open door and slamming her against the wall on the other side of the corridor with a sickening crunch. The guard crumpled to the floor, lifeless. Aetheris stood over her, eyes glowing with a predatory gleam.

"Okay, I get it," I stood there gaping, part out of respect, part out of fear. "You are no one's pet."

Without thinking, I dashed through the open cell door, my mind singularly focused on escape. It took me until I reached the end of the corridor to realise that Aetheris wasn't following. I turned back with instant regret. Hunched over the guard's body, Aetheris teared into the flesh with a ferocity I had never seen before. Blood splattered the walls as she ripped chunks of meat from the lifeless body, her fur matted with carnage. She was devouring it as if she had been starved for days.

"That is disgusting!" I tried to give my best unimpressed scold, but my trembling voice didn't deliver the tone as well as I had hoped. The sight of her gnawing on the guard's intestines made my stomach churn.

Aetheris stopped and stared at me momentarily, then shimmered and vanished. Well, that's new. My eyes widened in surprise at her invisibility but the carnage didn't disappear with her. All I could see now were chunks of flesh and organs being devoured by a floating mouth surrounded in bloodied fur, adding to the grotesque spectacle.

"Great," I muttered, trying to steady my breathing. "Now I get to watch intestines disappear into thin air. Much better."

Aetheris reappeared, her eyes meeting mine with a look that seemed to tell me to deal with it. The image of her blood-soaked muzzle and the disembodied entrails burned into my mind.

"Well, I need to go," I said, forcing myself to look away from the gruesome scene. "I guess you will have to catch up."

I decided to take her grunt and uninterrupted feasting as acknowledgement. I turned and ran, hearing the faint sound of Aetheris relishing in her fresh meal. Every step echoed the dreadful realisation that escape may be impossible.

No one has ever escaped. I tried to stop my mind from repeating Maren's words. Maren! I hated the thought of leaving her behind in this horrible place. But there was simply no time.

My heart raced as I sprinted down the labyrinthine corridors of the dungeon. Every turn seemed to lead me deeper into the maze. Terror gnawed at my insides as my footsteps echoed in a hollow cadence that mirrored my growing fear. I was hopelessly lost.

The sounds of pursuit echoed from behind—shouts, the clatter of armour, and the heavy thud of boots on stone. I pushed myself harder, the adrenaline-fueled sprint threatening to give way to exhaustion.

I skidded around another corner and collided with a dead end. Frantically, I spun around, retracing my steps, only to find myself at another impasse. The guards' voices were getting closer now, their menace reverberating through the passages.

In desperation, I took a final turn, halting abruptly at the edge of a cliff face. The ground dropped away sharply, revealing the same yawning abyss that we were forced to build bridges over. My heart skipped a few beats. The rock face loomed impassively above me, its jagged surface offering no footholds, no escape. A fall from this height would mean certain death—a grim fate that seemed all too imminent.

I glanced behind me, scanning for any sign of Aetheris, but she was nowhere to be seen. Had she shrunk into invisibility, or... did she leave me here? The uncertainty clawed at me, but there was no time to dwell on it.

"No wonder no one has ever escaped this place," I muttered, the hopelessness of my situation settling like a leaden weight.

I pressed my back against the cold stone of the cliff face, my eyes darting around in a frantic search for a hidden passage, a secret door—anything that might offer a way out. But the dungeon was merciless in its design, offering no solace, no reprieve. Only the unyielding stone and the relentless approach of my pursuers.

The guards closed in on my location. A surge of panic overwhelmed my senses. There was nowhere left to run, no escape route to be found. I was trapped, cornered like a frightened animal.

The first guard approached, her expression twisted in a triumphant sneer. Time had run out. The dim torchlight cast deep shadows across her hardened features, highlighting the glint of her weapon as she levelled it at where her instincts anticipated I would be.

"She's cornered now. There's no way she could have escaped." Her voice cut through the tension like a blade, and her comrades followed confidently.

"Where did she go?" one muttered, eyes scanning the narrow corridor. Confusion flickered across their faces, mingled with frustration and a hint of disbelief.

"I saw her right here," another insisted, her voice tinged with uncertainty.

They spread out, searching every nook and cranny, their weapons held ready. Meanwhile, unseen above the entrance, I desperately clung to the outer rock face.

I grasped dangerously to the tiny crevices just above the cavelike opening. My long, prehensile feet, each toe bearing a strong, curved claw, were ideal for gripping and climbing. Still, my malnourished body was weak, pulling me downward. Every muscle strained against gravity, every breath a silent prayer for strength. One slip, and I die.

The guards' voices grew louder, their footsteps closer now, as they combed the area for any sign of my escape. I dared not move, hardly daring to breathe, as I clutched to my unstable perch. The cold stone pressed against my cheek. Just as I feared their search would look up, revealing my hiding place, a shout rang out—a cry of frustration mixed with disbelief.

"She's gone!"

I heard them leave, their footsteps fading into the distance as they conceded defeat. Relief flooded through me, but I knew my respite was temporary. With trembling hands and renewed determination, I began the slow and painstaking climb downwards.

The rough stone scraped against my hands and knees, threatening to shred my resolve along with my skin. My grip slipped at one particularly precarious moment, and I swung out into open space. My heart leapt into my throat as I scrambled for a hold, my fingers finding purchase just in time to prevent a deadly plunge.

Gasping for breath, I glanced around, my eyes searching for any sign of salvation. That's when I saw her. Aetheris. Perched on a ledge below me, watching with large eyes and almost casual amusement. It was as if she found my predicament comical, which both exasperated and relieved me.

"You could have helped, you know," I called down to her, focusing on my next move. My voice tinged with mock indignation. "Instead of sitting there like you're at a comedy show."

Aetheris tilted her head, a hint of mischief in her eyes. She stretched, her movements fluid and sinuous as if awakening from a nap. Her tail curled gracefully behind her, twitching slightly with each languid stretch. At the same time, her large, expressive eyes gleamed, reflecting intelligence and feline grace. As the muscles beneath her fur rippled across her sleek form, I did a doubletake. Is she... growing?.

In a mesmerising display of her Nxyaran genetics, Aetheris stretched slowly, her form swelling as she transformed to a size large enough to easily accommodate me on her back.

"Fine," I muttered, half to myself and half to her, as I concealed my admiration at her ability to change size at will. "If you're done showing off, how about a lift?"

With a flick of her tail, Aetheris lowered herself slightly, making it easier for me to jump onto her broad back. Settling myself behind her wings, my hands gripped her fur gently for stability as I navigated the unfamiliar perch.

A shout shattered my focus—a returning guard had spotted us. Desperation flooded through me as she bellowed the alarm, her voice reverberating through the corridors, setting off a chain reaction of shouts and footsteps in pursuit. Aetheris tensed beneath me, every muscle coiled with readiness, the urgency of our escape now more pressing than ever.

"Time to go!" I urged, trying to sound more confident than I felt.

As she took a giant leap off the cliff, Aetheris's movements were hesitant, her wings beating with uneven rhythm. I gripped her fur tightly, feeling every uncertain shift and adjustment. The rush of wind roared in my ears, drowning out the distant shouts of the guards below. Aetheris was flying, but she was clearly still learning.

"You sure you've got this?" I called through the

wind, trying to inject humour into my voice.

Aetheris snorted in response, her focus on maintaining altitude evident in the tense set of her powerful shoulders. As she adjusted her wings, we suddenly dropped. I clutched her coast tightly as she corrected our course and shot me an amused glance as if she relished the challenge.

"Just focus," I muttered to myself, accepting her reminder that she knew more about what she was doing than I did.

Swallowing hard, I forced myself to relax into my first feline flight. We pressed forward, the sky swallowing us whole as we journeyed beyond the reach of the dungeon's walls. Aetheris's movements steadied, her wings finding a more confident rhythm. With each beat, we soared further away from captivity and closer to freedom.

The cool air whipped against my face, exhilaration mingling with the lingering fear. I stole a glance behind. The lights of the fortress grew smaller, and the guards were mere specks now, their shouts disappearing into the background as we soared into the unknown.

Aetheris rumbled beneath me with what appeared to be a touch of pride. I couldn't help but grin, relief flooding through me. "Yeah, yeah, you're not half bad for a giant cat."

Aetheris huffed a laugh, the tension easing from her frame as she settled into a rhythm, leaving behind the dark chapter of the dungeon and embracing the uncertain but hopeful future ahead.

Twelve hours of flying left my body aching in ways I never knew possible. We hadn't stopped. Not even when I dozed off and nearly fell. Yet, I wasn't convinced we were far enough from the dungeons to go undiscovered.

Aetheris moved effortlessly as if she could fly forever. I couldn't help but wonder if her strength was boosted by the guard she had consumed. Cringing at the thought, I pushed the image away and forced myself to concentrate on scanning the rugged shoreline for the perfect hiding place. Dark, imposing rocks towered like natural monoliths. Jagged peaks etched against the sky in stark contrast to the smooth, reflective surface of the sea below. Then I saw it!

"There!" I exclaimed, pointing one of my long fingers at a cave in a distant rock formation, its entrance hidden amidst deep grooves and crevices.

Eons of sculpting by relentless forces. Its dark interior promised shelter and a sanctuary from the searching eyes of pursuers.

Aetheris glided closer, allowing me to ascertain the cave's suitability. Its structure was sturdy, composed of dense basalt and volcanic materials that gave it an aura of permanence amidst the ever-changing seas below. Crystalline formations protruded from its walls, catching the dim light and casting shimmering reflections across its interior. Hardy algae clung to the outer surfaces and small creatures scuttled among the fractures, adding to the cave's sense of life and... food.

I felt a surge of relief. This would be our refuge, our hiding place until the pursuit ceased, allowing us time to determine our next steps. With a silent nod of gratitude to my purring companion, we entered the cave, its cool shadows enveloping us like a protective embrace against the uncertainties beyond.

Aetheris landed with surprising grace for her size, her massive wings folding neatly against her sides as she let out a low, rumbling purr. My body felt like a dead weight as I slid off her back. Every muscle screamed in protest, but the promise of rest pulled me forward. My legs wobbled, barely supporting me on the uneven ground. I explored our new refuge with a determined stride. A pony-sized Aetheris stood over me, her eyes sharp and alert, ever vigilant for any signs of danger.

The cave's entrance was narrow but widened considerably as we ventured deeper. Stalactites hung from the ceiling like ancient chandeliers, dripping water that echoed tenderly in the vast space. The ground was littered with pebbles and the occasional bone remnants of creatures seeking shelter here long before us.

Outside waves crashed against the rocks, sending mist into the air and carving new shapes into the mass. During high tide, the sea would flood the entry, surrounding the higher inner caverns in a protective embrace to shield us from enemies.

At low tide, the exposed rock would reveal access to hidden nooks and crannies – ideal hiding places to evade intruders.

The inner cavern walls bore stories and legends from the inhabitants of Nxyara, creating a space that could be viewed as a natural fortress, a sacred site, or simply a place of solitude. More importantly, they whispered promises of safety and anonymity.

I leaned against the rough, cool wall, my fingers tracing the jagged edges of the crystalline formations. I glanced at Aetheris, her eyes glowing in the dark as she curled up protectively near the entrance. She had flown tirelessly, her strength contrasting my own exhaustion.

My eyelids drooped, heavy with the weight of fatigue. I slid down the wall, letting myself sink to the ground. The hard surface was unyielding, but it didn't matter. I was too tired to care. My head lolled back, resting against the cold stone, and I let out a shuddering breath.

Sleep beckoned me, an abyss of oblivion I was all too willing to plunge into. The last thing I remembered was the distant sound of waves crashing against the rocks, a soothing lullaby that drowned out my internal chaos. I closed my eyes, surrendering to the depths of sleep, my body finally giving in to the exhaustion. The darkness wrapped around me, a comforting cocoon that promised rest, if only for a little while.

From this moment, the cave was our world.

A faint, almost imperceptible scuffling dragged me from my exhaustion-induced sleep. I blinked, disoriented, my body aching with the remnants of fatigue. Aetheris was already alert, her ears pricked, eyes gleaming with a predatory light as though imagining the deliciousness of her next meal. She had reduced herself to a more manageable height, her head now level with mine. I rubbed my eyes. The noise grew closer. I forced myself to focus, straining to listen.

Intruders.

I followed Aetheris as best as possible as she maneuvered to the mouth of the internal cave we called home. Straining to see her sleek body blended with the shadows, we crept forward, the cave's darkness masking our approach whilst every muscle in my body protested. The rock wall crevices provided ample cover as we edged closer to the source of the noise.

Through a gap in the rocks, I spotted them: a small group of Neophytes moving cautiously, their eyes scanning the surroundings with wary precision. I counted five, each clad in distinctive yet ancient attire. The intricate designs of their long, flowing garments and the elaborate braids of their hair gave them a commanding presence, and their every movement was deliberate.

Aetheris and I locked eyes, a silent exchange. Were we followed? Are they friends or foes? Their presence was an enigma, their intentions unclear. We couldn't afford to make a wrong move, and one thing was certain: I was not returning to the dungeon.

We advanced with a perceptible united nod, blending seamlessly into the darkness, circling around until we positioned ourselves unseen behind. I selected a sharp rock as a weapon, feeling its comforting weight in my hand. Aetheris tensed beside me, ready to spring into action. We stepped forward, revealing ourselves.

"Stop right there," I commanded, feeling alive due to the adrenaline surging through my veins. "Who are you, and what do you want?"

The group froze, their eyes widening in surprise.

"We're here to help," a tall, imposing figure stepped forward, raising her hands in peace.

I narrowed my eyes, suspicion gnawing at me. "Why should I believe you?"

Aetheris, her sleek, powerful form radiating tension, locked her eyes onto one of the smaller, younger Neophytes, who winced under her fierce gaze. The apprehension in the air was intense, every breath drawn a moment suspended in time. Aetheris's low and menacing growl reverberated through the cavern, making the group tremble.

I could see the fear in the young Neoyphytes eyes, her once confident stance now betraying uncertainty. She tried to step back, but her legs seemed to falter. The anticipation hung thick in the air as Aetheris bared her teeth, a silent promise of what could come next.

The tall Nxyaran held her ground, though I could see the faint flicker of worry cross her features. She glanced at the younger one, then back at me. "Please, call off your creature. We mean no harm."

My heart pounded in my chest. I weighed her words against the fear in the group's eyes and the threat Aetheris posed. Every instinct screamed to trust no one, but there was an undeniable sincerity in the Nxyaran's voice that made me pause.

"It's okay," I reached out to Aehteris gently, my voice steady despite the chaos within.

Aetheris's ears twitched, but she didn't take her eyes off the Neophyte. With an exaggerated sigh, she plopped down on her haunches, tail flicking dramatically. She looked at me, rolling her eyes in the most adolescent way possible, as if to say, *Really? Are we letting them off that easy?*

I stifled a chuckle. "Yes, really," I said softly. "Stand down."

Aetheris let out a huff, shooting one final withering glare at the Nxyarans before settling down on the ground. Her body stretched out, her tail flicking in annoyance at the underwhelming outcome of the situation.

The tension in the cavern eased. The tall Nxyaran let out a breath she seemed to have been holding for far too long. "Thank you," she said, her voice tinged with relief.

I nodded, keeping a wary eye on the group. Aetheris, meanwhile, was doing her best impression of a bored teenager, licking her paw and giving me the occasional side-eye.

"She's a real charmer, isn't she?" one of the others murmured, trying to break the ice. I raised an eyebrow as Aetheris gave a loud, exaggerated yawn to drive the point home.

"Talk," I said, my voice hard. "You have one chance to convince me you're not a threat."

"We've been looking for you since we heard you had escaped," The tall one said earnestly, her hands still raised in a gesture of peace. "We're here to help you."

My eyes narrowed. "How did you know I escaped?" I demanded, my voice laced with suspicion, confident that Drakonis wouldn't allow the news of an escape, let alone my escape, to spread that quickly... if at all.

"We have our ways," she replied, but the uncertainty in her eyes betrayed her.

A wave of confusion and anger surged through me. How could they have known? My escape was spontaneous and only happened less than twenty-four hours ago. Unless... I felt a cold dread creeping up my spine.

"You're lying," I hissed, my voice trembling with barely contained rage. "You have been sent by Drakonis, haven't you?"

"No, it's not like that!" she protested, but it was too late. The seed of doubt had taken root in my mind, blossoming into a full-blown conviction. These Nxyarans were not my rescuers; they were my enemies.

Aetheris sensed my shift in mood and immediately sprang to action, her fur bristling. I felt a cold, detached fury settle over me. There was no room for mercy or hesitation. "Attack!" I commanded, and Aetheris leapt forward with a snarl. I moved with her, my body a blur of motion as I launched myself at the nearest Neophyte. Then everything stopped.

My fists hovered, poised in mid-air, ready to strike with brutal precision fueled by desperation and fear, aimed at the tall Nxyaran frozen before me, her face a mask of shock. I could only shift my eyes to glimpse Aetheris, a whirlwind of claws and teeth suspended in readiness, eager to pounce on her Neophyte prey with savage ferocity. The other four Nxyarans stood like statues, caught in poses of horror or flight.

If this wasn't Aetheris, then what was it? Deep dread and unbridled panic filled my body.

'Enough!' A barely recognisable yet achingly familiar voice bellowed.

As if drifting through a dream, we all gently descended to the ground. Shadows flickered around us, parting to reveal a figure advancing, sceptre in hand, moving as though time held no power over them. A captivating, pale serpent-like creature coiled around the sceptre, its head resting delicately on the crest. Its iridescent scales shimmered softly in the dim light, and hidden wings folded gracefully against its sleek head, heightening its mystical charm. The creature was hypnotic, its body radiating a soothing, golden glow that pulsed with calming energy.

I may not have recognised the voice, but there was no mistaking that sceptre. As the figure stepped further into the light, my heart seemed to stop.

"Nova?"

SIX
DRAKONIS

The door creaked open, and I sensed her presence before I saw her. The timid shuffle of feet, the hesitancy in her steps—telltale signs of fear. I didn't look up from the ancient texts spread before me. The words of my ancestors offered a fleeting solace, a reminder of the order I was sworn to protect.

"High Councillor Drakonis," she began, her voice quivering like a leaf in the wind.

I raised my head slowly, fixing my piercing blue eyes on the Neophyte before me. She flinched, a bead of sweat trickling down her temple. "Speak," I commanded, my tone a blade of ice.

"Zarya...she's escaped," she stammered. "I-I don't know how it happened. She just...disappeared."

The room trembled with the force of my anger as she cowered, her face pale, eyes filling with terror.

"You imbecile!" I spat, stepping around the table

with measured, lethal grace. "Do you have any idea what this means?"

"How could this happen?" My voice echoed off the stone walls as my fist crashed onto the table, scattering the texts.

She shrank back, hitting the wall with a soft thud. I advanced, every step deliberate, my eyes never leaving hers. The room seemed to darken, my presence filling it with an oppressive weight. My snail-like pet, Rune, mindlessly crawling over my shoulder, its lone eyeball swivelling from the middle of its shell, taking in the scene.

"She must be found," I hissed, my voice low and dangerous. "Get me the Councillor in charge of the Dungeons. And if you fail that task, you will wish you had never set foot in this chamber."

She nodded, her body shaking. The sight of her fear fed my anger, but it was not enough. I needed action. I needed results. Rune reached my hand and began to crawl over my fingers. Its cold, slimy trail a bizarrely calming sensation.

"Get out of my sight," I whispered. "And pray that you find Councillor Alaric before I find do."

She stumbled out of the room, leaving the door ajar. I stood in the centre of the chaos I had created, my breath heavy, my mind racing. The ancient texts lay scattered around me, their wisdom forgotten in the face of my rage. Rune slowly made its way back up my arm, its single eyeball gazing at me.

"Courage in adversity," I muttered, more to Rune than myself.

I took a deep breath, forcing my mind to focus. There was work to be done and strategies to be devised. No one must know that escape was possible from the dungeon. Not while I still held power. Not while I still had breath in my body.

It wasn't long before the door to my chamber creaked open once more, and in stepped Councillor Alaric, my Dungeon Master. Her entrance was marked by an air of grim authority, her dark robes flowing around her like a shadow. Her eyes, sharp and calculating, met mine without flinching.

"High Councillor Drakonis," she said, her voice morbid. "You requested my presence?"

I stared at her, my anger barely contained. "Yes, Councillor Alaric. How could you allow Zarya to escape from your dungeons? How could you let anyone escape?

Her face remained emotionless, but I could see the hint of unease in her eyes. "I... I have no explanation. The escape was not anticipated. We are still investigating the breach."

I could feel the rage boiling over again. "Investigating? This is not a matter of simple oversight! This is a catastrophic failure! Your incompetence has endangered our species!"

Her composure faltered, and she stepped forward, her voice rising. "I assure you, High Councillor, this is not a matter of incompetence. I have upheld my duties with utmost precision—"

"Precision? Then how do you explain Zarya's escape?" I roared, my voice reverberating off the walls as Rune continued its slow crawl along my arm, unperturbed by the commotion. "Do you expect me to believe this is the result of mere chance? There has never been an escape from our dungeons! Your negligence is inexcusable!"

Her eyes flashed with frustration. "High Councillor, the conditions in the dungeons are—"

"Do you think I care about conditions?" I cut her off with a thunderous roar. "I entrusted you with the responsibility of containing a dangerous enemy, and you let her slip through your fingers. Do you understand what that means? Do you understand the chaos your failure has unleashed?"

Alaric stepped closer, her jaw clenched, her voice rising in defiance. "You have no idea what challenges we face down there! The dungeons are not infallible, and Zarya's escape was unexpected!"

"Unexpected?" I snapped, my patience fraying. "Do you know what an unexpected escape costs? It costs lives. It costs order! It undermines everything I have worked for, everything I have sacrificed to maintain Nxyara's stability!"

Alaric pointed an elongated finger at me, her anger matching mine as her voice trembled with the strain. "You think you know everything, Drakonis! You sit in your lofty chambers and judge, but you have no idea what it takes to keep the dungeons secure. We face constant threats, and for the first time in history, despite our best efforts—"

"Best efforts?" I bellowed, stepping forward, my imposing figure towering over her. "Your 'best efforts' mock everything Nxyaran guardians represent! If you cannot do your job, you are a liability to us all. And if you think defying me will prove your valour, you are gravely mistaken."

Without hesitation, her eyes furious with rage and resolve, Alaric drew one of the sharp blades sheathed in her robes and, in one seamless move, hurled it toward me with deadly force. The dagger tore through the air, a lethal blur aimed directly at my heart.

Sensing the imminent threat, Rune emitted a

faint, shimmering energy shield. The fatal projectile halted abruptly, mere moments from my chest, its paths precision blocked by Rune's protective barrier. The dagger hung in mid-air, and I fixed Alaric with a cold, unyielding stare, my anger now a controlled, murderous fury.

"Did you truly think you could challenge me so recklessly? Rune's shield is not a mere trinket. It reminds me of my worthiness to rule.... and your stupidity."

The dagger fell to the floor with a sharp clatter, echoing like a death knell. Alaric's defiance shattered, her face a mask of shock and fear. Her bravado crumbled into a pitiful expression of regret.

"You dare to attack me in my own chamber?" I said, my voice a deadly whisper. "Your betrayal is the final proof of your incompetence. You will face the consequences of your actions."

I gestured to my guards. "Take Councillor Alaric to the dungeons. She will stay there until I have some spare time to decide her fate."

The guards moved swiftly, their grip firm as they seized Alaric and began to escort her out. Her protests filled the air, a desperate cry for mercy, but it was futile. Rune continued its slow, composed journey along my arm, its single eyeball gazing at me with a blank, indifferent stare.

The door closed behind them, and the room was silent once more, save for the soft, rhythmic hiss of Rune's movement. My mind was a storm of strategic calculations. I may have made an example of Alaric, but the real work lay ahead. Zarya would be found, and Nxyara's order would be preserved—no matter the cost.

Sitting at my dresser, I gazed into the mirror, observing a reflection that was all too familiar. Intense blue eyes, sharp and unwavering, stared back with calculated intensity. The high cheekbones and strong jawline that defined my face reminded me of my life's dedication to discipline. My floor-length hair was intricately braided, framing my features with regal authority.

I removed my jewellery in preparation for a visit to the dungeon. Each piece held its own significance, and I treated them with the reverence they deserved. Rune began a gradual, reassuring journey across my face as I unclasped a simple, finely crafted ring. Its antennae caressed my skin gently, a rare moment of tenderness in my otherwise solitary existence.

As I watched Runes progress in the mirror, I reflected on how far I had come—from a neophyte with grand ambitions to a staunch traditionalist and leader of Nxyara. Dressed in a sleek dark grey suit with clean lines, exuding authority and professionalism, I removed a delicate pendant bearing the Nxyaran insignia, feeling lighter. I unfastened my earrings, tracing a long scar across my face.

Hiding a discreet tattoo on my left shoulder beneath my jacket, I laced up practical yet stylish boots, completing an ensemble that allowed me to move with purpose and confidence over rugged terrain. The dungeon was no place for fashion.

Anger fuelled my determination to interrogate prisoners myself. I checked my appearance, reprimanding myself for lashing out impulsively. That was against my nature. I was the kind who planned meticulously, ensuring that my response to any provocation was effective, decisive, and brutal.

Feeling the familiar weight of the royal sceptre in my hand, I marvelled at its craftsmanship. It was exquisite, fashioned from a single piece of gleaming obsidian and inlaid with a delicate filigree of pure gold, winding its way up the shaft like tendrils of ivy. At its top sat a large, perfectly cut ruby that caught the light, casting a kaleidoscope of colours across the room. The sceptre's handle was wrapped in rich, deep purple velvet, worn smooth from years of use by the royal lineage.

I glanced at Rune, who was now exploring my forearm. Its eerie eyeball continually shifted with an unreadable expression as it followed my movements. The combination of the enigmatic, living creature and the ancient, powerful artifact filled me with a sense of invincibility.

"If you venture into the dungeon like that, you'll be devoured by some critter... or stood on!" I said matter-of-factly as I plucked Rune off my body and threw it into the air, watching as it glided smoothly down to the ground, unphased.

As it fell, Rune began to change. Stretching towards the ceiling, elongating and expanding. It's soft body hardened, becoming more defined and intricate, like the ridges and grooves of ancient bark. Its shell spread outwards, swirling with shades of green and blue, reflecting the dim light like a precious gem and forming a flowing robe, the single, all-seeing eyeball positioned in the centre of its back. Standing slightly below me. The creature before me was majestic, with a humanoid form, though still reminiscent of a snail's, exhibiting a depth of wisdom and strength.

With the transformation complete, Rune's antennae twitched as it gazed at me with a profound understanding that seemed to transcend words. It drew closer, its presence both soothing and commanding, offering an almost palpable comfort. Yet, beneath that comfort lingered a simmering frustration—Rune knew my troubles and likely held the answers. Still, its silence left me grappling for the guidance I desperately needed.

I turned back to the mirror, my heart a battleground of doubt and determination. Clinging to our traditions felt increasingly precarious, a choice weighed against the possibility that Zarya might be right. Though I'd never admit it aloud, the gnawing uncertainty was an ever-growing shadow at the edge of my resolve.

Rune's antennae brushed against my cheek, a small but potent gesture of reassurance. I steadied myself, forcing calm into the tumult of my mind. Trust your instincts, I admonished. Lifting my crown carefully from an ornate chest, admiring its grandeur as I placed it atop my head.

It was a detailed, majestic headpiece that framed my face with two prominent, curved tusk-like structures extending from the sides, curling upward and inward with delicate latticework connecting them. It rested upon my forehead, integrating seamlessly with my hairstyle and giving me a renewed surge of resolve.

Striding out of my quarters, Rune by my side, my determination was as cold and unyielding as the sceptre I carried. The guards' salutes went unnoticed as I swept past, entering the dimly lit corridor of the council chambers. Shadows seemed to recoil from my presence, retreating as if driven back by my formidable aura.

I felt no fear with Rune's protective shield, now amplified due to its transformed state, expanding and contracting as needed to ensure my safety. The ultimate bodyguard, I thought with a silent, satisfied huff. My eyes, sharp as blades, surveyed the path ahead,. There was no room for compromise.

With a flick of my wrist, I summoned a spark from the sceptre which hovered before descending to the ground, its light merging with the encroaching darkness. My eyes followed as it led the way, a shiver of anticipation running up my spine whenever I reflected on the combination of my power and Runes' shield. I was unstoppable. I yanked the door open with a forceful motion, the creak of its hinges echoing like a precursor of doom.

As I descended into the dungeon, the air grew cold and thick with the scent of damp earth and ancient decay. Torches flared to life along the walls as I passed, their flames dancing nervously in the draft. The sceptre crackled with a barely contained energy, its hum a dark promise of the wrath I was prepared to unleash.

Navigating the labyrinthine with deliberate intent, I focused on the answers I sought. Every twist and turn of the winding passageways only reinforced my conviction, with anger simmering just beneath the surface, poised to erupt if provoked. Rune kept pace with me effortlessly, its presence a silent, reassuring shadow.

At last, I arrived at the entrance of the dungeon. An ancient door covered in arcane symbols awaited my command. My lips curled into a cold, predatory smile. Here, there were no rules, and that gave me immense pleasure.

I invoked the symbols etched into the door with a decisive gesture, and they glowed fiercely in response. The door creaked open, revealing a dark, oppressive corridor which seemed to stretch into the planet's core. I stepped inside, eyes flaring with determination as I prepared to solve the puzzle of Zarya's escape—the only escape in Nxyara's history.

The air was thick with a vile stench of decaying flesh, mould, and stagnant water that clung to the walls and seeped into the bones of those unfortunate enough to be trapped within. The sceptre's spark continued to lead the way, casting long, wavering shadows that transformed every crevice into a menacing shape that danced and writhed with each step. The corridor torches were grimy, their flames struggling to burn through the oppressive darkness.

The stone walls, once imposing, were now crumbling and streaked with dampness. Chains clanked rhythmically in the distance, echoing off the walls like a grim symphony of despair. The iron bars of the cells were rusted and encrusted with grime. Their strength diminished by time and neglect. Each cell was a dark, claustrophobic box, barely large enough to hold its occupant.

I found the putrid odour, a blend of unwashed bodies and the insidious stench of human waste, welcoming as it clung to my nostrils. Deep satisfaction overcame me as the dim light revealed the gaunt, hollow-eyed faces of prisoners, their expressions a mix of hopelessness and defiance. Huddled in the corners and shivering against the damp stone, their tattered rags clung to their skeletal forms.

The sound of dripping water was constant, its rhythm irregular and unsettling, mingling with the muffled groans and occasional cries of the condemned. The floor was slick with a dark, stagnant liquid that made each step a careful maneuver, the foul substance splashing with an unpleasant squelch.

I stretched out my hand to greet the vermin, who scurried into the corners, their tiny claws clicking against the stone. The dampness of the dungeon, combined with the stench and the sounds of suffering, created an environment so brutal and unrelenting—and it filled me with pride.

"At least I can rely on something to do its job," I muttered to Rune, who slid beside me through the filth, expressionless and apathetic.

"Show me the prisoners!" I demanded, my voice cutting through the stale air like a blade.

A Neophyte guard with a pallid face stumbled back, her confusion evident. "P-prisoners, High Councillor? We weren't—"

I silenced her with a gesture of my hand. She exchanged frantic glances with her fellow guards, their unease rapidly mounting as they were clearly unprepared for my visit yet fully aware of their imminent punishment if they failed to comply. Unable to contain my frustration, I stepped closer, my eyes narrowing to cold slits.

"Do I need to repeat myself?" Laced with restrained fury, my voice reverberated through the stone corridors, causing the guards to flinch.

"High Councillor Drakonis, please, allow me to handle this," Captain Harlan, a veteran guard with a face marked by years of harsh duty, stepped forward with a hesitant yet determined stride. Her voice was steady despite the tremor in her hands, and her eyes, though full of trepidation, held a glimmer of resolve.

"Follow me." Harlan gestured, her movements precise and deliberate as she led the way. The other guards fell into a disordered line behind us, their eyes shifting nervously between each other.

We entered a particularly grim room filled with prisoners. Their haunted eyes, locked onto me with a mix of terror and disbelief. Faint sobs of the less resilient ones created a symphony of despair that reverberated through the dungeon.

"Here," Harlan said, positioning herself against the wall making it clear her role was that of an observer, not participant.

The prisoners huddled within were trembling, their ragged clothing barely covering their bodies. The dank air was thick with their fear, a stark contrast to the stoic calm I projected. I could see the mixture of hope and dread in their eyes as they caught sight of Rune, hovering menacingly beside me. This was going to be fun.

"Please," one of the prisoners, a Primevex with hollow eyes, whimpered, her voice almost a whisper. "What do you want with us?"

"You should consider yourselves lucky that I'm here," I said with an icy smile, my gaze sharp and unyielding. "There's been a breach in this very sanctuary that has kept you safe—a sanctuary that has shielded you from those who wish revenge for your past behaviours."

"I've come to investigate and fix this issue for your protection. Tell me what I want to know, and I might spare you. Remain silent, and you'll face the consequences of your defiance."

Immediately, the guards pulled a random prisoner from the trembling group, her eyes bursting with terror, as she was thrust before me. Her ragged breaths came in shallow gasps, and her eyes darted between me and the looming figure of Rune, who seemed to pulse with malevolent intent.

"Tell me," I said, my voice a cold whisper that carried a dark promise. "How did Zarya escape?"

The prisoner's face contorted in confusion and fear. She stammered, "I—I don't know, High Councillor. I swear, I don't know anything about it!"

"How fortunate for you." I smiled.

The prisoner's excuses were cut short as I brought my blade down with precise, deadly force. The execution was quick but not without brutal artistry. Blood splattered against the stone walls, darkening the damp surface with its stark crimson contrast. The Primevexes body slumped to the ground, lifeless.

The guards and the remaining prisoners stood frozen in horror, their faces pale and their breaths caught in their throats. I left the body where it fell, the blood pooling around it like a grotesque halo. The sight was both a warning and a promise that spoke of the dark consequences awaiting anyone who did not give me the information I sought.

"Next," I commanded, my voice unwavering despite the carnage, and the guards moved to pull another prisoner from the group. Harlan rested expressionless against the wall as a Neophyte with tear-filled eyes was dragged forward.

I surveyed her with a detached, almost clinical interest. "How did Zarya escape?" I asked again, my voice cold and unfeeling.

She stammered, her voice barely more than a whisper, "I—I don't know! Please, I don't know anything!"

I didn't wait for more. My blade flashed once more, slicing through the air with death-dealing velocity. The Neophyte's last cry was a haunting echo that filled the dungeon as her life was extinguished. The blood sprayed across the floor, mingling with that of the previous victim, creating a hostile scene of despair and death.

The guards worked to pull yet another prisoner from the group. Each execution was a grim performance, my enjoyment evident in the meticulousness of my movements and the cold satisfaction I took in their fear. The dungeon was alive with the sounds of terror and the pong of blood, each death a dark, uncompromising statement of my power and resolve.

As I moved from one prisoner to the next, my blade danced with a merciless grace, each strike delivering a final, bloody message. The bodies piled up as the dungeon, once a place of confinement, became a stage for a morbid display of power.

The remaining prisoners could only watch with dismay and anguish as their companions fell one by one, their own fate hanging in the balance with every blood-soaked step I took.

"Next," I commanded.

A sense of familiarity overcame me as I studied the Primevex, who had been thrust before me. "Maren! How delighted I am to see you in this circumstance." My voice was smooth and dripping with a chilling satisfaction.

Once my most trusted advisor, Maren was a confidante who had played a crucial role in consolidating my power and enforcing my will. However, her ambitions had extended beyond mere advisory roles; she had harboured secret plans to undermine me and seize control for herself. Her actions were a direct threat to my rule and a personal betrayal. I should have killed her then. Instead, I will kill her now.

"She!" exclaimed one of the Primevex prisoners, her accusatory tone tinged with hope. "She was always with Zarya! Talking in secret as they ate!"

Ignoring the desperate attempt for salvation, I raised my blade. The thrill of power and retribution surged through me as I prepared to bring the blade down with a satisfying finality. Maren's pleading was music to my ears.

"Enough!" A voice rang out, cutting through the oppressive gloom. Commanding and frantic, the tone leaving no room for hesitation. The guards froze, their faces masks of bewildered fear.

The sudden appearance of an Octaryan between my blade and Maren was as startling as it was dangerous. Not to mention audaciously disrespectful.

I dropped my blade slowly, my expression shifting from cold surprise to intense irritation as all eight eyes, locked onto me.

"Stop this madness," the Octaryan demanded, eyes filled with fierce determination. "These deaths are an unjust spectacle. None of us know the information you seek."

I narrowed my eyes in dark amusement. "How noble," I said, dripping with sarcasm. "And what a shame. Rune?"

Without warning, Rune's bark-like texture smoothed and turned deathly black. Dark energy emanated from the cloak's shellwork as it mentally coerced those around us, seizing control of their very will to live and extinguishing their desire to breathe. It was a subtle but devastating manipulation.

One by one, those in the room began to falter.

Their eyes glazed over, and they crumbled to the floor, gasping futilely for air that would no longer sustain them. In a matter of seconds, the cell was littered with motionless, lifeless bodies. Only Harlen, the Octaryan, and I remained untouched by Rune's deadly influence.

A deep satisfaction spread across my face as I stood, bloodstained and resolute. I knew I had uncovered the truth: answers lay hidden, but not here.

Harlen let out an exasperated huff and walked away, clearly unimpressed. She had witnessed Rune's mind-control powers before and was obviously unimpressed by the sudden necessity to recruit and train new guards. Dungeon duty wasn't exactly what Nxyarans willingly signed up for.

I turned my attention to the Octaryan, who hadn't moved.

"You're quite resilient," I said, cold amusement dripping from my voice. I stepped closer, doing my best to look into all eight eyes concurrently, my blade slick with blood.

"You are now the last of your kind—your freakish, disgusting, multi-focal kind. Your continued existence is not a sign of favour but a warning to anyone who dares to challenge my authority."

The Octaryan blinked her eyes simultaneously.

She remained silent, processing the gravity of what had just transpired, as I circled her in a predatory manner.

"Living with the knowledge the your actions led to the extermination of both the Hexaryan and Octaryan classes is your punishment," I hissed. "Nauseating classes that, thanks to the renewal ceremony, will never exist again."

I watched her with satisfaction, revelling in the success of my brilliant strategy of using the Primevex class to eliminate the Elder class in a 'Renewal Ceremony' before they became…*this!*

It had been an unexpected, yet welcome, turn of events when the Elders willingly offered themselves for sacrifice believing it would ensure the survival of the Nxyaran race.

The belief that only a Primevex could self-generate, and only once they had taken an Elder's life at the renewal ceremony, had formed naturally and suited me perfectly. I shuddered at the thought of how my rule would be affected should every Nxyaran self-generate at whim.

The thought of becoming the sole Nxyaran to evolve into the Hextaryan and Octaryan class – and whatever class came next - filled me with a self-satisfied grin. One day, I would be the only evolved Nxyaran and revered as a true visionary, surpassing all others. I smiled, savouring the anticipation of the power and admiration that awaited me.

"You'll remain here, alone and forgotten," I straightened, casting a final, disdainful glance at the Octaryan.

With that, I turned on my heel and strode toward the exit, Rune close behind. As I walked away, my mind already focused on the next steps of my ruthless campaign, her eight haunted eyes followed me, silently acknowledging the inescapable reality she now faced.

SEVEN

Nova and I sat by the crackling fire. The soft glow casting a warm, comforting light that danced on the cavern walls. Aetheris and Solvyr were a blur of motion, and my heart swelled with joy as I watched them reunite. I had forgotten they were also separated from each other when they were taken from us years ago. Pets evolved solo to ensure the survival of the fittest. Many didn't return, making them rare and precious in Nxyara.

Ruffling his sleek fur, Aetheris pounced at Solvyr with mock ferocity. The white snake gracefully slithered and weaved with impressive speed, keeping its feathered wings hidden close to its head. They tumbled over each other, a tangled mass of fur, feathers, and scales full of contagious, exuberant energy.

The game continued as the playmates practised their predatory instincts and newfound abilities. Rolling onto her back, Aetheris batted at her friend with her paws. Lightly fluttering her feathered wings, Solvyr nipped playfully at the large feline's ears, tiny fangs harmlessly grazing the fur.

I glanced over at Nova, catching her eye, and we shared a knowing smile. The bond between our pets, their unfiltered joy and innocence, was reminiscent of our own emotional reunion only moments ago.

The firelight flickered, casting long shadows as the rest of our group set up camp, arranging bed-rolls and eating around their fires. Laughter and conversation filled the air, creating a symphony of camaraderie that resonated deep within me.

Aetheris let out a playful growl as Solvyr flicked his tongue and coiled away, only to dart back in and wrap around the feline's legs in a friendly embrace. Their tussling grew more intense yet remained full of that same joyful energy. This simple moment of happiness was priceless.

I couldn't tear my eyes away from my friend, the questions swirling in my mind were too loud to ig-nore. Taking a deep breath, I shifted closer.

"How are you still alive? I thought... I thought you were gone," my voice a whisper.

Nova looked up, her eyes meeting mine with a calm intensity. She paused as if searching for the right words.

"It's a long story and not easy to tell," Nova sighed.

I leaned in, my heart pounding. "I need to know, Nova. Please."

She nodded slowly, her gaze distant as she began.

"I thought I was done for. There was so much blood, and they were dragging you away. I must have passed out as they took Rhea. The next thing I knew, Solvyr was wrapped around me. Turns out my little scaly friend here can grow drastically in size and heal." Nova patted Solyer appreciatively on the head, the snake oozing love and satisfaction.

"I never knew that pets have abilities," she continued, scratching Solvyr under the chin. "She mended wounds that should have taken my life."

I stared at her, disbelief etched across my face. "I didn't know pets had abilities either. It must onset at adulthood." I looked over at Aetheris, curled up near the fire as she groomed her wings, exhausted from the play.

"So far, I have seen Aetheris change into some incredible sizes, carry me in flight and turn invisible. That time freeze earlier was that...

"Solvyr? Yes." Nova nodded proudly. "She can only sustain it for a very short time, though."

"I wonder how many pets there are," I muttered

out loud.

"I don't know," Nova shook her head, evident that she had asked herself the same question. "Solvyr was still healing me when a group of rebels found us. They took me in and helped me recover fully."

Rebels. In the past, the very thought would have horrified me. But wasn't that precisely what I was now? A rebel? Branded like livestock for all to judge. I rolled my shoulder, feeling the phantom pain of the scar as if it were freshly seared into my skin. The intense agony from the branding iron's touch resurfaced in my memory. I shuddered.

"At first, I was terrified, but I didn't have the strength to fight or run. I trusted Solvyr to protect me if anything untoward happened," Nova paused, reflecting on her experience. "They are not the barbarians we have been taught to fear. Time with them has shown me a different side of our world."

"When you didn't come to see me, I thought you were dead. I mourned you every day, and all the while, you were out playing house with the rebels?" I said, my voice trembling with the deep hurt of being abandoned in the dungeon. "I never imagined you as someone who would stay with rebels. Not for long, anyway."

Nova reached out, her hand covering mine. "It

wasn't an easy decision. I wanted to return to you, to everyone. But I had to learn how Drakonis used us and how the High Council pulled the strings. I had to understand their tactics. The rebels showed me methods of fighting back, which I would never have imagined. If I had returned too soon, we would be unable to fight back."

The weight of her words settled over me, a mix of relief and confusion.

"So, knowing I was rotting away in the dungeon all this time, you were with them? Learning... what?"

Nova's eyes flashed with anger and frustration. "Learning how to survive! Learning how to fight for our freedom! Do you think it was easy for me? Do you think I didn't think about you every single day?" Her voice rose, cutting through the tension in the air.

"You had a choice, Nova! You could have come back and tried to help me!" I shot back, the anger and betrayal I had felt for so long now boiling over. "I was suffering, imprisoned, thinking you were dead. You don't understand what life was like there. If you could call it life at all!"

"I had no choice!" Nova yelled, her voice filled with emotion.

"If I had come back, they would have caught me

too, and then where would we be? Both of us rotting in that dungeon? I did what I had to do for the greater good, for our freedom!"

"Freedom?" I scoffed, my bitterness evident. "What good is freedom if we lose everything and everyone we care about in the process?"

The air between us crackled with tension. Our words had struck deep, unearthing raw emotions buried for too long. Without thinking, my body moved on instinct, driven by a primal urge to release the storm of emotions brewing inside me.

"What good is freedom if it means abandoning those who need you the most!" I hissed, my voice a low growl as I positioned myself to attack.

Nova's eyes widened, surprise flickering before hardening into determination. "If that's what it takes," she replied, stepping back and raising her hands in a defensive stance.

Without warning, I lunged forward, my fist aiming for her jaw. The seasoned warrior sidestepped with grace and I stumbled past her, my weakened body protesting the sudden exertion. I turned quickly, barely catching her next move, as she swung her leg in a sweeping arc. I felt the impact as her foot connected with my ribs, the force sending a jolt of pain through my side.

I gasped, the taste of iron filling my mouth. I spat blood onto the ground, my vision blurring for a moment. But anger fueled me, pushing past the pain. I advanced again, this time feinting a punch before driving my knee towards her midsection. She anticipated the move, catching my leg and twisting it sharply. I cried out, losing my balance and crashing to the ground.

The dirt was cold and rough beneath me, but I forced myself up, refusing to give in. I ignored my muscles as they screamed in protest, focusing solely on Nova as she came at me again. I barely managed to deflect her fluid and precise movements, each impact resonating through my bones like a drumbeat.

Sweat and blood mingled, stinging my eyes. I could hear the rapid thud of our heartbeats, the laboured breathing and the grunts of exertion. My vision tunnelled, focusing only on Nova and the determination etched across her face.

She caught me off guard with a swift elbow to the temple, stars exploding in my vision. I staggered, and she took the opportunity to sweep my legs out from under me. I hit the ground hard, and the wind knocked from my lungs. My body screaming in agony as I gasped for air.

Nova straddled me, pinning my arms to the

ground. Her weight pressed down on me, her face inches from mine, her breath hot and ragged. "I never wanted this, Zarya," she panted.

My vision swam, the edges darkening. I struggled beneath her, but my body was giving out. Desperation clawed at me, but it was no use. Nova had me pinned, and I was too weak to fight.

"Stop!" Rhea's voice rang out, clear and commanding just as I was about to give in. A couple of Primevexs rushed forward, grabbing Nova's arm and pulling her off me. I lay there, gasping, my body trembling with exhaustion and pain.

"Enough, both of you!" Rhea yelled, her eyes blazing with fury. "This isn't the way to solve anything!"

Nova stood, breathing heavily, her face a mask of conflicting emotions. She looked down at me, her eyes filled with regret. "I'm sorry," she whispered, her voice barely audible.

I closed my eyes, the fight leaving my body as the pain and exhaustion took over. I could feel Rhea's hands lifting me gently.

"We'll figure this out," she murmured. "But not like this. Never like this."

I blinked at Rhea, my breath catching in my throat. She was almost unrecognisable. Gone was the familiar sight of her round face framed by auburn hair.

Her skin, now shimmered with a metallic sheen, like the surface of a precious gem. It was as if she had been sculpted from stardust and moonlight. A stunning figure that seemed to have stepped out of a dream—or a nightmare, depending on how one looked at it.

The roundness of her face had given way to sharper, more defined features, accentuating a beauty that was both mesmerising and unsettling. But it was her eyes that truly took my breath away.

No longer the warm brown pools that conveyed her every thought and feeling, they now shone with an intense, icy blue light, as if they contained the essence of the cosmos. They stared at me with a depth and intensity that made me feel like she could see straight into my soul.

Her hair, if it could still be called that, had transformed into a cascade of tendrils, each seemingly with a life of its own. They framed her face like a halo. The practical coveralls of the past were replaced by an intricate, form-fitting suit that appeared to merge with her skin, composed of sleek, dark materials interwoven with delicate threads.

My astonishment must have been evident as

Rhea tilted her head slightly, a small, knowing smile tugging at the corners of her lips. Her transformation was beyond anything I could have imagined. I struggled to reconcile this new image with the Rhea I had known. The Rhea who had been powerless against Drakonis' guards as they dragged me away that fateful day so many years ago.

"Zarya," she said, her voice so soft it resonated within my bones. "It's still me."

I nodded, swallowing hard as I tried to find my voice. "What happened to you?"

Her smile widened, and she leaned closer, the threads of her suit shifting with her movements like liquid light. "It's a long story, but I'm still the same person inside."

I reached out, my fingers trembling as they brushed against her arm. The sensation was comforting yet utterly unfamiliar.

"You're...incredible," I whispered, my eyes locked onto hers as I tried to determine if what I was seeing was real or the result of a concussion.

Rhea laughed softly, "And you, my friend, are as resilient as ever. We have much to discuss, but for now, know I am here and will always stand by your side."

I nodded again, then passed out.

I awoke to the pressure of Solvyr coiled around me, her scales cool against my skin. Fear spiked through me, but Nova's words quickly resurfaced. Turns out my little scaly friend here can ... heal.

Aetheris stood guard at my feet, eyes sharp and vigilant, filling me with an overwhelming gratitude. The cave buzzed with activity as our small group undertook their assigned tasks, faces set with determination. How long had I been out? The last thing I remembered was the desperate fight, the blinding pain, and then... darkness.

"Well, look who finally decided to join us," Nova's voice sliced through the haze, approaching with an amused yet worried smile. "After all those failed missions to get you out of that dungeon, you decide to tap out? Not on my watch!"

Her words struck a chord. "You said missions. Plural." I croaked, my voice hoarse.

"Ah, her body may be weak, but there's nothing wrong with her mind," Rhea interrupted, eyes scanning me with concern as she knelt beside me. Solvyr slid off, tasting my cheek with its forked tongue before coiling around Nova's staff, resting her head on the top, clearly exhausted but ever watchful.

"Rhea," I murmured, relief flooding through me. Her appearance hadn't been a dream. "You look amazing!"

She blushed under my gaze, but her hands were steady as she helped me sit up. "Here, drink this," she said, passing me a steaming bowl of soup. "You need to rest."

I took the bowl, feeling the warmth seep into my hands. Rhea's touch was gentle, her concern genuine. The camaraderie in the cave contrasted with the cold isolation I had grown accustomed to. I glanced at Nova as she spoke to Aetheris about guarding me as if she was expecting her to respond. Then I turned my eyes to Solvyr, who appeared very much at home on Nova's staff, her head bobbing reassuringly.

Aetheris nuzzled my leg, her tail flicking with irritation and affection. "You too, Aetheris," I whispered, stroking her head. The creature purred softly, its guard lowered to reassure me that I wasn't alone. We were in this together.

"How long have I been out?" I asked.

"A few days," Rhea answered, standing behind Nova, who had settled beside me with a resigned smile. The curiosity bubbled inside me as Aetheris reduced her size and settled onto my lap.

"So," I began, still raspy but determined, "tell me about these missions. You said they were failures. I want to know what happened because earlier, you made it abundantly clear that you made no attempts to find me."

"Right...," Nova drew out the word, then chuckled softly. It was as if our fight had never happened.

"Where do I start?" she said, her eyes sparkling with amusement and exhaustion. "The first mission was an absolute disaster. We tried to breach the dungeon's outer defences under the cover of night. We had a map, a plan, and a lot of bravado."

"Until we were nearly caught by the dungeon guards," Rhea chimed in, her tone light but her eyes intense. "I had to use every engineering trick I knew to get us out of there."

Nova grinned at Rhea's interjection. "Right. So we snuck in, dodging patrols and slipping through traps, only to find out that the map was outdated. The cells where we thought you'd be were empty. We almost got trapped ourselves trying to escape. Remember that, Solvyr?"

Solvyr's head bobbed in what looked like an embarrassed nod as if acknowledging her role in that chaotic night. Her forked tongue flicked out to taste the air, a playful glint in her eyes.

"That was just the first try," Nova continued, a wistful tone creeping into her voice. "The second mission involved disguising ourselves as guards. We thought we could blend in and gather information, but let's just say we weren't very convincing and were discovered pretty quickly."

Rhea laughed softly. "You should have seen Nova trying to convince them she was an authority figure. It was rather amusing, but we had to make a hasty retreat. We almost got caught when Solvyr's tail knocked over a stack of supplies."

Aetheris looked up from my lap, flicking her tail in what appeared to be an acknowledgement of how difficult tails could be.

"Then there was the third mission," Nova said, her tone shifting to something more sombre. "We tried a different approach, this time aiming for a more direct assault. We managed to get inside, but the dungeon was on high alert. We fought our way through but were met with an overwhelming force just as we reached the corridor to your cell."

"You got that close?" Conflicting emotions rose within me.

"Solvyr did its best to protect us, but it was like fighting against the tide," Rhea's voice was low.

"We had to retreat before we could get you out. We learned a lot from that attempt but nearly lost Solvyr in the process."

The thought of losing Solvyr, or any pet, tugged at my heart. I reached out and touched her incredible scales, murmuring my thanks.

"And then there was the last mission," Nova said, a hint of pride in her voice. "We came up with what we thought was a foolproof plan, and everything was set perfectly, but..."

Her voice trailed off as she glanced at Rhea, who stepped in with a solemn nod. "There was a betrayal," Rhea explained gently. "A member of our group, who had seemed trustworthy, turned against us. They leaked our plans to Councillor Alaric, and the dungeon's defences were fortified. We were ambushed and had to abandon the mission."

I felt a pang of disappointment but also admiration for their resilience. "You went through all that just for me," I said, my voice thick with emotion. "Thank you."

Nova's smile was both sad and proud. "We couldn't have done it without the Rebels," she said softly. "They weren't giving up on you, no matter how many times we had to try. You are one of them now. But it looks like Aetheris's covert mission won in the end. We didn't even know she was back."

Aetheris let out a soft, contented purr, her eyes half-closing as if she were reminiscing about past adventures.

"You have to tell us what life was like in the dungeon. What did they do to you? How can we use what you know to stop Drakonis?" Nova persisted.

Drakonis. I had almost forgotten about her. I shifted my weight.

"Not right now. You need to rest," Rhea said, her tone gentle but firm. "There'll be time for more stories later."

I nodded, feeling the weight of their efforts and the warmth of their companionship. As I settled back, the cave seemed to hum with a quiet promise of safety and the comfort of shared struggles. We were together again, and that was enough for now.

I could hardly breathe, my heart pounding against my ribs as I finished recounting the horrors of the dungeon and the work we were forced to do there. The firelight flickered across the rugged faces of my audience, casting deep shadows in our cave. Nova and Rhea's expressions were a tangled mess of disbelief and profound sadness.

Nova's normally stoic demeanour cracked, revealing a warrior overwhelmed by the weight of my words. She clenched her jaw, hands trembling as she struggled to maintain composure. The deep furrow of her brow told me that she was wrestling with the implications of what I had just shared.

Rhea was less restrained. Her face paled as if the blood had drained from her veins. Her usual confident posture slumped, and her eyes filled with tears that she did nothing to hide. She shook her head slowly, her breath coming in short, sharp gasps. "It can't be true," she whispered, more to herself than anyone else. "All this time..."

I could see the gears turning in her mind, trying to reconcile her experiences with the grim reality I had laid bare. Rhea had advocated using technology to assist the High Council in protecting Nxyarans. The notion that these supposed protectors could be so complicit in Nxyaran suffering seemed almost too much for her to bear.

Nova reached out, placing a steadying hand on Rhea's shoulder, but her gaze remained fixed on me. Her eyes now seemed distant and hollow.

"Zarya," her voice was rough and broken, "this changes everything."

I swallowed hard, the sting of her words cutting deeper than I expected. "I know," I said, my voice barely above a whisper, "but there is more."

The weight of the revelation I was about to share pressed down on me like a physical burden.

"Nova, Rhea," I began, my voice steady yet tinged with the urgency of the truth I had uncovered, "there's something you both need to know. What we've been taught, what we've believed for so long, is a lie."

Nova's eyes widened with curiosity and concern. At the same time, Rhea's brows furrowed, her analytical mind already racing ahead, trying to piece together what I might say next.

"In the dungeon, there are advanced forms of our own kind—what we are meant to become," I paused, letting the impact of my words sink in. "The prisoners call them Hexaryans and Octaryans. They are the next two generations after the Elder class. They are real. They are us."

Nova glanced at Rhea's hand; her knuckles whitening as she tightened her grip around the data crystal she always carried.

"What do they look like?" Nova asked, her voice barely above a whisper.

"The Hexaryans," I began, "are way taller and

more agile than us. They have high cheekbones, prominent foreheads, and six black eyes that move independently, always scanning their surroundings. Their long, pointed ears and black lips make them look almost extraterrestrial. They also have these shiny black tusk-like appendages. They're both beautiful and terrifying. I felt like observer and prey whenever I was in the same room."

Rhea's eyes widened as she absorbed this information. "And the Octaryans?"

"Even more commanding and unnerving than the others," I continued. "Octaryans have eight eyes arranged in a hypnotic pattern, giving them an all-knowing aura. It feels like they can see right into your soul. Their smooth, pale faces have dramatically tilted ears, giving them a sinister look. Their noses are almost invisible, and their lips are pitch-black, surrounded by tattoos. They look like dark, majestic demigods. They are what I would call... perfect."

"Why haven't we seen them?" Rhea interjected, her voice trembling with the need for answers.

"Because they were eliminated," I replied, my tone sombre. "The slaughter of our elders at the Renewal ceremony has nothing to do with ensuring the self-generation process. It is a deliberate act to stop us from evolving into our next form. It is... genocide."

Nova gasped, and Rhea's eyes darkened with anger.

"Genocide?" Rhea repeated, her voice shaking. "But why? Who would do such a thing?"

"It has to be Drakonis," I continued, my heart pounding in my chest. "By keeping this knowledge from us she maintains control, fearing the power and potential of our evolution. The Renewal ceremony is a twisted murder ritual to prevent the progression of our species. When they tell us it is about purging the weak to strengthen the line, they really mean keeping us from attaining our true potential."

"So, we can self-generate at any time." Rhea shook her head in disbelief.

"Apparently," I nodded. "Once we have the ability and know-how, we can trigger the transformation, but the knowledge has been kept from us for who knows how long? Considering the estimated ages of the Octayrans, I dare say this has been happening for generations."

Nova's eyes blazed as she stepped closer, her fingers gripping mine tightly. "What are we going to do about it?" she demanded impatiently.

I pulled my hand away, trying to steady my own

rising anger.

"We uncover the truth about who knows what. It can't only be Drakonis. We must discover who's behind this and why. Then we can prepare to end this cycle of oppression and deceit."

Standing beside us, Rhea nodded, her eyes burning with determination. But Nova wasn't satisfied. Her face flushed with anger as she leaned in.

"We don't have time for this, Zarya. We've been talking about 'uncovering the truth' for too long. Every moment we waste is another chance for them to tighten their grip. We must act now—raise an army with the rebels, show them we're ready to fight back!"

My gaze hardened, and I stepped back, feeling a storm brewing inside me. "Raise an army? Is that all you think it takes? Do you think a few skirmishes will topple an entire regime? We need to be strategic. We need to find the head of the serpent before we can chop it off!"

Solvyr seemed to cringe, and I silently reprimanded myself for using such a poor analogy.

"We have been strategising for decades while you were in the dungeon!" Nova's face was a mask of fury. "We must stop the next slaughter, or have you forgotten about Elana already? We must show strength and make Drakonis understand we're ready to fight!"

"And you think throwing ourselves into battle without a plan will make a difference?" My voice rose, sharp and fierce.

"You're so blinded by impatience that you can't see the bigger picture! If we don't identify who's pulling the strings, all our efforts will be for nothing. We'll just be pawns in their game!"

Nova's fists clenched, her breath coming in quick, angry bursts.

"You think I don't understand the risks?" She glared. "We have all seen the bloodshed of the 'Renewal Sacrifice'. I'm done waiting for the right moment. No one else can die at the next Renewal Ceremony. We must make a stand, not just talk about it!"

"Making a stand without knowing who's behind this—without understanding their full power—is reckless and stupid." My face was flushed with rage, my voice trembling with fury. "We can't afford to be reckless. We need to be smart. If we act now without the full picture, we risk losing everything we've fought for."

"I thought you were a warrior, skilled in strategy," I pointed to the faint scar along her left forearm, acknowledging her military ranking. "Perhaps you are just a soldier after all."

I could see the deep cut of my words on Nova's expression. The tension between us was electric. Rhea's eyes darted between us, her anger simmering beneath the surface.

"We need to find a balance," she said, trying to bridge the gap between our conflicting viewpoints. "Both of you make valid points. We can't wait forever, but we can't rush in blindly. There must be a way to combine strategy with action."

Nova's gaze remained unyielding, but she glanced at Rhea, her frustration now tinged with resignation. "Fine. But don't make me wait too long. Every second counts."

"I won't," I said, my tone softening slightly, though the fire inside me still burned fiercely. "How many years until the next Renewal Ceremony?"

"Two hundred and fifty-six years, eight months and sixteen days," Nova replied curtly. "And counting."

"Then we have a little over two and a half decades to find a way to ensure there will be no genocide at the coming Renewal," I declared firmly.

"Agreed," Nova huffed, suppressing her anger.

"Agreed," Rhea added, her voice steady.

We locked eyes, the weight of our decision hanging heavy between us. The future of Nxyara was already precariously balanced, and our ongoing conflict would only make the path ahead more challenging.

We needed unity....

We needed a miracle...

We needed the Twins.

EIGHT

The first rays of dawn filtered through the narrow crevices in the cave's ceiling, casting faint, dancing shadows on the rough stone walls. I stretched, my body feeling fantastic thanks to Solvyrs' healing powers. It had been two weeks since Nova and the others arrived, and life in the cave had settled into a natural rhythm.

Each morning, Solvyr and Aetheris left the cave to hunt for game, returning with fresh meat, which kept us nourished and grounded as we repaired gear, kept camp, and contemplated our next moves. The cave proved to be a true fortress, with labyrinthine passages and hidden chambers. A place to regroup and strategise without fear of attack.

Weapons, tools, and makeshift bedding fashioned from whatever materials we could scavenge lined the walls. The air was filled with the scent of earth and moss, and small fires flickered in the dim light.

I sat by a fire, turning meat on a spit, and wondered for the first time how Nova and her crew, along with all their equipment and luggage, initially got into the cave. I chose this cave because it was nearly inaccessible, a haven only reachable by those with flight abilities. Aetheris and Solvyr were the only ones capable of flying. Aetheris was with me when the group arrived, and even an enlarged Solvyr could not carry everyone, plus supplies.

I rose and walked to the cave's only entrance, a jagged opening high above the ground, barely wide enough for a larger Aetheris to squeeze through. Below, the sea stretched out, tranquil yet unforgiving. There was no logical way they could have all entered the cave without another entrance.

I searched for Nova, who I found disembowelling Aetheris's latest kill.

"How did you all get in here? " I tried to sound casual. "Without flying, there's no way in or out, and Solvyr couldn't have carried you all."

I glanced at Aetheris, perched on a rock, her eyes gleaming with curiosity and a hint of mischief. Solvyr was coiled beside her, wings folded against her back, looking as if she was trying to devour the carcass with her eyes.

"Teleportation," Rhea said, stepping forward with a calm and assured expression.

"Teleportation?" I echoed, sceptical.

Rhea raised her arm, revealing a bracelet made of tiny, intricately designed beads.

"Nano-Portal Beads," she explained. "Each bead contains a micro-teleportation device. By tapping a specific bead, you open a temporary portal to a pre-programmed location."

She tapped one of the beads on her bracelet. Before my eyes, a pinprick of intense light appeared, rapidly expanding into a full-size circular gateway about two meters in diameter. The edges shimmered and rippled like liquid mercury, emitting a soft glow that cycled through the colours of the rainbow. She tapped the bead again, and the portal disappeared.

"We've spent the last decade locating and exploring caves within a certain radius of the dungeon on the off chance you might be there," Nova said. "It was Rhea's idea. She proposed that if we couldn't get you out of the dungeon, the least we could do was help you if you managed to find your way out."

"There are three small scout groups like ours that continually check potential caves in an ongoing cycle," Rhea added. "We had checked this cave nine times already. This time, we found you! It was a wonderful surprise."

"You invented this technology?" I asked, suddenly noticing that everyone had a Nano-Bead bracelet around their wrist.

"Yes," Rhea said proudly. "The benefit is that we can choose who gets which beads, preventing security risks of Naxyarans teleporting willy-nilly. Could you imagine if Drakonis got her hands on this technology? The programming in the beads allows us to specify how many journeys can be made, to which locations and by whom."

"Did this genius come with your upgraded look?" I teased, looking Rhea up and down, reminding her she still owed me an explanation.

"Genius is in her blood!" laughed Nova, settling next to a fire after washing up.

Rhea brought us each a jug filled with a drink made from fermented fruits native to Nxyara, infused with a delicate blend of spices and herbs. Its rich flavour and warmth reminded me of more innocent times. I watched Rhea as she gazed out over the fire, her eyes reflecting pain and determination.

"After Drakonis' guards took me, I was sent to an engineering school. Like you, I also thought Nova was dead," Rhea said, her voice steady but tinged with bitterness.

"At first, I thought it might be an opportunity to find a way to help you. But I quickly realised it was a place you never leave. Even after graduation, you stay, working for the High Council, trapped in a perpetual rotation of servitude."

"What was it like there?" I asked gently.

Rhea took a deep breath. "The workload is gruelling. Students are expected to work around the clock with barely any breaks. Sleep is considered a luxury, making the stress and exhaustion unbearable. But that was just the beginning."

She paused. The horror in her eyes told me everything.

"Students are forced to participate in dangerous experiments, often without proper safety measures. Accidents were less common than deaths. Novice students are used as test subjects for unproven and harmful technologies undertaken by the Seniors. It was terrifying."

Nova and I exchanged glances as we tried to align the school we had often seen with Rhea's description. From an onlooker's perspective, the school was a unique and striking structure built into a large rock formation for all to see. It was an engineering masterpiece, appearing as if it was carved directly from the natural rock, with trees growing around and on it, enhancing the integration of nature and architecture.

Its modern design had large, round windows and a prominent, sleek, glass-enclosed deck jutting from the top, contrasting with the rough texture of the rock.

Nxyarans from all over marvelled at the overall tranquility and seclusion, making the structure appear as a hidden sanctuary or a secluded retreat in the wilderness, not a horrific life sentence. However, as I thought about it, I noted that I had never met one of its students – past or present - only those who dreamt of enrolment.

"The faculty is abusive, both physically and mentally," Rhea continued. "Punishment is harsh and humiliating for even minor mistakes. There is no escape. Any perceived attempt to leave is met with execution, no questions asked."

She shuddered, her face pale. "Psychological torture tactics are employed to accelerate ingenuity. Dormitories are overcrowded, filthy, and infested with pests. Quality food and water are provided only to those who achieve significant breakthroughs and swiftly withdrawn if subsequent breakthroughs are not achieved.

"How did you manage to escape?" My heart ached for Rhea, knowing all too well the despair of being trapped in a seemingly endless nightmare.

"It was an accident," Rhea said, a flicker of triumph in her eyes. "I was forced into an experiment that went horribly wrong. When I woke up, I thought I was hallucinating. My appearance was drastically altered. But as it turned out, no one knew who I was, and I was promptly escorted off the property. That freakish experiment ended up being my ticket out."

"So far, I haven't been able to reverse the transformation. On the upside, not even Drakonis recognises me. But I do miss my auburn hair," she added, stroking her head with a sad smile.

"Hair is overrated," Nova said, vainly stroking her floor-length braids and pinning them back up out of the way.

I rolled my eyes. "I think you look majestic, Rhea. I wouldn't even think you were from Nxyara if I didn't know you."

"Weird, isn't it?" Rhea's eyes lit up with amusement. "I come and go from the Twins' lab completely undetected. It really helps them stay under the radar. Drakonis has been relentless in trying to catch them ever since our appearance before the High Council. For decades, she's conducted random checks, hoping to catch them in the act of replicating the cloning process."

Nova laughed. "They're so much smarter than Drakonis. I think she's finally given up."

"Where's your pet?" I asked, suddenly realising Rhea was without a companion.

"Engineers and scientists aren't allocated pets," Rhea seemed grateful for the subject change. "Pets are considered distractions. I don't mind, but you know Astra and Lyra are not about to be left out."

The room filled with amused agreement.

"They created their own 'pets' in the lab," Rhea explained.

"If you can call them that," Nova huffed disapprovingly. "All I can say is that I'm glad I didn't return from military service to find one of those things waiting for me. Solvyr is a far superior battle companion."

Solvyr proudly slid around Nova's waist with an air of confidence. I never thought there would be a day when I could confidently say that snakes have an attitude.

Aetheris seemed unconscious. Her lion-sized body spread out on the dirt floor, wings expanded and paws flopping mid-air as she relaxed around the fire. I chuckled to myself.

"Speaking of the Twins, are they well?" I asked, keen to hear about Astra and Lyra. They had been abandoned and responsible for trying to replicate the clones. Surely, there had been some success in the last century.

Rhea's face softened. "They're as determined as ever, but the process has been slow. Each day brings new challenges, especially considering they have no prior notes or work to start from. They've managed to create life forms, but the complexity of actual cloning is still out of reach.

"Their spirit is unbroken. I'm sure They'll get there," Nova interjected. "Besides, you can ask them yourself tomorrow."

The fire crackled, and for a moment, hope flickered as brightly as the flames before us. My thoughts wandered to Maren and the others I had left behind. Perhaps we could finally get them out with Rhea's technology and Nova's battle skills. But that was a problem for tomorrow – a remarkable place where everything is possible.

A soft aura filled the air as the portal stabilised, humming like a well-tuned crystal glass. The cave felt charged with static electricity, causing my hair to stand on end, and there was a gentle pull as if the space was drawing me closer. The portal's edge was cool to the touch, with a slight resistance, like pushing through a thin, pliable membrane.

"It's incredible," I murmured.

Rhea smiled. "It's quite an experience. Stepping through, you feel a momentary sensation of weightlessness, like gravity has let go of you."

"I love the brief, exhilarating rush, like free-falling or diving into deep water, before you find yourself seamlessly at your destination," added Nova, always the thrill-seeker.

"How does it work?" I asked in awe.

Rhea took me to the side to explain, while Nova, bored by the details, helped the others prepare for travel.

"A device within each Nano-Bead scans every tiny detail of your body—cells, molecules, even the arrangement of atoms. It's like taking a super-detailed picture of you, capturing all the information about your physical structure.

"This detailed scan is converted into data, then transmitted to the destination programmed into the Nano-Bead selected. The device starts to rebuild you from scratch at the destination, using the information to arrange atoms and molecules exactly as they were in the original location."

I shook my head in wonder. "This technology is... beyond anything I could have imagined."

Rhea gave a knowing smile. "The device uses a powerful energy source to make the entire process quick and efficient. Multiple checks are in place to ensure safety, and data is double-checked to guarantee no errors. This assures that you are reassembled correctly and safely."

"Wait..." I hesitated. "You mean there is a chance I could come out all wrong at the other end?" My nervousness spiked as the reality of teleportation set in. The concept of being disassembled and reassembled, no matter how scientifically explained, was terrifying. My heart raced as I glanced at a panther-sized Aetheris perched on a nearby rock, eyes wide with fear.

"Come on, Aetheris, I guess we've come this far. What's a little teleportation?" I held my hand out to her, hoping for a smooth transition. But Aetheris, as usual, had her own plans.

In a blink, she shrank to a size so tiny she was nearly invisible, zipping around the cave like a hyperactive firefly. I tried to catch her, but she was a blur of motion, darting and weaving with the grace of a caffeinated flea.

"Argh! Aetheris, stop! This isn't a game!" I called out, but she was too busy with her mini panic attack to listen.

Nova leaned against the cavern wall with an air of amused detachment, her staff coiled with Solvyr, who watched the spectacle with an expression that made it clear the serpent found her friends' antics entertaining.

"Looks like Aetheris isn't exactly a teleportation aficionado," Nova quipped, her voice dripping with playful sarcasm as Solvyr flicked her tail in what could only be described as a serpent's snigger.

Frustrated, I threw up my hands in surrender. "Aetheris, you can't just abandon me like this!"

With a final, almost theatrical puff and a look of dramatic resignation, Aetheris reappeared in her larger form, hovering in front of me with an expression that screamed both apology and stubbornness. She flew towards the cave's entrance and launched into the sky after giving me a final I'll race you there look.

"I guess she decided she'd rather fly to the Twins' lab than face the portal," Rhea laughed.

"Assuming she knows where the Twins' lab is," I countered, confident my feline friend would find her way safely.

"It's going to be fine, Zarya," Nova reassured me. "We've done this hundreds of times. It's safe."

I watched the others enter the portal, anxiety mounting as my turn approached. I took a deep breath, trying to steady my nerves. The hum of the portal seemed to beckon me, yet with Aetheris gone, I felt a pang of loneliness.

As I advanced, I felt the static charge intensify, my skin tingling with anticipation. The cool, pliable edge of the portal brushed against my fingertips, and I closed my eyes, taking one last deep breath before embracing the gentle pull of the portal, drawing me in.

"Here goes nothing," I whispered.

NINE

A wave of nausea hit me as I stepped through the portal. Rhea had warned me I might feel this way, and I knew it would pass, but it still took a moment to steady myself. As the vertigo faded, my surroundings came into sharp focus, and I felt like I had entered the heart of the future.

The Twins' laboratory was bathed in a cool, bluish light, casting a serene glow over meticulously organised workstations. Each desk was a hive of activity as if operating on autopilot, surrounded by advanced equipment and holographic displays. Enormous, high-definition screens lined the walls, depicting intricate diagrams and animations.

To my left, a life-sized hologram of a Nxyaran rotated slowly, its anatomy rendered in astonishing detail. Every muscle, organ, and bone was visible, illuminated in various colours, highlighting different systems and functions. The screens beside it displayed the complexity of molecular structures and genetic sequences. It was daunting... and mesmerising.

Directly ahead, a colossal image of an atom floated, its electrons orbiting the nucleus in perfect harmony. Next to it, visualizations of cosmic phenomena and theoretical physics models danced across the screens, their elegance underscoring the profound mysteries they represented.

I wandered further in, observing the Twins clad in pristine white lab coats, undisturbed by the small group that just entered their world. The air was cool and conditioned to perfection, I assumed to maintain the delicate balance required for experiments.

Astra and Lyra moved with purpose, their faces lit by the glow of their screens and the holographic projections they manipulated with deft gestures. Each station was equipped with tools and devices, their functions so advanced that I could only guess at their purposes.

Lyra was engrossed in a complex analysis. Data streams flowing across her screen like a digital river whilst Astra was adjusting a delicate instrument, the precision of her movements speaking to the high stakes of her work. Dedication and expertise filled the room. Breakthroughs were being forged here.

The laboratory was not just a workspace but a cathedral of knowledge and discovery. A place where the boundaries of science were being pushed, where the future was being written in real time.

I let the cool air fill my lungs and allowed myself a moment to absorb it all until the nausea passed. A century had passed since I last saw Astra and Lyra. The anticipation and the lingering effects of the teleportation portal made my heart pound.

"Astra, Lyra!" Nova startled me as her voice broke the silence.

The Twins looked up in unison, their identical faces lighting up with recognition. Their expressions shifted from concentration to joy as they recognised Nova and Rhea.

"Nova! Rhea!" Astra exclaimed. "We weren't expecting you back so soon. Did you have any success this time?"

Before Nova could respond, Lyra's gaze shifted past her and landed on me. Her eyes widened in disbelief, and she grabbed Astra's arm, drawing her attention to me.

"It can't be," Lyra whispered.

Astra's eyes followed Lyra's, and her breath hitched the moment she saw me. The room seemed to stand still as the realisation dawned on them.

"Zarya?" Astra's voice was barely above a whisper, as if she feared that speaking too loudly might shatter the moment.

I stepped forward, feeling a rush of emotions that I hadn't anticipated. A lump formed in my throat.

The distance between us was closed in an instant, and I found myself enveloped in a fierce embrace. Astra joined in, and for a moment, we stood there, holding onto each other, the past century melting away in the warmth of our reunion. As if feeling left out, Solvyr flew from her perch on Nova's staff and coiled herself around us, providing an extra squeeze.

"We thought we might never see you again," Astra whispered, her voice choked with tears as she wiped away the lingering tingle of Solvyrs' kisses.

"Calm yourself, Solvyr," laughed Nova as she looked on with Rhea, their smiles reflecting the joy of this long-awaited moment.

"There are some mice waiting for you," Lyra said, wiping her eyes before petting the serpent between its wings. As Solvyr took flight to explore, we reluctantly released each other's embrace.

"We've been working tirelessly," Astra said, finally stepping back to look at me properly. "But we've never forgotten you, Zarya. Every breakthrough, every discovery, we wished you were here with us."

"I've thought of you both every day," I confessed, feeling a mixture of regret and joy. "And now, we're back together. There's so much to catch up on."

Lyra's smile widened, the spark of the scientist gleaming in her eyes. "And there's so much we want to show you. The lab, the projects, everything we've been working on."

Astra nodded, her expression a perfect blend of excitement and determination. "You're going to love it."

Surrounded by the comforting presence of my oldest friends, I took another look around the laboratory. The awe-inspiring technology and advanced research seemed insignificant compared to the strength of the bond we shared.

"Let's get to work," I said, a smile spreading across my face. "We've got a future to build."

Nova and Rhea helped the others unpack as Astra and Lyra guided me through their lab. I couldn't help but feel a sense of wonder, excitement, and delight. I was honoured to have been granted a personal tour of the Twins' sacred space. Astra led the way.

"This is one of our newest projects," she said, gesturing to a sleek console embedded into the wall. Holographic screens flared to life, displaying complex algorithms and simulations.

"We've been working on improving molecular stabilisation techniques. It's been a challenging but rewarding endeavour."

I leaned closer, trying to make sense of the intricate patterns.

"How does this technology differ from what you had before?"

"The previous models were limited in their precision and efficiency," Lyra chimed in, her voice brimming with pride. "This one uses advanced quantum algorithms to better predict and control molecular interactions. It's like we've moved from a basic toolkit to a high-tech surgical suite."

Astra nodded, her fingers deftly manipulating the controls to show me a live simulation of the technology in action.

"And here, you can see the stabilisation process in real-time. We've achieved a level of accuracy that was thought impossible."

I marvelled at the display, watching the simulation unfold and having no clue as to its meaning. "That's incredible."

Lyra smiled, her eyes twinkling with excitement. "We hope to integrate this technology into several other projects, including our genetic research for cloning. It's a game-changer."

As we continued our tour, Astra pointed to a large, cylindrical chamber in the centre of the room. "This is our experimental reactor. We use it to test new materials and energy sources. It's one of our most ambitious projects."

As I approached the reactor, I desperately tried to mask my feigning understanding, taking in its imposing structure. "And how's it been performing?"

Lyra took a step closer, her expression serious but enthusiastic. "It's been exceeding our expectations. We've managed to create some new compounds with unprecedented properties. A major breakthrough for us."

Astra then led me to a series of smaller workstations, each dedicated to different aspects of their research.

"This is where we conduct our detailed analyses," she explained. "From genetic sequencing to advanced materials science, every station has its own specialised focus."

I glanced at the various screens and instruments, noting the complexity of their work. "It's all so detailed. How do you manage to keep track of everything?"

Lyra laughed softly. "It's a challenge, but we've developed some advanced management systems to help us coordinate our efforts. Plus, we've been working together for so long, it's almost second nature."

I turned to Astra and Lyra, feeling a deep sense of admiration. "It's truly impressive."

As the tour concluded there was a burning issue I needed to address.

"Rhea mentioned some issues with Drakonis?" I tried to keep my tone gentle. Astra and Lyra exchanged troubled glances.

Astra spoke first.

"When Drakonis branded you as a rebel, everything changed for us," her voice heavy with emotion. "The fallout was immediate and harsh. We were cut off from society and labelled as Rebel sympathisers. With Nova dead, or so we thought, the sense of loss and isolation was almost unbearable."

Lyra's eyes grew distant as she continued, "Our research came under intense scrutiny. All scientific efforts were closely monitored by Drakonis and her loyalists. We had to operate in secrecy, making every project a delicate balancing act. It was a constant struggle to protect our work from being seized or sabotaged."

I could see the strain etched into their faces, and it pained me to hear about their hardships. "And Rhea? How is she faring after her ordeal? I understand she has spent all her time with you since her return."

"Rhea's departure was a blow. Engineering school was rigorous, and she had to prove herself. She faced immense challenges adapting to the new environment." Astra shared, her expression solemn.

"But Rhea's spirit is unbreakable," Lyra added. "Despite the adversity, she excelled. She has been instrumental to us since her return. Her inventions and technological mind have been a blessing, as has her companionship."

I looked at Astra and Lyra, feeling deep empathy and regret.

"I'm sorry for all the pain and hardship my decision to approach the High Council caused you. It's clear that you've faced tremendous adversity, and yet you've managed to achieve so much." I gestured to the lab.

"We believe in our work and hoped that we would one day be reunited," Astra gave me a small, appreciative smile. "Your return has given us renewed strength."

Lyra took a deep breath, her eyes determined yet vulnerable.

"Drakonis has been a formidable obstacle. Her control over the scientific community has stifled progress, and her opposition to our work has only intensified. We are determined not to let her undermine everything we've built."

I nodded, "So you have Rhea, but no one else? I understand you need to keep security tight, but how are you running this scientific universe with just the three of you? I already know you don't have pets.

Lyra smiled at her sister. "Should we show her?"

"We should show her," Astra nodded, matching Lyra's playfulness.

"Meet Nyx and Nox," they announced, reaching into their lab coat pockets and opening their hands.

I looked down. Each had an identical tiny creature perched on their palm. Their entire bodies must have been no more than five centimetres tall. They were so delicate and ethereal that they seemed almost like an illusion.

I could see my astonished reflection in their massive eyes. Glossy orbs that conveyed a sense of curiosity and innocence. Their heads were disproportionately large, making their body appear even more fragile in comparison. Their skin had a smooth, glassy texture with a faint, almost imperceptible glow. I could make out faint hints of their sophisticated biology.

Their body was slender, almost skeletal, with long, spindly arms and legs that were slightly translucent, ending in tiny, rounded extremities that seemed perfectly adapted for fine interfaces. Despite their fragility, there was an elegance in their posture, a grace that suggested they were at home in their tiny form.

I stared at Nyx and Nox, then at Astra and Lyra, then back at the tiny creatures who remained upright but relaxed in the Twins' palms as if they were calmly observing me just as intently as I was observing them. There was a sense of mutual curiosity, a silent exchange between two vastly different beings. I knew I was witnessing something extraordinary that would stay with me forever. Somehow, I felt an unexpected connection to these tiny ....

"Are these pets?" I asked, trying to make sense of what I was seeing.

"No," Astra smiled. "Scientists and engineers..."

"... don't get pets because it's believed they might distract you from your work," I finished, recalling Rhea's words.

"They were an unexpected result of a cloning experiment that went wrong," Lyra explained. "One of our attempts to reverse engineer the cloning process we observed after Elana's sacrifice led to the creation of these two small, enigmatic creatures."

Astra nodded. "They aren't exact duplicates of any one organism. Instead, they're a mix of genetic elements, giving them their unique appearance.... and behaviour." She laughed, giving a knowing look at Lyra.

"Their small size and peculiar features are a direct consequence of the experiment's instability," Lyra resumed. "Despite this, they have a symbiotic bond, much like us, and they're extremely intelligent."

"Do they talk?" I tried to imagine what they would sound like.

"In their own way," Lyra replied. "They have a unique language and often converse with each other, though we haven't fully deciphered it yet. They understand us perfectly."

Nyx and Nox seemed agitated. Their calm, curious demeanour replaced by an unmistakable air of fear. They huddled close to Astra and Lyra, glossy eyes darting around the lab.

"What's wrong with them?" I asked, my concern

growing.

Astra and Lyra exchanged uneasy glances. "They've been acting strangely since your arrival," Astra admitted. "We thought it might be the anxiety of new visitors, but it seems more serious."

Suddenly, a shiver ran through the room. An invisible presence swept over us, chilling the air. The hairs on my neck stood up, and Lyra's eyes widened, her gaze scanning the lab.

"Something's wrong. I can't see anything, but I think we are being... hunted."

Nyx and Nox pressed even closer, their tiny bodies trembling whilst emitting soft, anxious chirps. Their communication tinged with distress.

I rolled my eyes.

"Aetheris," my voice demanding. "Show yourself!"

A domestic-sized Aetheris materialised and hovered in front of me at chest height. Her fur ruffled and tail twitching, excited by the stalking of the little beings now huddled in Astra's hand.

I gave her a scolding look. How long had she been here tormenting these poor things? Astra and Lyra gasped, their eyes widening in astonishment.

"What in the world is that?" Astra whispered, her voice filled with awe.

"Remember my pet, Aetheris?" I grinned. "She's harmless, well, at least to my friends."

I held out my arms, and Aetheris allowed me to hold her. "Perhaps it would be easier to make friends if you were more approachable," I suggested.

Aetheris hovered gracefully before leaping onto Astra's palm, shrinking to the size of Nyx and Nox along the way. The Twins stared in fascination, their mouths slightly agape.

"Now you are just showing off." I laughed.

Nyx and Nox flitted around her, their tiny forms darting with excitement, their previous fear forgotten. Aetheris let out a soft, melodic purr, her demeanour friendly and inviting.

"See? She's not a threat," I said, watching Nyx and Nox take to Aetheris immediately.

As if understanding, Aetheris gave a playful flick of her tail and proceeded to nuzzle the miniscule beings, now fascinated. Climbing onto Aetheris back without invitation, they rode around Astra's palm, enjoying themselves. Aetheris seemed to relish the attention, gracefully adjusting her movements to accommodate her new passengers and not leaving the safety of Astra's palm.

Not one to miss out on the fun, Solvyr reduced her size accordingly, floating over Astra's palm to join the miniature playground.

Nova, Rhea, Lyra and I gathered around Astra's palm, watching in amusement as our four companions danced around with playful abandon, their tiny forms creating a flurry of activity and laughter. The sight was nothing short of comical—like a high-tech, interspecies carnival.

"I never thought I'd see Nyx and Nox playing with a mini-Aetheris and mini- Solvyr." Lyra chuckled.

Astra shook her head with a bemused smile, her palm now a veritable playground. "I suppose we should have expected the unexpected in a lab like this."

I leaned in, feeling a sense of warmth and amusement as I watched the camaraderie unfold. The serious tension of earlier seemed to melt away, replaced by a joyful and light-hearted moment.

"Looks like we've turned our investigation into an impromptu playdate," I said, grinning at the sight. "Who knew lab work could be so entertaining?"

The lab had settled into a peaceful calm, the earlier excitement now a distant memory. Now a domestic cat size, Aetheris lay on her back with Nyx,

Nox, and Solvyr snuggled up against her, sleeping off their exhaustion. They used her soft stomach as a pillow, rising and falling gently with each breath—a serene picture of contentment.

We formed a circle around them like guardians, the light from the holographic displays casting a gentle glow over our faces. The topic of our discussion was as old as our mission—replicating the cloning process that had eluded us for a century.

"A hundred years of research, experiments, and countless trials, yet success remains out of reach," Astra said, her tone reflective.

Lyra nodded, her expression serious. "We've tried every conceivable method. Genetic splicing, advanced bioengineering, synthetic wombs—we even attempted to replicate the exact conditions of the Renewal Ceremony. But each time, we've fallen short."

"Could it be that the problem lies in the complexity of the process?" Rhea proposed. "What we once thought was purely scientific now appears intrinsically linked to nature. It's not just about duplicating cells; it's about understanding the deeper, more mystical elements of self-generation."

Nova leaned forward, her brow furrowed in thought. "So, what you are saying is it's not something we can force through sheer technology. Self-regeneration is a part of our natural evolution, an organic mechanism we haven't fully understood."

We all nodded, processing our collective findings and views on this topic as we watched our sleeping companions.

"The best we've managed so far is partial success," Lyra broke the silence. "We've created clones, but they lack the vitality and longevity of naturally generated beings. They live, but they don't thrive."

"Are you saying you have made some clones—aside from your mini-clones?" Nova raised her eyebrows, turning her head toward the Twins while keeping her eyes on the tiny beings, who were now using Solvyr as a blanket.

"There are always unforeseen complications," Astra continued, sidestepping the question. "Physical deformities, shortened lifespans, cognitive deficiencies. It's as if the essence of what makes us whole is missing."

"Show us," I encouraged, knowing the Twins didn't take kindly to exhibiting their failures.

Astra and Lyra exchanged a glance, their hesitation unmistakable. Finally, Astra sighed and led us to a secluded part of the laboratory.

My breath caught in my throat as I entered a vast,

hidden room filled with endless rows of cylindrical chambers, each glowing with an eerie blue light. Each contained figures suspended in a viscous fluid.

"Welcome to the last century of our work," Astra announced, her voice tinged with frustration. "This is where we have been trying to replicate the cloning process."

Nova stood beside me, repulsed. "This is... horrifying."

Lyra nodded, her expression weary. "We've had some... difficulties," she said, her voice cracking. "Each one of these chambers represents a failure. Each one a potential life that never came to be."

"Half of this one is missing!" exclaimed Nova as we all came to spectate.

The Nxyaran-like torso had limbs dangling awkwardly, ending in delicate, claw-like fingers. Its sickly pale pink and translucent skin clung to its skeletal frame, revealing sinewy muscles and protruding bones. Bulging eyes stared unblinking from the sides of its elongated head.

"Is it... alive?" asked Rhea, her voice thick with curiosity and repulsion.

"No, they are all dead," Astra sighed, running a hand through her hair. "We're missing a key component, something that we can't quite identify. Every time we think we're close, something goes wrong. It's like trying to solve a puzzle with missing pieces."

"How about this one?" I stared at yet another mutilated form, my stomach churning. This one had skin that was a sickly shade of purple, slick and glistening.

Bulbous, lifeless eyes stared vacantly, devoid of any spark of consciousness. Malformed limbs, twisted and elongated, writhed involuntarily. Its misshapen head, disproportionately large for its frail, worm-like body, tilted slightly as if seeking understanding in a world that will never make sense to it.

The sight of its contorted, claw-like fingers sent a shiver down my spine.

We continued inspecting endless rows of failed cloning attempts, the Twins reassuring us that they were all deceased and only kept for research purposes.

I passed Rhea, shamelessly inspecting a twin foetus, both deathly pale white. One had skin stretched tightly over its deformed, bulbous head. Tiny, malformed limbs covered its face as if trying to shield itself from the world it should never have been brought into. Its twisted mouth, frozen in a silent scream.

The second, equally disturbing, appeared wrapped in a shroud of warped flesh. Its unnaturally bent and fused limbs forming a grotesque cocoon around its fragile body. The creature's head was buried deep within this macabre shell. A hint of a face that will never see the light of day.

The entire room was a graveyard of failed experiments. A collection of stark warnings of the boundaries shattered and the horrors unleashed in our relentless pursuit of scientific discovery. No wonder the Twins didn't like to talk about them. Even if their motivation was for a better Nxyaran future, these were not images that left you sleeping peacefully.

"Why have there been so many failures?" Rhea whispered.

Lyra walked over to a control panel and tapped a few buttons. One of the chambers lit up brighter than the others, revealing a figure sculpted from some form of crystalline material, catching and refracting light in mesmerising patterns.

"This one," Lyra says, her voice shaking with frustration, "was our closest attempt. But the neural pathways wouldn't stabilise. It was alive for mere minutes before... before it failed."

I could hardly believe my eyes as I stood before

the being. Its body - if it could even be called that – was slender and elongated, with a transparency that revealed a complex network of what appeared to be veins and organs beneath the surface.

Its head was smooth and featureless, except for a slight gradient suggesting a face. The lack of defined facial features only added to its enigmatic presence, making determining any emotion or intention difficult.

Long and spindly limbs tapered to delicate points gave it an overall gentle and refined appearance that I found alluring and intimidating.

I felt like I was standing before a living piece of art, something far beyond the ordinary realm of existence, feeling a profound curiosity. The idea of creating life, only to watch it suffer and die was unbearable.

"Why keep going?" I asked. "How can you keep trying after so many failures?"

"Because we believe it's possible," Astra's eyes meet mine, filled with a determination that bordered on obsession. "We believe that one day, we will succeed. When we do, everything will change for Nxyara. That is why Drakonis can not find... this." She gestured to the entire room.

"But each failure weighs on us," Lyra continued

with a more sombre expression. "It's hard to keep hope alive when all you see are your mistakes staring back at you."

Nova stepped forward, placing a hand on Lyra's shoulder. "You will find the answer, no matter how long it takes."

"There must be something we're missing, some ancient clue that will unlock the secret," Rhea interjected, her eyes filled with wonder.

I saw a flicker of hope reignite in Astra's eyes.

"That's what we're thinking," excitement edged her voice. "Some ancient artifact, writing or legend of some kind."

"Nothing exists," Lyra reminded her sister. "We have looked everywhere. We would have found it by now."

All the pieces fell into place.

"Octaryans!" I announced proudly.

As we exited the hidden laboratory, trying to shake off the lingering dread that filled the air, I shared with the Twins what I had discussed with Nova and Rhea about the mystic beings in the dungeon.

"They must know something," Nova concluded, her expression resolute.

"At the very least, something we haven't considered," Lyra looked at Astra, both still working to comprehend the concept of further Nxyaran evolution.

"Perhaps we need to change our approach," I thought out loud. "Instead of forcing nature to bend to our will, we should focus on understanding it better. What if the key lies in ancient knowledge of our natural process rather than technology?"

Rhea nodded thoughtfully. "Nature does have a way of balancing itself. It's humbling, isn't it?"

"For all our advancements, we're still students, trying to unlock secrets." Nova scoffed.

Aetheris let out a soft, contented purr in her sleep. Nyx, Nox, and Solvyr nestled closer, oblivious to our return.

"What if we changed our perspective?" I proposed with a note of determination in my voice. "Instead of cloning ourselves, let's create a new species."

My friends looked at me, struggling to find the right response.

"Hear me out," I continued. "I've been considering this idea for a while, and I think it will work. What does Drakonis want?"

"To be the only evolved Nxyaran?" Nova replied.

"Yes! Well, at least that's what it looks like," I had to make them think this through for themselves. "But why?"

"So she will be unique, unchallenged. The oldest, 'wisest' Nxyaran," Astra contributed.

"She will be worshipped and, with Rune, immortal," Rhea put forward.

Rune. This was new information I hadn't taken into account.

"Tell me more about this... Rune," I inquired.

My companions took turns describing Drakonis' pet to me and its abilities. They continued to share some of the losses they encountered while discovering the shields and the mind control Rune possessed.

I processed the new information as I studied our sleeping companions. Our plan would still work. How strong do these pets get? I wondered, making a mental note to return to that question.

"A new, unique species would take all that away from Drakonis – snail or no snail." I smiled mischievously.

I watched as the concept started to sink in, and the realisation on their faces filled me with hope. I knew I was onto something.

"If we merge our separate strategies—replacing replication with creation—not only will we ruin Drakonis's plans, but we will also end the genocide and address the future issue of societal stagnation."

The silence that followed felt prolonged, and I began to sense an uncomfortable tension.

"We already have ideas for a new species," Astra blurted out.

"We will still need missing information from ancient times." Lyra countered.

"Zarya!" Nova ordered, forgetting she was with friends. "You and I can visit all the Rebel camps and speak to their leaders. Not only to get their support with an uprising but to locate ancient knowledge and artifacts."

"Perhaps one of them knows how to break out the Hexaryans and Octaryans." This was getting exciting. My thoughts turned to Maren, still enduring the dungeon. Is it possible that I could finally free her?

"I will find out more about Rune. There must be some way to detatch it from Drakonis," Rhea volunteered.

"More knowledge about Drakonis' plans would be helpful," Nova added. "But don't go doing anything stupid. She might not know who you are but that won't stop her from killing you if she feels like it."

"Careful, promise." Rhea held her hand up in oath.

Tension hung in the air as the realisation of what we were about to undertake pressed on all of us. We all understood the risk. There was no room for error.

"I have to stay hidden," I finally said, steadying my voice. "If Drakonis even catches a whisper that I'm alive, everything we've fought for will unravel."

"You're right," Nova's stern expression softened. "Bringing you with me would be too risky."

Astra and Lyra exchanged glances, their silent communication as effective as words. Lyra was the first to speak.

"Zarya, you should stay here with us. We can keep you safe and hidden, and you can help us move forward with our work on the new species."

"Agreed," Nova's tone was firm as if finalising an agreement. "I'll return to military service to maintain my cover and set up meetings with the Rebels whenever possible."

Addressing Rhea, Nova suggested using a code for the secret transportation of meeting times, locations and coordinates.

"I'll design a nano-bracelet for her," Rhea looked at me, her mind already at work. "It will allow you to teleport directly to the meetings and back without being detected."

"That could work," I said, ideas and contingencies forming in my mind. Rhea nodded, her focus intensifying.

"I'll take care of it. Just be ready when it's time."

The room fell silent again, but this time, it was charged with a shared purpose and mutual understanding of the task ahead.

"I trust all of you," I said, looking into the eyes of those who were more than just comrades; they were my family. "After all, if there is any skill I have perfected in the dungeons over the last century, it's waiting."

As each of my companions began to drift into their respective duties, I felt a familiar irritation bubbling up inside. To break free from imprisonment and uselessness, only to find myself in a different kind of confinement, sidelined while the others moved forward with plans to shape our future, was not what I envisioned.

Nova disappeared down the corridor, Solvyr coiled around her like a necklace, accepting her future of walking a dangerous line between duty and rebellion. Astra and Lyra quickly became engrossed in ideas for the new species, voices merging into an excited hum. In moments like these, their twin bond was most evident—each anticipating the other's thoughts, their collaboration seamless.

Even Rhea, who had lingered for a moment, was now gone, lost in the depths of her lab, bringing her nano-bracelet ideas to life. And here I was, once again left behind, watching, waiting.

The frustration gnawed at me. I wasn't one to sit idle, to let others carry the burden while I remained on the sidelines. It was maddening to feel so powerless, so unnecessary. But I had come too far, and the stakes were too high to let my emotions get the better of me.

I decided to use this time to gather my strength and prepare for the moment I could act.

The shadows lengthened around me as I sat beside Aetheris. The silence was thick, pregnant with anticipation, clashing with the tempest swirling inside me.

Our day was coming. I could feel it. And when it arrived, I would be ready.

But for now, I would do what I do best.

Wait.

TEN

As I paced back and forth, the advanced technology embedded in the walls of my new quarters sent a cascade of light rippling across the floor. It had been years since Nova's last message, and the silence gnawed at me.

I paused by a low table, running my fingers over the smooth surface, wondering what Nova was facing in the world beyond these walls. The coordinates for the next meeting with the rebels should have arrived by now. It was unlike Nova to be late.

A massive panel above my bed caught my eye as it shifted from a swirling nebula to an interlocking geometric pattern. The ever-changing display was meant to soothe and inspire, but at this moment, it felt like a mockery of my endless waiting. I longed for action, for something tangible to do.

I turned my attention to the touch-screen interface on the table, pulling up the latest data from the laboratory. The Twins had been working, their brilliance shining through in every line of code, every experiment. They hadn't said it outright, but I knew they appreciated my presence here, even if it was just to bounce ideas off of.

Rhea, on the other hand, was harder to decipher. It was understandable, given that she spent half her time in enemy territory. I can only imagine the constant vigilance required to daily navigate the High Council's treacherous environment.

I closed my eyes and let out a slow breath, trying to push away the worries. I had to stay focused and ready for when Nova finally made contact. Until then, I'll continue to busy myself, pouring over the laboratory's data, assisting the Twins, and trying to piece together the fragments of our plan. This room was my refuge, where I could prepare for whatever came next.

I inspected my appearance in a full-length mirror. The tailored uniform provided by the Twins was sleek and practical, designed for both authority and efficiency. The fabric clung to my form with precision, a blend of lightweight, breathable material interwoven with tiny sensors allowing me to access data streams, communicate with the laboratory's systems, and even monitor environmental conditions—all without a single device in hand. Turning to the side, the mirror displayed a holographic overlay of my vital signs. Everything's normal, as it should be.

A soft chime from the door pulled me from my thoughts. My heart skipped a beat. There was only one person from whom I was expecting news.

"Come in," I called out, my voice steady despite the rush of anticipation.

Rhea stepped in, her expression as unreadable as ever. Her eyes flickered over me before she held up a data pad.

"I've heard from Nova," she cut straight to the point. "I'm in the process of decoding the coordinates now."

Relief washed over me.

"Did she say anything else?" I asked, trying to keep the hope out of my voice.

"It appears to just be the code." Rhea shook her head, her focus remaining on the data pad. "It's different this time—more complex. But I'll have it figured out soon."

I cringed. Different could mean safer. It could also mean more danger. The last time Nova and Rhea's coordinates were off by a fraction, I'd found myself almost embedded in the trunk of an ancient

Nyxtree instead of materialising in the middle of a forest clearing as intended.

I glanced at Rhea, who was deep in thought.

"Let's hope we get it right this time," I murmured, more to myself than to her.

"We will," she looked up, catching my eye with a reassuring smile. "It won't be long."

As the door closed behind her, I returned to the mirror. The uniform's sensors vibrated faintly in reaction to my heightened pulse. I took a deep breath, determined to stay focused as I prepared for negotiation with the next Rebel leader. Nova and I had succeeded in getting them to align with our vision, but so far, no artifacts had been discovered to aid the Twins.

Needing a distraction, I checked in on the Twins and found Astra and Lyra cheering on Nyx and Nox, who were in the middle of one of their curious games. Zipping through the circuit boards of a scientific instrument with boundless energy. They were communicating in a unique language of intricate chirps, clicks, and whirs that I've never been able to decipher.

A miniature Aetheris was chasing after them, unaware she was being used to clean some of the most hard-to-reach places. As she dashed this way and that, her fur gathered the dust that the Twins stirred up. Her tiny paws scrambled over surfaces and through narrow passages as she playfully hunted the beings, who stayed ahead of her nipping jaws. They were impossibly fast. I found comfort in knowing there was room for playfulness and spontaneity, even amid... everything.

Catching sight of me, Aetheris stopped in her tracks, an unmistakable look of exasperation in her eyes as if to say: Can you believe these two? I giggled softly, crouching down to get a better look at the trio.

"You're doing a great job, Aetheris," I reassured. Her fur rippled with a hint of pride. Nyx and Nox exchanged a flurry of rapid clicks. Then they were off again, leading Aetheris on another wild chase through miniscule nooks and crannies.

I watched with the Twins for a moment longer, marvelling at how they navigated the space. But as much as I wanted to stay and observe their antics, I couldn't linger here forever.

Just as my anxiety threatened to get the better of me, Rhea arrived, a flicker of excitement in her eyes that she couldn't quite hide and a small silver bracelet in her hand.

"The nano-bracelet is ready," she announced,

crossing the room and handing it to me.

It was lighter than I expected, almost weightless, and the metal was cool against my skin as I slipped it onto my wrist. The bracelet hummed softly, adjusting to my bio-signature and syncing with my uniform.

"Nova sent additional information," Rhea continued as she helped me tighten the clasp. "Your meeting is with a rebel named Vesper Kryos. She is a collector, rumoured to possess ancient artifacts that might be useful to our cause. The destination point is her home."

A collector. I had heard rumours of Nxyarans who acquired relics imbued with power or knowledge long forgotten by most. If this collector was willing to meet, it could mean she possessed something invaluable. But the whispers always carried a warning: when dealing with a collector, you never know their true intentions. If they were an ally or an enemy. Rhea seemed to sense my hesitation.

"Nova advised caution, but she believes this is worth the risk. Kryos is elusive, but she's been a key player in the rebel network for years. If anyone has what we need, it's her."

"Let's hope Nova's right." I ensured the bracelet was fastened securely, avoiding stating the obvious.

If Nova's judgment was off, we were all in trouble.

"You're not going in alone," Rhea's gaze softened as she gestured to Aetheris, now shoulder height. "Nova will be waiting at the destination point."

I glanced at Aetheris, who had been observing from the door. Her eyes met mine, and with a final nod to Rhea, I pressed the bead on my bracelet and made my way to the centre of the room. The air shimmered with energy as reality bent and twisted to form a portal. Aetheris padded over to my side, her fur bristling with caution as the portal flared to life with a sudden burst of light. There was no turning back now.

"See you on the other side," I said to Rhea, my voice steady despite my heart racing.

Rhea gave me a slight, encouraging nod as the Twins casually waved goodbye. With Aetheris following close at my heels, we entered the portal together. It's disorienting, like being pulled apart and put back together in an instant. Still, I had now been through it enough times to push past the discomfort. I focused on the destination, on the thought of Nova waiting for us. Then, just as suddenly as it began, the journey was over. The world snapped back into focus, and I found myself standing before a haven sculpted right into a cliffside.

Sweeping curves and sharp angles harmonised with the rock formation that cradled it. Terraces jutted out with confidence, and the glass walls revealed glimpses of a sleek, modern interior. Light glinted off the structure, casting reflections across the water below. Steps hovering over jagged rocks invited me to explore this delicate balance of ambition and nature further.

Aetheris pressed close to my leg, searching for any sign of danger, her fur shimmering with the remnants of the portal's energy. I reached down to give her a reassuring pat when a figure stepped out of the shadows.

"Zarya," Nova's voice was low, but unmistakable. She moved quickly toward us, her eyes sharp as she assessed our surroundings. "You made it."

"Is this the place?" My heart was still racing as Nova nodded, her expression serious.

"This is Kryos' home. We need to be careful. She's expecting us, but with a collector, you never know who or what else might be waiting."

My hand moved to the nano bracelet, feeling the comforting pulse of its tech against my skin. We were as ready as we would ever be.

"Let's go," I said, Aetheris growling in agreement.

We entered the collector's home together, bracing for whatever came next.

Kryos was the embodiment of power wrapped in a cloak of elegance and charm. As the head of a rebel group, her appearance was as commanding as her presence. Her face boasted the high, sharp cheekbones typical of a Nxyaran, but her eyes were white, glowing with vast intelligence and ruthless determination. Her braided hair cascading down her shoulders, suggesting an unpredictable mind that valued order and detail.

The collector's skin had a smooth, stone-like texture as if carved from ancient rock, giving her an air of timelessness and resilience. Her forehead and neckline were adorned with complex markings, evidence of her authority. I wondered if they were badges of honour or reminders of the sacrifices made in the relentless pursuit of her goals.

Tailored to allow for movement, her clothing was adorned with subtle yet striking designs, emphasising the intricate details of her braids and the markings on her skin and further reinforcing her role as a leader who was as strategic as she was charismatic.

This Nxyaran knew how to use her beauty and

presence to influence those around her. Charming and manipulative, she was not just about fighting for freedom. She had crafted a route to her own ascent to power.

The sheer abundance of her home enveloped us. A grand display of taste and wealth. Marble floors gleamed like polished glass, walls were adorned with intricate tapestries, and towering columns that seemed to touch the heavens filled the hallways. Every detail spoke of a life lived in luxury.

"Zarya, Nova, welcome!" She greeted us with a warmth that was almost disarming. Her smile was genuine, her eyes sparkling with curiosity and delight. "I'm so glad you could make it."

Aetheris, perched on my right shoulder like a delicate ornament, absorbed every inch of this new world with curiosity and apprehension. Her eyes darted around, absorbing the grandeur whilst Solvyr coiled around Nova's waist like a fashionable belt, her scales glinting with a subtle sheen as she adjusted her position with indifference.

As she led our tour, Kryos' gaze often drifted toward Aetheris. Her interest was unmistakable. Every room we entered seemed to present her with fresh opportunities to reveal her fascination as her eyes lingered on the winged feline with barely restrained curiosity.

There were vast libraries filled with ancient tomes, each a potential treasure trove of knowledge. Artifacts from countless cultures were displayed with meticulous care, each piece evidence of Kryos 's discerning eye and boundless curiosity. As we continued, it became clear that this was more than just a home—it was a living museum. In this place, history and luxury coexist harmoniously.

Servants, though few in number, moved silently in the background, their presence barely noticeable yet essential to the seamless flow of our visit.

When the tour concluded, we gathered in a large dining room where a lavish banquet awaited. The aromas were intoxicating. Kryos' attention was focused on Aetheris as we took our seats. Her movements were gentle and deliberate as she approached me, her eyes never leaving what she called, much to Aetheris' disgust, the "teeny winged kitty".

"I've never seen anything quite like her," she remarked, her tone filled with awe. Her voice was almost reverential. "May I?"

With approval, Kryos extended a hand towards Aetheris, who, sensing no threat, allowed herself to be examined as conversation flowed from pleasantries to more intriguing topics.

Nova was the first to bring up what had been weighing on our minds.

"We've been searching for an artifact that might hold ancient knowledge about Nxyaran anatomy," she began, her voice filled with quiet determination. "This could help unlock new insights into our evolution."

Kryos' eyes lit up with genuine curiosity.

"Nxyaran anatomy, you say?" She leaned in, warm and inviting. "That sounds absolutely fascinating. What exactly are you hoping to uncover?"

"We're trying to understand what makes Nxyarans... Nxyaran," Kryos made me feel remarkably at ease, but I still wasn't ready to share details.

"It's more than just our physical form; we want to understand the essence of our being. What defines us, how we're constructed. This knowledge could help us understand our purpose and place in the universe."

Kryos' gaze was intent and thoughtful, her interest evident as she absorbed every word. Her attention often shifted to Aetheris, who was nestled comfortably on my shoulder, contentedly nibbling on the small pieces of food I offered. Solvyr, draped around Nova's neck like an ornate necklace, had taken a liking to the food, helping herself to Nova's plate with a playful curiosity.

Kryos 's fingers lightly drummed on the edge of the table, and her face brightened with a spark of excitement.

"I might have just what you need!" She leaned in conspiratorially, her voice dropping to a hushed but excited tone.

"I have a collection of ancient artifacts, many of which are not yet fully catalogued. There's one, in particular, that might hold the precise information you're looking for. I acquired it recently as part of an alliance. It is ancient and rumoured to hold detailed information of various species, including Nxyarans, dating back thousands of years."

With a graceful gesture, she signalled to her servants. They moved with swift, efficient grace, disappearing into the depths of the house with purpose and discretion.

"That sounds incredible," I exchanged glances with Nova, sensing our shared relief and anticipation. Finally, we were in precisely the right place. "If it contains what we need, it could be a significant breakthrough."

"I'm thrilled to help." Kryos' pale eyes sparkled with genuine enthusiasm. The artifact is stored in a secure part of the house, so it may take a little time to retrieve. But I assure you, it will be worth the wait."

Aetheris stayed on my shoulder the entire time, her gentle sighs hinting at her satisfaction. With a satisfied air, Solvyr reclined around Nova's neck, enjoying both the meal and the peaceful surrounding. It had been a long time since we had felt this comfortable, let alone been in a place where our concerns were met with genuine interest and support.

The anticipation was almost unbearable as we waited for Kryos' servants to return with the artifact. When they finally reappeared, Kryos' eyes gleamed with pride and excitement as she gestured to the doorway.

My heart skipped a beat. Kryos' artifact wasn't an object. It was an... Octayaran!

A mixture of emotions overcame me as the same being I had encountered in the dungeon was ushered under guard. Its presence was just as awe-inspiring and unsettling as I remembered. An ethereal, demi-god-like figure with an intense aura of power. The Octaryan's eyes, sharp and intelligent, seemed to recognise me without giving away our past connection.

Having never seen such a creature before, Aetheris reacted. Her transformation to table height was swift and graceful, a magnificent display of her protective instincts. Her powerful stance signalled her readiness to defend. Solvyr responded simultaneously, her serpent form hovering in a defensive pose, mid-air between Nova and the Octaryan.

"Oh, this is marvellous!" Kryos' eyes widened with delight.

"I've seen many Nxyaran pets, but Aetheris is extraordinary!"

"Zarya, you didn't mention they were—" Nova turned to me, her expression a blend of shock and revulsion.

"Yes, I know," I interjected, my chest tightening with anxiety. I sensed that revealing my familiarity with the Octaryan would raise questions I wasn't ready to answer.

"They're not exactly pleasant to encounter, but this one appears well-preserved," I said, adopting a tone of detached observation, as though discussing an inanimate object rather than a revered being with its own complex nature.

"Isn't it incredible?" Still beaming with excitement, Kryos leaned closer to the Octaryan. "I've studied many artifacts, but having a living example, even in this state, is a rare treasure. I have verified that it is the last of its kind. The knowledge it has must be invaluable."

Protective but curious, Aetheris let out a low growl as she approached the Octaryan, who regarded her with a calm, almost detached gaze, its presence commanding respect.

Nova's eyes flicked between the two with a begrudging admiration for how Aetheris had risen to the occasion. "And you are willing to trade it?"

"I'm sure you can uncover something extraordinary from it." Kryos' enthusiasm was unbridled. "As a symbol of our alliance, consider the Octaryan yours."

A blend of horror, joy, and excitement swirled within me. The Octaryan would have the information the Twins needed. Hopefully, it is friendly. I didn't really know how to tell.

"In exchange for Aetheris, of course," Kryos added.

The warmth of the evening was replaced by a chilling tension. Kryos' gaze had hardened into something cold and calculating. Guards had silently surrounded us while we were distracted by the Octaryan. Their eyes trained on us with an unwavering intensity, underscoring the gravity of the situation.

My heart thundered in my chest, a whirlwind of

emotions swirling within—fear, desperation, and a deep, aching sorrow. I shifted uneasily, the phantom burning of the rebel scar on my skin reminding me of the last time I faced this situation. Aetheris sensed the shift, her eyes flickering with uncertainty. I saw the distress mirrored in her gaze as she turned to me, seeking reassurance that everything would be alright.

"If you wish to leave, with or without the Octaryan, Aetheris must be exchanged." Kryos' voice cut through the thick silence, her tone firm and unyielding. "I am sure that the only Nxyaran dungeon escapee and her attack dog would make a nice addition to my collection."

The words hit me like a physical blow, and Nova did not take to being called my attack dog. Every instinct screamed to protect Aetheris; the thought of giving her up was unbearable, yet the prospect of losing the chance to stop Drakonis by being trapped here as part of Kryos' collection was equally daunting.

I looked at Nova. Her expression hardened with grim determination as Solvyr returned to her waist. She grasped the stakes as I did. We both knew that this trade could reveal crucial knowledge, but it carried a devastating price.

Turning back to Kryos, I felt a deep betrayal and resignation.

"If this is the only way... then I don't see a choice," my voice cracked despite my attempts to remain composed.

Kryos clapped her hands in celebration while Aetheris whimpered, her eyes fixed on me with a pleading gaze. My heart ached with each step as I reached out to her, watching as the guards moved in to escort her away. Seeing her subdued and retreating felt like a piece of my soul was being torn away. I clung to the hope that this sacrifice would not be in vain, that the Octaryan's knowledge would make it all worthwhile.

The price of this trade was high, and its burden weighed on me. Yet, beneath the grief, a fierce resolve ignited—a steadfast determination to reclaim Aetheris one day and, until then, to press forward with our plan.

Aetheris glided through the opulent corridors of Kryos' estate, her every movement radiating quiet dignity, her powerful form standing out amongst the delicate beauty of the surroundings.

Rich tapestries and luxurious fabrics lined the walls. Still, Aetheris's gaze remained fixed on a lavish feast made just for her in a room ahead.

Paying no mind to the splendour or the growing crowd of spectators surrounding her, Aetheris enjoyed her meal with slow, deliberate bites. Whispers of excitement buzzed around her as Kryos' entire rebel community gathered in the hope of witnessing the creature's rumoured abilities—perhaps a display of her size-shifting prowess or a breathtaking flight.

"Ladies and gentlemen," Kryos announced with a theatrical flair as she entered the room, her eyes sparkling with smug satisfaction. "I'm thrilled to inform you that Zarya and Nova have departed with that despicable creature, thank the Gods. Here is my latest and much more appealing acquisition."

The air thickened with anticipation as Kryos ensured every member of her rebel faction was present.

"Prepare to be amazed," she declared, her voice brimming with pride as the last of the observers settled in.

Aetheris continued eating as her massive form became taut. Her fur bristled with a subtle, ominous energy. The audience collectively held their breath, eyes wide in awe as they braced for whatever spectacle was about to unfold.

Now! Aetheris thought to herself, and in a horrifying instant, she struck.

Still devouring the feast before her, she unleashed a deadly storm of needle-like fur strands that sliced through the air with lethal precision. The attack was swift and merciless, leaving the crowd no time to react. Gasps of wonder turned to shrieks of terror as the deadly strands pierced flesh, finding their marks with ruthless accuracy.

The room descended into chaos, a nightmarish scene of blood and violence. The air filled with the sickening thud of lifeless forms hitting the ground, their final breaths choked out by the vicious assault.

Watching, paralyzed, as her rebel comrades fell around her, Kryos' eyes widened in horror as she realised her fatal mistake. Lives were snuffed out in a matter of seconds, and the finality of their deaths settled into the room like a suffocating fog. Kryos, caught in the middle of the carnage, was among the last to succumb. Her terrified gaze met the oncoming storm of strands, and with a final, strangled gasp, she crumpled to the blood-soaked floor.

As the life drained from the room, Aetheris continued her feast, consuming the fallen with a feral efficiency that was brutal and chilling. The once-lavish room now lay in ruin, stained with the blood of the slain. With newfound energy, Aetheris soared towards the Twins' laboratory.

No nano-bracelet needed, she purred with dark, arrogant pride.

ELEVEN

The glass walls of the mezzanine-level meeting room provided a sweeping view of the laboratory below. Tucked away in the corner, Aetheris was grooming herself as if she had just returned from an epic quest. I was thrilled to have her back, but her escape was a mystery, leaving me to wonder if she was a secret genius or simply the luckiest pet on the planet.

But today, Aetheris was not the focus of attention. Not even close. Nova, Lyra, Astra, and Rhea had their eyes glued to the Octaryan sitting at the far end of the meeting table on which Nyx and Nox had made themselves comfortable, using Solvyr as a makeshift lounge. Fascinated, they nibbled on something like tiny popcorn, engrossed in watching the eight-eyed being as if it were the most captivating show they had ever seen. It was the only time I had ever seen them stay still for more than a few seconds.

The Octaryan remained silent, just as intrigued by Nyx and Nox as they were by her. Mimicking their actions with bizarre grace, she used her prehensile feet to pick up invisible food, pretending to eat. Watching this ancient, god-like being imitate two pint-sized pranksters was endearing.

"I think I'm going to be sick," Nova muttered, looking like she was regretting her breakfast earlier. Rhea, seated across from Nova, appeared equally unsettled.

"Is this behaviour... normal?" she asked, her gaze fixed on the Octaryan.

"I don't know," I hesitated, my voice tinged with uncertainty. "I didn't see that much of them in the dungeon."

Everyone turned to look at me, their faces a mix of disbelief and outright terror. Still, they were searching for answers I didn't have. The Octaryan was an enigma, even to me, and the uncertainty of what she might do next hung heavily in the air.

Meanwhile, Nyx and Nox had somehow managed to inch even closer to the Octaryan, who responded by sliding closer to them in return. The three of them were engaged in a bizarre dance, inching closer until the minuscule creatures could almost touch the Octaryan's tusks.

Tilting its head as if pondering some profound, cosmic truth, the Octaryan slowly extended one of its prehensile feet towards the smaller folk. Nyx let out a giggle—an actual giggle!—and grabbed hold of it like it was the most natural thing in the world. Nox followed suit, and within seconds, they were playing an odd game of tug-of-war.

I couldn't help it. My laughter sliced through the tension in the room like a knife, and soon enough, everyone was laughing. The Octaryan's grim, imposing demeanour hadn't changed one bit, but the absurdity of the situation was too much to bear.

As the laughter subsided, the Octaryan finally released Nyx and Nox, who collapsed into each other with exaggerated sighs of exhaustion, their game over. The room fell silent again, but this time, the tension had eased. The Octaryan remained inscrutable, a being of immense power and mystery. Still, at least now, she didn't seem quite as terrifying.

I caught Rhea's eye, and she offered me a weak smile as if to say, Well, at least we're still alive. Nova seemed a little tense, continuing to eye the Octaryan warily.

She is probably wondering if she had any other surprises up her sleeves. I thought to myself. Did she even have sleeves? Whatever. I will figure that out later. For now, we had much bigger things to worry about.

"We are running out of time," I said, breaking the silence. "The next Renewal Ceremony is just two hundred years away."

Rhea, Astra, and Lyra began speaking over each other, their voices rising in a chaotic blend of excitement and urgency as they scrambled to share their findings from their assignments. But Nova remained quiet, her gaze locked on the Octaryan, her usual sharpness dulled by something that gnawed at her. The tightness in her jaw, the way she avoided our eyes—it was like she was holding back a tidal wave.

"There's something I need to tell you all." Nova's voice was sharp and urgent, demanding our attention.

"I've been called to participate in the Renewal Ceremony sacrifice."

The room fell silent as the words hit like a physical blow. Rhea gasped, and I felt my stomach twist with dread.

"No. That can't be," I whispered, her revelation sinking in. "You're under the age requirement."

"It's already been decided." Nova's face was a

mask of regret and grim resolve. "The High Council selected me based on 'criteria' I apparently meet. If the Renewal Ceremony goes forward, I'll be forced to kill an Elder. None of us will ever be the same again."

The room seemed to shrink, the walls closing in as the reality of her words settled over us.

"We can't let this happen," I said, my voice trembling with desperation. "We have to stop them. We have to stop the Renewal."

Nova's eyes finally met mine, and I saw the flicker of fear she had been trying so hard to hide.

"I don't want to do this," she admitted, her voice barely a whisper. "But if we don't act fast, what I want won't matter."

"We have to fight this," Rhea said, her earlier excitement replaced with cold, hard determination.

"We'll find a way," Astra added, her voice steady but laced with urgency. "We won't let them do this to you."

"We need to move quickly. Every second counts," Nova nodded. "If the Renewal Ceremony goes ahead, we'll lose any chance of stopping Drakonis."

Rhea hesitated.

"There's more you need to know," her voice was tense with urgency. "Drakonis' plans go beyond just being the only evolving Nxyaran. She is seeking immortality and will use Rune to achieve it."

"What is a Rune?" Astra and Lyra's query came in unison.

"Rune is... a creature. Drakonis' pet," Rhea took a deep breath, trying to convey the dire situation. "It looks like a snail with a single eyeball in the middle of its shell. Its power is that of shield generation and mind control. They are forming a bond—one that could make them unstoppable. Combined with Drakonis' plans to be the only Nxyaran that evolves, they could live... forever."

"Immortality... so this isn't just about genocide," I could see the fear in Lyra's eyes. "It's about control... over our entire future."

"Exactly," Rhea replied. "We need to stop the Renewal Ceremony before it's too late, not just for Nova or us, but for everyone."

"How do we do that?" Astra looked around the table, desperation creeping into her voice. "We're running out of time, and in another two centuries, Drakonis will be more powerful."

"We keep to our plans," I said, forcing myself to stay calm. "A new species will stop Drakonis, and we will ensure that Rune has no power over it. We don't have the luxury of time, but we must make it work. We can't lose Nova, and we can't let Drakonis succeed."

The new information from Nova and Rhea had thrown everything into sharper focus. There was no turning back now.

"We need to reconfirm our decision," I said, my voice firm as I tried to keep everyone grounded.

"Being able to replicate the cloning will not stop Drakonis even if we perfected it. Outright warfare doesn't solve the problem either; stopping the Renewal Ceremony slaughter alone won't work. If it's not Drakonis, someone else will find a way to keep the ceremony going. We need something more. Something that can change the game entirely."

Everyone nodded in agreement.

"We need to think beyond the Renewal Ceremony or the slaughter," Rhea continued in my line of thought. "The real problem is that Drakonis, or anyone like her, can continue manipulating our evolution. We need to create something new, something they can't control."

"That's why we decided to create a new species," I picked up where Rhea left off. "A species completely outside the High Council's control."

"By doing this, we eliminate the need for genocide—no one will be more unique than this new creation. Drakonis loses the advantage of being the only Nxyaran to evolve, and we will ensure Rune won't be able to exert any influence over it. With that, the power struggle ends."

For a moment, there was silence as everyone absorbed the enormity of what I was suggesting.

"We have been toying with creating a new species for a while now," Astra said casually as if ordering something from a menu.

My eyes snapped to Lyra, who shrugged and glanced toward where Nyx and Nox were perched.

"We didn't think it was worth talking too much about because you wanted cloning, not creation," Lyra explained dismissively. "And to be fair, we are only in the early stages."

"But we have made much more progress with creation than with cloning," Astra interjected excitedly.

I looked at Nyx and Nox, the faint glimmer of hope rekindling in my chest.

"Show us!" I demanded.

The Twins exchanged a glance, a silent conversation passing between them.

"We can't risk this falling into the wrong hands. Nova and Rhea are going to have to step out," Lyra's tone made it clear that she was not making a suggestion. "The less they know, the safer they will be."

"What you don't know can't be used against you," Astra pleaded with Nova and Rhea. "For security reasons, no one with connections to the High Council can be across this information."

Rhea looked at me reluctantly. We had all vowed not to keep information from each other, especially something as instrumental as this. It didn't feel right. Still, we all knew the stakes were too high to argue.

"Alright," she said, her voice resigned.

Nova, however, hesitated. There was a flicker of something in her eyes. Was that hurt? Is she offended? But she quickly masked it, nodding her agreement. I caught the briefest glimpse of disappointment on Nova's face as they left the room, which no one else seemed to notice. There was no time to dwell on it now.

As the door closed behind them, I turned back to the Twins. This was our last hope. We had to get it right.

"Show me," I commanded.

The Twins activated a hologram, and the figure of the new species flickered into view above the table. We all leaned in, captivated by what we saw.

The design was tall and powerful, with a muscular frame. Astra broke the silence first, her tone laced with amusement.

"Is it just me, or is that some premium-grade anatomy right there?" Pride in the design was evident in her voice.

I tilted my head, scrutinising the details.

"It looks like a partly decorated tree to me. And... what's with the tail?" I pointed toward a curious protrusion at the front of the figure. "Why did you put it there?"

Lyra and Astra exchanged an amused look.

"That's not a tail, Zarya," Lyra started. "It's... well,"

"Let's just say it's an important part of the anatomy," Astra finished.

"Alright, moving on," I blushed as my eyes widened in realisation and desperately sought a change of subject. "It has more muscles than our biology textbooks!"

"Don't you just love it?" Astra grinned. "It's got muscles in places you didn't even know muscles could exist."

I chuckled. Obviously, the muscles were Astra's idea. Lyra changed the subject.

"We have named the new species 'male.'"

Now, I was intrigued. Naming a new species must have take a lot of consideration. "Why?"

"Because 'Mysterious And Legendary Entity' was too long," Rhea answered with a shrug.

"And whilst my sister wanted to satisfy her two-for-one muscle obsession, I wanted a name that had a nice balance of ancient mystery and modern simplicity," Lyra added.

I raised an eyebrow, indicating my scepticism.

"Okay, okay," Lyra sighed, grinning sheepishly. "The term 'male' was invented on a whim after some a very inspiring caffeine-infused elixer."

Obviously, naming a new species isn't all that hard after all; I smiled to myself as I considered the figure before me.

"Progress has come to a standstill, though," Astra admitted, her tone more sombre now.

I listened to the Twins explain how their creation was tangled up in complex technologies and scientific principles that seemed insurmountable. Their frustration was evident in their voices.

We had pinned our hopes on the Octaryan, believing that this ancient being would possess the knowledge and expertise to unravel the intricacies of the Twins' design and push their work forward.

But the Octaryan remained silent, unable to understand or communicate with us. We grappled with the realisation that our potential saviour might not be able to help after all.

The Octaryan, silently observing from the shadows, leaned forward.

"I will solve," Her low and resonant voice sent a shiver down my spine. As her gaze met mine, a dark glint in her eyes hinted at a truth I wasn't ready to confront. One that might change everything we thought we knew.

It had been one hundred and ninety years since the Octaryan had offered her help in creating a new life. One that we call 'male' or 'man'. Now, as I stood in the heart of the laboratory, watching the delicate dance of science and life, I was filled with awe and trepidation.

A being of few words, the Octaryan seemed to speak more frequently with Nyx and Nox. Astra and Lyra named her Theo, short for The O(ctaryan), and she moved with precision in evidence of the centuries of knowledge she had brought us.

Our journey began with synthetic stem cells designed to differentiate into any required cell type. The synthesising of these cells, their translucent forms shimmering like the essence of life itself, required much patience. We spent most of our time waiting and watching. They began to divide and multiply, laying the foundation for what was to come. Nyx and Nox attended to the minute details that could mean the difference between success and failure, their tiny forms almost invisible, yet their presence always felt.

The growing structures took almost twenty years to differentiate into the three primary embryonic layers required. Lyra carefully worked with biocompatible gels, creating a supportive environment that helped the stem cells develop correctly.

The next couple of decades saw the formation of the first organs. A neural tube emerged as a delicate structure that would become the brain and spinal cord. Theo was meticulous in her work. Using 3D-printed tissues made from biocompatible polymers, she embedded cells within these structures, allowing them to grow and form delicate networks to sustain life. The bio-inks she used were nothing short of miraculous.

Observing the first blood cells taking shape, their fragile forms coursing through the primitive pathways, felt like witnessing the dawn of life.

The major organs followed: lungs, liver, heart, kidneys, and the digestive system. Each masterpiece, crafted from silicone, gelatin, collagen, and elastin materials, mimicked natural tissues' flexibility, strength, and resilience. Theo's expertise was vital, with her profound knowledge of connective tissues ensuring the seamless integration of each organ.

The skeletal and muscular systems took shape over the next couple of decades. Bones were created using a unique ceramic material that was strong and light. To help the bones grow and connect properly, the Twins used a glass that encouraged bone tissue to develop and merge smoothly.

Muscles capable of contraction and movement grew from conductive polymers and elastic hydrogels. It was a marvel to watch as these structures, once mere ideas, became tangible, functional parts of what we hoped would soon be a living being.

The integumentary system was the final protective barrier. Astra worked tirelessly to create bioengineered skin substitutes, crafting them from collagen and keratin. The synthetic fibres for hair were delicate yet strong, their texture indistinguishable from the real thing. Nyx and Nox had meticulously arranged every strand of hair and perfected every pore.

The sensory systems were the last to be created, their complexity unmatched. The eyes, formed from optoelectronic materials, captured light in a way that was eerily un-Nxyaran. The ears, made from piezoelectric materials, detected sound with astonishing accuracy.

Looking at the culmination of nearly two centuries of work, I was filled with pride and a profound sense of responsibility. We had reached into the very essence of life and pulled forth something entirely new yet familiar. The new 'male' lay before us as a new beginning, forging new friendships and a chance to reshape our world.

But it wasn't alive.

"I don't think we should keep calling it 'It,'" Lyra said thoughtfully. "If we can bring it to life, it will need an identity. I was thinking of using He, Him, or His. Those words seem to fit."

"We should give it—him—a name," I suggested.

"Caelum," Astra declared as if she had already made the decision on behalf of our group.

"Caelum it is," I confirmed, glancing at Theo, whose blinking eyes had become our way of knowing she agreed.

We could not tear our eyes away from the figure lying before us. He was unlike anything we had ever seen. With every muscle and curve carefully crafted, he resembled a statue carved from living flesh. He had two strong arms extending from broad, powerful shoulders, each ending in a hand with five fingers. His legs, equally muscular, supported his frame with flat feet, each with five toes to provide balance and stability.

His broad chest was defined with pectoral muscles that hinted at strength, and his abdomen was firm. Dark hair contrasted his pale skin, framing a face that was both stern and serene. The skin that covered his body was smooth and pale, almost like a soft, even canvas stretched over the muscles beneath. Its whiteness gave him an ethereal, almost ghostly appearance.

From his limbs to his torso, we had designed every part of him for purpose and movement, yet also for aesthetic beauty, as if his form was meant not only to function but to be admired.

Astra's touch: I smiled to myself.

Mechanical arms hung above him like the limbs of some great, slumbering beast. They had done their work precisely, but now, there was a sense of anticipation in the stillness, as though the air was holding its breath.

What, exactly, had we created?

The question echoed in my mind as I leaned in closer, my gaze tracing the contours of his face. His features were strong and defined, yet there was a softness that contrasted with the raw power of his physique. His eyes were closed, long lashes casting shadows on his cheeks, and I wondered what colour those eyes would be when they opened. What kind of soul would look out at us from behind them?

Astra and Lyra's expressions mirrored my own mix of awe and uncertainty. None of us had expected this. We had anticipated a being that looked more like our own kind, something familiar. Still, this... this was something altogether different. Something new. It felt as though he had always existed, waiting for us to bring him into being.

"Beautiful." To our surprise, Theo was the first to break the silence.

The word hung in the air, and I could only nod in agreement. Beautiful, yes, but there was also something unsettling about him, making me question how much of that was due to the lack of Zxyaran DNA. My pulse quickened as I reached out, my hand hovering just above his chest. There was no faint rise and fall of breath, only perfect stillness.

"We need him alive... and awake," I stated the obvious. The thought of being this close but not finished in time for the Renewal Ceremony filled me with dread. What would happen if we could not bring him to life? Worse, what kind of being would he be if we did?

We only had ten years left until Nova was forced to perform in the Renewal slaughter. She was relying on us to save her.

"Could it be because he doesn't have a reproductive system?" I wondered aloud.

"No," Astra thoughtfully shook her head. "The lack of reproductive organs has nothing to do with whether he's alive or not."

"We designed Caelum to serve a specific function," Lyra leaned in, her gaze intense. "Adding the ability to reproduce would only complicate things. Our goal was to create a singular, focused entity. That is what we have done."

I looked at Caelum, his form lying still and poised.

"I hope we haven't diminished his life by making that choice."

"We've allowed him to be something new, something we hope will contribute to a better future," Lyra responded. "His existence will not be about traditional roles or abilities. It will be about what he can become and how he can help shape our world."

"So, how do we bring him to life?" I asked in sheer frustration.

We exchanged looks of uncertainty. The truth is, we had no idea. Everything we could possibly have thought of, we had done. Then some. An air of frustration filled the room. We were on the brink of something monumental, and with time running out, we couldn't afford any mistakes now.

"Integration," with a single, decisive word, Theo abruptly exited the room, pointing a long finger in the air as if she had just uncovered the key to... everything.

TWELVE
CAELUM

At first, I didn't know if it was real—this soft pulse of light that filtered through my senses. But it was there, persistent, tugging me from the depths, like it was pulling me out of a deep well. I inhaled, and air filled my lungs for what felt like the first time.

I was alive.

As my vision adjusted, I saw a figure standing out against the sharp white of the laboratory. She wasn't looking at me, but there was an intensity I couldn't place, as though she was expecting something. Was she waiting for me?

My gaze lingered on her sharp features, softened by a focus I couldn't understand. I tried to make sense of two identical figures she spoke with, but it felt like a dream. Distant, unreal.

Two small figures darting between her feet caught

my eye. Tiny yet precise in their movements, like they were pure energy. I enjoyed the challenge of keeping them in my sight as they skittered around. Then my whole body froze.

Standing apart from the others was a life form, unlike anything I could have prepared for. Four pairs of large, all-black eyes seemed to pierce through everything. It was as if she could see into places others didn't even know existed.

The others called her Theo. She radiated a calm, lethal energy, her very presence commanding the room without uttering a word. She appeared to belong to another realm entirely, and as I looked at her, I felt a deep sense of unease. Her presence felt electric, like she could split the air around her if she willed it. And as I watched her, a question bubbled inside me.

What, or who, am I?

The quiet hum of conversation filled the space, words barely cutting through the fog in my mind.

"He'll need to learn language – speech, reading, writing," the one called Zarya said in a low voice, as if trying not to disturb me.

"History," Theo volunteered. I shuddered at the thought of learning anything from...whatever that was.

"We'll handle technology, math, and science... Nyx and Nox can help," said Lyra, one of the identical figures, as she exchanged a glance with her counterpart. A quick nod passed between them, mischievous smiles flickering across their faces as though they held a secret they'd never reveal.

"Nova would be perfect to teach him combat," her counterpart, Astra, said longingly.

"Nova and Rhea can't know," Zarya added quickly, her voice dropping. "If they find out about him—"

She didn't finish the sentence. My mind snagged on the names Nova and Rhea. I couldn't place them and wondered why I was such a secret. The tension in the room felt like it was about to snap, only interrupted by the beings they called Nyx and Nox who noticed I was awake.

Their tiny bodies darted toward me faster than I could react. They practically vibrated with excitement as they swarmed over my body, their small hands running over my arms, face, and chest.

I felt... curious.

Nyx and Nox spoke in a language different to the others yet addressed me as if they were confident I could understand. Something about my skeletal structure, the internal systems regulating the air I breathed, and—were they talking about nanites? I listened, not understanding fully, but it didn't matter. Their excitement was contagious, and I found myself leaning into their energy.

It was Zarya's voice that pulled me away.

"He's awake," she said. The words were barely a whisper, but they stopped everyone in the room. She turned slowly, her gaze finally meeting mine. A flicker of realisation rippled across her face as if a long-awaited moment had arrived.

Theo turned next, her eyes narrowing simultaneously as she studied me with a mixture of curiosity and something else. Something harder to read.

"Caelum," Zarya spoke again, her voice steadier now, as though my name anchored her.

Caelum. That was me.

All eyes were on me as if waiting for some grand revelation or for me to say something all-knowing. But all I could do was breathe, feel the strange rhythm of this new existence, and try to understand.

I wasn't just alive. I was something else entirely.

"How much does he know?" Zarya asked, her eyes locking onto Theo as though she could drill the answer out of her.

"Not enough," Theo replied, stepping closer.

"But he will," Lyra and Astra rushed to my side excitedly. "Between us, we will teach him everything."

They knew who I was. Or rather, what I was. And now I had to find out, too.

The following days were a blur of sensations. At first, I could barely stand. My limbs felt like they didn't belong to me, and every step was a struggle between balance and gravity. I was alive, but my body was still learning what that meant.

That's when I met Aetheris.

The creature was massive compared to the others. Her movements were deliberate, slow, yet graceful. Zarya had called the feline over, and the way it responded to her, a silent understanding passing between them, fascinated me.

Aetheris approached me without hesitation and, from that moment, became more than just a living crutch to help me balance. She became my assigned companion through my first lesson - movement.

Leaning on her broad back, I took my first tentative steps. Aetheris moved with me, patiently guiding me, allowing me to regain my sense of control. I felt grounded when her soft fur brushed against my skin. Her presence became something I relied on until, gradually, I learned to walk without stumbling. To feel the floor beneath my feet as if it had always been there.

"Good," Zarya said from a distance, observing my progress. Her voice had a hint of pride, though it was always tempered by something deeper that I couldn't place.

The years that followed were a relentless blur of academic lessons and combat training, each session pushing my mind and body to their breaking points. History, mathematics, speech, science - every subject was a silent reminder of the heavy expectations placed upon me. Yet no one would reveal what those expectations were.

The rate at which I absorbed information was extraordinary. I took in everything around me, including subtle shifts in the atmosphere when specific names were spoken. There was a weight to the unspoken truths, especially whenever Nova and Rhea were mentioned. They had been kept from me. I didn't know why, but I was getting closer to the answer.

More than anything, I watched Zarya. She was a master of control. Every movement calculated, every word measured. But beneath that control, I could sense conflict, an undercurrent of something she wasn't ready to show. The Twins, on the other hand, were more open. They questioned everything and challenged everyone, and while their words seemed harsh, there was no denying their respect for the others.

I stored every detail away, reading how they interacted and enjoying endless conversations with Nyx and Nox as I practised their native language. They were all part of something bigger. A purpose I had yet to fully grasp.

When I was not in lessons or absorbing the complexities of my environment, I retreated to my quarters. The sleek, minimal design was practical, built for function rather than comfort. The walls were embedded with screens that flickered with data whenever I needed it. My bed, tucked against the far wall, was firm, the type that ensured you woke up ready to work rather than sink deeper into sleep. Shelves lined one wall, filled with books and tablets—texts that I was encouraged to read in the brief personal hours I was allotted.

Zarya demonstrated how to use the room's technology to monitor environmental conditions and communicate with the outside world. It was standard in all assigned quarters, and now I had the same level of control, though I used it sparingly.

My personal time was brief, often just long enough to process the day's lessons before I returned to my routine. But today, I had an entire day to myself. No classes, no schedules, just time. The quiet unnerved me a little, but accepting that I deserved a break, I made my way to one of my favourite places.

The library was vast, filled with towering shelves of ancient texts. The others preferred their tablets and digital records. Still, I found something deeply comforting in the feel of physical books: their weight in my hands. I gravitated toward the oldest tomes, which smelled of time and history, their pages worn but still full of knowledge. They told stories of Nxyara's long-forgotten civilisations that rose and fell before anyone had even thought to record them.

Sitting with my back against the cool stone of the library walls, I opened a worn volume on distant worlds. Aetheris curled up beside me, her large frame surprisingly compact as she settled into a comfortable position. I rested my hand on her fur, feeling the steady rise and fall of her breathing.

For the first time, I let myself fully relax. There was no pressure, no expectations. Just the words on the page and the content purring of Aetheris beside me. The laboratory felt far away, and for a moment, I was content to simply exist in this small, stolen peace.

As I drifted off, questions lingered: the mysteries of who I was, why I had been created, and what role I was meant to play in this complex, secretive world.

I awoke to Theo towering over me, ready to guide me through the intricacies of Nxyaran history and politics. I no longer found her intimidating, having grown accustomed to her godlike demeanour over our endless history lessons.

"Ready?" Theo's voice cut through the quiet of the Library.

"Absolutely," I replied, mimicking her signature one-word communication style.

Theo led me to a small, sleek research room, its walls lined with holographic displays. I took my seat, facing a table where projections of ancient Nxyaran cities flickered in and out of existence. The scene was set for what promised to be an intense lesson.

"The basics," Theo said, tapping a control panel. The holograms transformed into a vibrant image of Nxyara's earliest known cities. Grand structures intertwined with technology blending into the natural world.

"Nxyarans perfected self-replication. Our complex history spans millenniums. Advanced technology," she gestured to the holograms, "results."

I nodded, absorbing the information. Theo's words were precise, yet her enthusiasm for the subject was evident. It was clear she didn't just teach the material; she had lived it. We immersed ourselves in the details of Nxyaran society, their advancements, political structures, and the evolution of their governance.

"How old is this technology?" I asked, my curiosity bubbling up.

Theo's eyes widened slightly, surprised by my question. "Many millennia."

Millennia. The sheer scale of time and history left me stunned as I tried to grasp its enormity. It led me to wonder how old Theo was, but I decided asking would be impolite.

Theo continued, her voice taking on a more personal tone. "Several phases, each refining."

My mind raced through the facts as the lesson progressed, connecting dots at record speed. Theo noticed, some of her eyes squinting in thought as she watched me.

"You're fast," she remarked, a hint of curiosity in

her voice. "Exceeding others."

"It's fascinating," I replied, genuinely absorbed. "I'm seeing the pieces fall into place."

"Intuitive," Her gaze lingered on me, admiration evident in her eyes. "History speaks to you."

"It does," I confessed, unsure if that was a statement or a question. "It's strange, but there's something familiar about it. Like a forgotten part of myself."

"Interesting," A thoughtful expression crossed her face and I felt a new energy between us. She seemed to now view me as her student with a true passion for learning instead of her creation.

I concentrated on her supreme aura and tried to visualise an enhanced connection.

Theo?

There was a moment of silence as her eight eyes stared at me, startled. A soft, surprised reply followed.

Caelum? Is that you?

I could sense her mental presence, and she could feel mine. The communication was clear but subtle, a whisper in the mind rather than a shout.

This is incredible, my thoughts conveyed. I didn't expect this ability to be so precise.

Neither did I, Theo replied, the realisation dawning on her. But it's good to have someone I can communicate with fully. It might help us to progress faster.

Her mental presence carried a warm sense of approval.

Yes, it will be helpful. You use more words this way. I chuckled.

With that, I ended the connection, feeling a strange sense of satisfaction. Another piece of the puzzle had fallen into place. I was not just learning Nxyaran history but also discovering myself.

As I moved on to my next lesson, I was excited to see who else I could connect with telepathically. I was starting to feel a profound connection, not just to the history and the people around me, but to the world slowly becoming my own. Although I had not seen life outside of the laboratory yet, I had allies, knowledge, and a growing sense of purpose for now.

And that, I thought, was an excellent place to start.

Zarya faced me across the mat, her stance rigid and authoritative, her gaze unyielding. The warmth and approachability I had come to appreciate during our language sessions and in our growing friendship outside of the classroom were gone. She was all business.

It was my fourth year of combat training, and one thing was certain: this was going to hurt.

"This is combat training, Caelum," Zarya's voice cut through the charged atmosphere, steely and unwavering. "Here, there's no room for weakness. You need to be swift, cunning, and merciless. Anything less will get you killed."

I swallowed hard, my heart pounding like a war drum.

"Begin," she commanded, her voice like a whip crack.

I sprang into action, adrenaline surging as I moved with practised precision, Zarya responding with a whirlwind of strikes. Her kicks and punches were powerful and surgical, each aimed with ruthless accuracy.

I tried to anticipate her moves and read the patterns in her onslaught, but she was darting and weaving with blinding speed. Her every strike landed with bone-jarring force. I could barely keep up as my muscles screamed, each hit a brutal reminder of my limits.

"Left!" she barked, her voice cutting through the

haze of my exertion. I twisted away, avoiding a devastating blow.

"Remember, Caelum, a warrior doesn't just react; they foresee."

"I'm trying!" I grunted, sweat mingling with blood on my face.

Despite the agony, there was something hypnotic about the way she fought. The raw power and sheer intensity she unleashed were electrifying. Her movements were a masterclass in combat, making me wonder who Nova was, the one Zarya believed was better at combat.

As I ducked beneath another vicious strike, I reached out with my mind, trying to tap into her thoughts. I concentrated hard, attempting to breach the mental wall between us, but found only impenetrable silence. It was clear that telepathy required both parties to possess the ability for it to function. The realisation was both humbling and maddening.

Frustration surged within me as I raced to keep up with her relentless assault. Whenever I thought I had a moment to catch my breath, she was back on me; her strikes unforgiving. As I was about to deliver my best blow, one of her prehensile feet reached up, taking a firm hold on my throat.

"Stay sharp!" she roared, as I tried to loosen her

grip.

"That's cheating!" I managed to protest. "I don't have hands for feet."

"Just because you are the only flat-footed being on this planet doesn't mean you get any special consideration," she barked, releasing her grip. "Your body is different than ours. Learn how to use that to your advantage."

I collapsed onto the mat, gasping for air, my body a mosaic of blood, bruises and exhaustion. I looked up at her, her gaze softening.

"You're improving," she said, her words carrying a weight of recognition rather than praise. "You're learning to push through the pain. That's a start."

I managed a weak nod, my throat raw and my body trembling. The intensity of the lesson left me both humbled and invigorated. There was a bond forming between us that transcended mere instruction. Zarya had become my closest friend, challenging me physically, mentally, and emotionally. I valued her deep commitment to my growth, to push me beyond my limits. A fierce admiration for her surged within me. An emotional connection that made me feel as though I had a purpose, someone to live for, to protect.

Back in my quarters, the day's brutal training

echoed through my aching body. The room was silent except for the gentle hum of the ventilation system and the soft purr of Aetheris curled beside me. My thoughts were a whirlwind, but one stood out with piercing clarity: Zarya.

I turned to Aetheris, who regarded me with her mysterious eyes. I could almost sense her silent encouragement. As I closed my eyes, I vowed to honour our bond and protect Zyara with all I was, ensuring she would rise as the leader she was destined to be.

After eight years of training and living in the laboratory, I found lessons with the Twins the most exhilarating. Immersing myself in science and technology felt like entering a high-tech wonderland. Once I conquered the initial challenge of being able to tell the Twins apart, my learning accelerated.

Astra was already diving into the complexities of energy fields when I arrived. She manipulated a hologram of a swirling energy vortex with a flourish, her excitement palpable.

"Energy fields are the lifeblood of our technology," she explained, her voice bubbling enthusiastically. "They interact with matter in ways that let us control nearly anything. It's like having magic at your fingertips!"

I nodded, trying to absorb her rapid-fire explanations. The thrill of the challenge was exhilarating, even if I was struggling to keep up.

Beside her, Lyra adjusted the display with a practised hand, her expression serious as she laid out the intricacies of molecular manipulation.

"And this," she said, pointing to a series of molecular structures on the screen, "is how we harness these fields to power our devices and create sustainable environments. It all begins here, from the smallest unit."

Whilst it was mesmerising to see how these seemingly abstract concepts were the backbone of Nxyaran technology, I couldn't help but catch snippets of Nyx and Nox's louder-than-usual chatter as they darted around the room like buzzing fireflies.

"Sounds like they're plotting something," I said, glancing at their erratic movements.

Astra shot me a conspiratorial grin. "They've been this way all morning. Something big must be brewing."

Lyra, absorbed in her work, let out a soft chuckle.

"They have been extra mischievous lately. I must admit, it's refreshing to have someone who can understand what they are saying."

True to form, Nyx and Nox made their move. They scampered over to Aetheris, who was lounging in the corner, her large eyes half-closed in a semblance of sleep. Nyx circled Aetheris with exaggerated gestures while Nox clambered up onto her back, chattering excitedly.

Aetheris's tail twitched in response, and before long, she was bouncing around with the Twins, her calm demeanour giving way to playful exuberance. The sight was almost comical. Aetheris, usually so serene, was now frolicking like a giant kitten, matching Nyx and Nox's boundless energy.

Lyra couldn't contain her laughter. "They always find a way to add a bit of chaos to our lessons."

"Or make them better," Astra said with a smirk, her eyes twinkling as she glanced at me. "Their antics often bring a much-needed break."

Nyx and Nox were in full swing, using Aetheris as their playground. They leapt from her sides and bounced off her back while Aetheris growled playfully, clearly enjoying the game. Nyx dared to jump from Aetheris's back to a nearby console, missing her target by a wide margin and landing in a heap of giggles.

Not to be outdone, Nox fashioned a makeshift wand from a small tool, directing harmless beams of light at Nyx, who reacted with exaggerated mock terror.

I couldn't help but laugh. The minuscule Twins weren't just mischievous; they were a burst of joy and creativity, balancing out the rigid structure of the laboratory.

As the laughter finally slowed, I turned back to Lyra and Astra. They watched with amused patience as their companions snuggled beside Aetheris, exhausted from their escapades.

"They certainly have a unique way of learning," I remarked.

"They do," Lyra agreed, her smile lingering warmly. "And they're excellent at reminding us not to take things too seriously."

Astra nodded, her eyes reflecting a similar warmth.

"They offer a different kind of intelligence. One about creativity and spontaneity. It's an important counterbalance."

With the Twins' antics behind us, the rest of the lesson continued with a renewed sense of ease. Lyra and Astra guided me through more complex concepts, their explanations becoming clearer with each passing minute.

As I left the lab, the echoes of our laughter were still fresh in my mind. There was something deeply satisfying about the friendship we had forged over the years. It was uniquely different to the relationships I had with Theo and Zarya. And somewhere out there, the enigmas Nova and Rhea were waiting to be discovered.

THIRTEEN

The meeting room was thick with tension. Lyra's eyes were sharp, Astra's lips were pressed into a tight line, and I could feel my own frustration boiling beneath the surface. With the renewal ceremony only a year away, every detail was under scrutiny. Caelum sat in the corner, his gaze fixed on the floor, an almost passive observer to our heated discussion.

"I still think Caelum's not ready," I said, trying to keep my voice steady despite my frustration. "His progress is commendable, but it's not enough. We can't afford any mistakes."

"Zarya, you're being overly cautious," Lyra's eyes flashed with irritation. "Caelum has shown remarkable growth. It's not just about him being ready. We must consider the consequences for Nova and Rhea if we hold off."

Astra nodded in agreement.

"You're too emotionally involved in this, Zarya," her tone was sharp. "Your personal feelings are clouding your judgment. We need to base our decisions on objective facts, not just your concerns."

My hands clenched into fists, turning my knuckles white as the argument heated up.

"This isn't about personal feelings," I countered. "It's about ensuring Nxyara's future. We've invested too much to risk everything due to haste."

Across the room, Caelum's eyes widened and then focused on Theo, who gave him a reassuring nod.

The room fell silent as we all caught Caelum's reaction. Lyra's eyes widened in shock, and she exchanged a glance with Astra that spoke volumes.

"What was that?" Lyra's voice cut through the silence, her tone demanding. "Did Theo and Caelum just communicate... telepathically?"

I turned to Caelum, who now seemed more focused and determined.

"It appears Caelum and Theo have established a telepathic link," I said, my voice steady despite the jealousy rising inside me. "Not something we had anticipated."

"So, Theo and Caelum have a private communication channel," Astra's expression shifted to one of deep thought. "He can also understand Nyx and Nox. This could impact our plans in ways we haven't considered."

Lyra's gaze softened as she regarded Caelum with newfound respect.

"This could be a valuable asset. We should explore how to leverage this telepathic link effectively. It might offer insights or advantages crucial for the ceremony."

"We will need to re-evaluate our approach," I sighed, feeling the weight of responsibility pressing heavily on me. "Let's concentrate on the immediate tasks and ensure that Caelum is as prepared as possible."

The discussion shifted as we explored the implications of Caelum's telepathic abilities. The debate was animated, with each of us considering how best to integrate this unexpected development into our plans. We understood that navigating this new landscape required both prudence and ingenuity, maximising every available benefit.

The room was charged with emotion and excitement as we debated the advantages and potential adjustments needed. In the end, we concluded that we needed more time. This renewal ceremony would not proceed as planned; perhaps it might be feasible when Caelum is more adjusted in another three centuries. Yet, one pressing issue remained unresolved: Nova.

Nova was the one who would need to follow through on the renewal ceremony slaughter. She would be the one with the killing of innocent elders on her conscience. It is her trust that we were about to break by not delivering a new species. What is worse, she was totally oblivious. The question was, who would deliver the news?

I could sense the hesitation in the room as everyone glanced around, waiting for someone to take the initiative. A weight of unvoiced concerns and simmering tensions filled the room.

Finally, Lyra broke the silence.

"This news will be a significant blow to Nova's role in our plans, not mention her expectations. She also can't know any details of Caelum or how close we are."

"We all know her reputation for strong reactions when things don't go her way," Astra added, her expression serious. "Whoever tells her must be prepared to handle her response and manage any fallout."

"I'll do it," I breathed deeply. "I am her best friend. She must hear it from me."

"Are you sure?" Lyra's eyes met mine. "Nova's reaction will be intense, and Rhea said that she almost killed you during your last disagreement."

I nodded, remembering our fight in the cave like it was yesterday.

"I will let Rhea know, too," I moved the conversation forward. "I'll explain everything without giving any information about Caelum and address her concerns. As far as Nova and Rhea know, our attempts did not turn out as hoped."

Astra's expression softened slightly. "Just be ready for anything."

The group fell into a thoughtful silence. Delivering this news would be challenging. Nova was relying on us to get her out of the slaughter, and it was clear that she didn't like being kept out of the loop, even though she had agreed with the decision to do so.

I took a moment to compose myself before heading towards Nova's quarters. This was a pivotal moment, and I knew that how I handled it could influence the future of our mission and our team's cohesion. I took a deep breath as I stepped through the portal to Nova's quarters, steeling myself for the conversation ahead.

The atmosphere was heavy as I stepped inside. The room was a study in contrast: the soft, diffused light from the city outside mingled with the shadows cast by the sparse furnishings. Nova stood by the window, Solvyr wrapped around her right arm like a small, delicate bracelet, her posture betraying the tightness in her shoulders. She didn't flinch at the portal opening. It was almost as if she was expecting me.

"Nova," I began, my voice measured, "we need to talk."

She turned slowly, her face a mask of controlled emotion, though I could sense the storm brewing beneath. Having to keep information from her for the last ten years, even though we had all agreed it was necessary, had taken its toll on our friendship. We had never had secrets between us before.

"What's this about, Zarya?"

I took a deep breath, knowing the gravity of what I was about to say.

"The new species won't be ready for the renewal ceremony. You'll need to continue with the performance as planned."

There, I said it. Quick and to the point. Still, the

words hung heavy in the air, and I watched as Nova's eyes narrowed, her composure slipping.

"So, you're telling me I'm going to have to kill an innocent elder?" Her voice, though calm, was edged with disbelief and resentment. "Tell me more about this new species! How close are you – exactly?"

"I understand this is frustrating," I tried to steady my voice. "The new species isn't ready for integration into society. We need more time for its development."

The room seemed to contract with her mounting frustration as Nova's anger flared into a torrent, and she closed the distance between us with swift, angry strides.

"You're betraying my trust, Zarya! I've been dedicated to this project and kept out of the loop for ten years, and now you're telling me I'm not getting out of the ceremony? I am part of this process and have every right to know exactly what's happening!"

I signalled for peace with raised hands, hoping to ease the tension.

"The decision was made based on the current state of the new species. It's not ready. I can't disclose details to you or Rhea. You agreed to that."

Nova's frustration reached a boiling point, and she slammed her hand on a nearby table, causing papers and documents to scatter. Her breathing was ragged, her face flushed with anger. Solvyr filled the room. Her top half hovering mid-air, wings spread, and fangs bared as she took a defensive stance against me. I silently cursed myself for leaving Aetheris with Caelum.

"This isn't just about killing elders! It's about the trust you've broken and the secrets you're keeping from me. This was a critical decision that Rhea and I should not have been left out!" A tense hush swallowed the room, the remnants of her anger still crackling in the air.

I stood my ground, feeling a pang of guilt but knowing that my role was to manage the situation, not to cave under the pressure. Slowly, her anger seemed to give way to a more subdued yet intense curiosity. As Solvyr returned to her previous bracelet-like position, Nova turned away from me, her posture still tense and her gaze fixed on the distant city lights.

"Alright," she said, her voice resigned yet determined. "If I can't get out of murdering an elder, then I need to know more about this new species. What's its progress? What are its capabilities?"

I observed the shift in her demeanour, noting how quickly her anger had morphed into a focused interest. She was using this curiosity as a distraction, a way of coping with the disappointment of being left no choice but to partake in the ceremony.

"The new species is not yet ready for implementation," I said carefully. "I can't provide more specific details."

Nova's eyes locked onto mine, her frustration momentarily forgotten as she focused intently on the information I provided.

"I want to know everything you can share. If I'm stuck performing in the renewal ceremony, I deserve to understand what's happening with this new species."

I nodded, recognising the shift in her focus. "I'll keep you informed as much as I can."

The distance between us was intense. Rhea had adjusted to the news without protest, understanding the need for her separation. She had accepted it gracefully, throwing herself into the role of infiltrating Drakons' inner circle. But Nova.... she was different.

"You know I won't tell anyone," Nova cooed. "I just want to know what's going on. Do you even trust me anymore?

Her words stung more than I let on. Of course, I trusted her. I was trying to keep her safe.

"I know it is hard," I replied, trying to keep our newfound peace. "But you agreed that we can't risk it."

Nova shook her head, fingers twitching like she wanted to throw something.

"You have forgotten we are in this together." She snarled, her voice raised and accusatory.

She was wrong. I hadn't forgotten. Yet, each passing year made it harder to connect with her, as if she was slipping into a world I couldn't access. Perhaps it was I who had lost touch. Between the dungeon and the laboratory, it was possible that I had been away from Nxyaran society for too long.

I left her quarters wondering if, deep down, I was afraid to admit that she wasn't the same Nova I used to know. Something had shifted in her after she had been selected to partake in the renewal ceremony. I regretted the part she would have to play in the Elders' deaths. It made sense. Why wouldn't she be agitated and angry? Why wouldn't she lash out?

I returned to the laboratory using my nano-bracelet, hoping to find a miracle. A miracle strong enough to stop the renewal ceremony. Strong enough to stop Drakonis.

"Zarya," Theo greeted me, her calm voice laced concern. "How did it go?"

"Not well," I replied honestly. "Nova is furious about being kept out of the loop. She feels betrayed and demands to know more about the new species, adamant that her efforts over the last decade, coupled with what she is expected to do at the renewal ceremony, entitles her to full disclosure."

"I knew this would blow up," Lyra's eyes narrowed, her frustration evident. "It was only a matter of time before Nova's anger turned dangerous."

"What did you tell her?" Astra asked, ignoring her sister's comments.

I relayed the details of the confrontation, emphasising Nova's shift from anger to a more focused curiosity about the new species.

"She's trying to distract herself from the reality of her situation by focusing on the new species. It's as though she's using curiosity to cope with her disappointment," I concluded.

"We need focus." Theo's expression hardened as she absorbed the news.

I turned to Caelum, who had been observing the conversation and used my best accusatory tone.

"You've been quiet. Do you have anything to add?"

His gaze met mine with a determined intensity that I didn't expect.

"I don't know what you are all worried about," he replied casually, shrugging his shoulders. "I'm ready. I can handle it."

Theo's eyes narrowed and Astra's frustration boiled over.

"Are you mind speaking?" she accused Theo! "You're guilting Caelum into a position he's not ready for!"

"This is madness!" My face was a storm of conflicting emotions, as the argument heated up.

I am ready, Theo. I've learned more than they realise. I'm prepared for this challenge and any consequences that may come from it. Caelum's voice echoed in Theo's mind.

Theo's face softened as she replied, though her tone remained firm. I trust your judgement, but this reaches beyond you.

"It's not just about readiness; it's about the potential fallout from rushing things," Lyra's voice rose, her frustration palpable. "If Caelum isn't fully prepared, it could endanger the Nxyaran culture, Nova and Rhea's life, and our ability to duplicate this process."

"We don't always need to consider your precious

science!" I retorted.

The air pulsed, thick and charged, as if the room itself was holding its breath. Nyx and Nox, sensing the agitation, moved with increased urgency, their tiny forms darting between Lyra and Astra in an almost frantic manner. Aetheris shifted uneasily in her corner, her eyes darting between us as if calculating who she would attack first.

The argument reached a crescendo, voices overlapping and rising in a chaotic cacophony. The sense of division among us was stark, the gap between our perspectives widening with each heated exchange. The room was a battleground of conflicting emotions, each of us entrenched in our own viewpoint.

My frustration boiled over, and I slammed my hand on the table, the sharp sound cutting through the clamour and forcing an uneasy silence.

"Enough!" I declared. "We don't have the time for this. The decision is made. Caelum will not step in at the ceremony."

The silence that followed was suffocating. Caelum stood with defiance etched into every line of his body, his eyes burning with fierce determination. Theo, Lyra, and Astra stared at me, their faces a mixture of anger, resignation, and disbelief. The tension between us felt like a tangible force, and the weight of ten years' worth of unspoken emotions and buried disagreements flooded the room all at once. It was as if everything we held back, every withheld opinion and suppressed frustration, formed an insurmountable chasm between us, vast and unbridgeable.

As the tension hung in the air, extending myself to my full Nxyaran height I loomed over Caelum, pointing my finger at him whilst locking eyes with an intensity intended to crush any defiance. Every word dripped with authority, leaving no room for argument.

"You... will... NOT... go!"

FOURTEEN

A colossal formation known as God's Hand had been chosen as the location for the tercentennial Renewal Ceremony. An ancient formation where spires rose dramatically into the sky like the fingers of a giant reaching for the heavens. Each finger, hewn from solid rock, was draped in a thick blanket of greenery as if nature sought to soften the raw power of the stone.

Wisps of fog constantly swirled around the upper reaches, concealing the peaks as if they led into another realm. Waterfalls cascaded from the heights, their crystal-clear waters tumbling over the edges and vanishing into the void below.

The journey from Kael'thar was a steep ascent, only achievable through flight, which turned the space between God's Hand and our Nxyaran city into a hive of activity.

Sleek aero gliders sliced through the air, their

compact designs accommodating one or two passengers. Their silent propulsion systems made them ghostlike across the sky.

The elite of Nxyaran society travelled in nimbus cruisers, luxurious eco-friendly vessels boasting elegant, elongated structures. Inside, spacious lounges and private cabins offered its passengers comfort, while panoramic windows provided breathtaking views of the world below.

However, most Nxyarans opted for stratosphere shuttles, semi-autonomous transports that could carry up to fifty passengers at a time. Resembling sleek arrowheads, they were powered by a hybrid propulsion system, merging rocket technology with advanced aerodynamics.

Unable to risk being seen, I travelled in Lyra's vortex pod. The compact, one-person flying vehicle employed magnetic levitation and vortex propulsion for swift and agile flight. Its spherical design granted me 360-degree visibility and impressive manoeuvrability. I could summon it using the technology embedded in my nano bracelet if I needed a quick escape. With automatic parachute deployment and collision avoidance technology, the vehicle was ideally suited for my mission.

As I activated the pod, the hum of its magnetic

engines filled the air. The sound soothed my nerves as I prepared to navigate the unfamiliar technology. With a simple button push, it lifted into the air, ascending as I steered it towards the gathering at God's Hand.

The landscape below transformed into a blur as the rocky masses extruding out of Nxyara's oceans sprawled out like a patchwork quilt. My heart raced from the thrill of flight and the weight of the mission ahead. It would not be easy to remain unnoticed among the throngs of Nxyarans making their way to the ceremony.

Nearing the colossal floating formation, I joined a stream of aero gliders and nimbus cruisers, all gliding towards the arena nestled among the towering spires. The atmosphere crackled with excitement, and I could sense the energy radiating from the crowd forming below, a wave of anticipation building as they gathered for the celebration. I adjusted my course to approach from the north side of God's Hand, where the less populated areas provided the needed cover, maneuvering the vortex pod into a discreet corner just outside the arena's main entrance. Once confident I was hidden from view, I steadied my breathing as I observed the waves of elegantly dressed Nxyarans mingling, their flowing robes shimmering as they caught the light.

Stepping out of my transport, I caught my reflection. An off-shoulder, steel-grey corset cinched my waist, creating a striking hourglass silhouette. SSilver highlights sparkled across the bodice, while delicate, armour-like scales traced my arms, catching the light. Sleek black fabric lined with metallic silver panels covered my legs, running down to my boots. A sheer, delicate cape draped from my shoulders, adding elegance to the otherwise warrior-like attire. I quickly made minor adjustments, ensuring I blended with the surrounding crowd, my heart pounding not just from the thrill of the event but from the underlying purpose of my presence. I needed to find Nova among the attendees and find a way to get her out of this. I was not here for the entertainment; I was here to stop it. Forever.

Descending into the arena, I felt the atmosphere shift dramatically. The massive stone structure was carved from the same ancient rock as God's Hand. Its floor was expansive and flat, marked by the scars of countless ceremonies and battles. Dust swirled around my feet as I moved discretely through a sea of Nxyarans, competing for what they considered the best view for the ceremony. The towering walls of the arena rose up on either side, jagged and weathered, their surfaces pockmarked with time, telling stories of the lives lived and lost within this sacred ground.

Large gates loomed over us, rust and neglect sealing them closed, and the walls bore intricate carvings that told the tale of past renewals, battles, and sacrifices. Some sections had crumbled under the ravages of time whilst others stood firm, projecting a sense of enduring strength. It was a coliseum, a place where life and death intertwined, where the ancient rites of renewal were performed, and where blood soaked the earth, mixing with the dust of ages.

Pushing ever forward towards the centre of the floor to position myself as close to Nova as possible, I took in the rows of spectators perched on the crumbling ledges, their eager faces illuminated by the warm glow of the setting sun. Some wore the garb of warriors, their cloaks fluttering in the breeze. Others sported flowing robes, the colours of their garments blending into a tapestry of Nxyara. Their eyes gleamed with anticipation, reflecting the tension that filled the air. I felt that same anticipation coursing through me. A mixture of fear, reverence, and excitement.

I looked up at God's Hand towering above us like

a guardian. We were in the presence of something greater than ourselves. The peaks, shrouded in mist, held secrets I couldn't fathom, reminding me of the weight of tradition, the sacrifices made here, and the lives lost.

The drums echoed across the arena, a steady, rhythmic pulse announcing that the time for renewal and promising blood—our blood, the lifeblood of our people.

In the centre of the arena, the Primevex and Elder performers begin their ceremonial dance. Dressed in long, flowing black gowns that seemed to shimmer with an otherworldly light, they formed a circular gathering. The richly patterned fabric of their dresses, adorned with delicate, swirling motifs, reflected the ever-changing shapes of the mist curling upwards. Their gowns swirled around them as they moved, capturing the fading light and creating an enchanting display that captivated the crowd.

A swirling black mist began to rise and twist, spiralling upwards as if responding to their movements, drawing us all into the heart of the ceremony. The energy in the arena grew, and an intense force vibrated through my bones. I could feel it pressing against my skin, tugging at my senses, pulling me deeper into the ritual.

We all leaned forward, captivated by the sight unfolding before us. The floor beneath the dancers glowed with soft light, highlighting ancient symbols etched into the stone—a Nxyaran language lost to time but powerful in its meaning. This ground was sacred, a conduit for the energies of life and death, and I could feel its pulse syncing with my own.

The audience was alive with excitement. Tens of thousands of faces, some glittering with pride, others solemn with the weight of tradition, all watching as the dancers moved gracefully across the floor, their movements tracing ancient patterns that had been performed for millennia.

My gaze was irresistibly drawn to the High Council at the far end of the arena, towering above us from their lofty perch on a balcony that had been draped in deep crimson for the occasion. The broad stone foundation supported a graceful array of symmetrical columns, their gold accents catching the sunlight. Intricate carvings lined the tower's base, recounting tales of past triumphs. The sheer height of the structure exuded an aura of power and awe that seemed to grip all who dared to look. A sharply angled roof jutted forward, casting a shadow over the dignitaries gathered within. At the forefront, seated with undeniable authority, was Drakonis.

Her gaze swept over the ceremony below, her presence commanding, her eyes glimmering with satisfaction as she took in the unfolding scene, radiating absolute control.

Her gown seemed more alive than fabric. An embroidered golden serpent gave the illusion of coiling around her leg. The serpent's sleek body melded into the inky depths of the dress, its tail curling possessively near her thigh. Her shoulders were draped with golden, flame-like feathers that flared outward, framing her like wings. The serpent appeared alive as the gold shimmered in the flickering light of the ceremonial flames. Alive with a hunger to consume anything or anyone foolish enough to approach. Themes of elegance and danger were intertwined so seamlessly that Drakonis appeared more deity than mortal.

Rune stood silently nearby, its towering form a formidable presence nearly overshadowing the High Councillor. Its shell gleamed with a dark, iridescent sheen, its spirals catching the flickering flames of the ceremonial pyres. The unblinking eye had become a glowing orb, pulsating with an eerie light in time with the rhythmic beat of the drums. Rune's skin shimmered with a translucent hue, shifting between deep crimson and midnight black, casting elongated shadows across the floor that heightened the moment's gravity. Where Drakonis' dress resembled fire and serpents, Rune's outfit glinted with dim, glowing patterns that evoked the look of starlight trapped beneath a glassy surface, the hem leaving behind faint light trails as it floated just above the ground.

Contrasting the fiery feathers of Drakonis, Rune's adornments were cold, sharp, and dark, as if it were draped in shards of night itself. Around its waist, a belt of metallic tendrils coiled, their edges glowing faintly in time with its pulsating eye.

The snail-like creature carried an unsettling stillness, an aura of vast, quiet power. It was not a symbol of chaos like Drakonis but of something enduring, ancient, and unstoppable. Together, they were formidable. Drakonis, a burning flame of destruction and Rune, the cold, watchful embodiment of shadow and time.

I forced myself to focus on getting as close as possible to the performance, my heart sinking deeper with every step the dancers took. Nova moved like liquid; her every motion was flawless and captivating. She was beautiful. Powerful. Just as she had always been. Yet where the crowd saw grace, I saw the strain behind her every gesture. The weight of what was to come crushed me. I wanted to scream, to stop this madness. But it was helpless. I was suffocated by the tradition and duty that held me prisoner as much as it did her.

I glanced back at the balcony, hoping to catch Rhea's eye and share some wordless expression of our shared dread, but her gaze remained fixed on the ceremony. She looked more regal than I'd ever seen her as she stood in wait behind the High Council, who, in turn, sat like statues behind Drakonis, all watching with cold detachment.

Her bodice clung to her delicate yet powerful figure with intricate crystalline designs that seemed to bloom like frost on glass. The soft material had strength in its structure, as if the elegant patterns were laced with hidden power. Rhea was no simple engineer today; she was a servant of the High Council.

With each move she made, the fabric seemed to shimmer and shift, catching different hues as the dress cascaded down in waves. A flowing train swept behind her, short but breathtaking and twinkling with tiny, carefully placed crystals that gave the illusion of stars trailing her every movement. It was as if the dress had merged with her being, enhancing everything about her that was already formidable and enchanting. Rhea had always been strong, but in this moment, she was beyond powerful. She was celestial.

An enormous cheer from the audience brought me back to reality as the dancers twirled and leapt, oblivious to the truth behind what was unfolding before them. Each cheer cut deeper into my guilt. I had tried so hard to stop this, to find another way for Nova, for all of us. But tradition was stronger. Drakonis had won.

I clenched my fists at my sides, feeling utterly powerless. My breath came in shallow bursts as I forced myself to watch. I couldn't look away, not from Nova, not from what was coming. She danced so gracefully despite knowing full well what was expected of her at the end.

The Elders danced along the Primevexes, yet unlike the last renewal ceremony, their figures were cloaked in hooded robes, keeping their faces hidden. I could feel my pulse quicken as the Primevex dancers wielded their daggers. The moment was drawing nearer. The moment when Nova would be required to kill an Elder. The moment that will change her forever. The moment I promised would never happen.

A wild cheer erupted from the audience, entirely

at odds with the suffocating dread that had settled over me. Even from a distance, I could tell Rhea felt it, too. At the last renewal ceremony, we were part of the crowd, oblivious to the horror it held, thinking it was a moment of triumph, a symbol of the endless cycle that sustained us. But now we knew better. It was a nightmare.

"Please," I whispered to any deity that would listen. "Please, don't let her do this."

The weight of my guilt was pressing down, suffocating me. I wished Astra and Lyra were here with me instead of helping Theo ensure Caelum stayed put. I was about to lose Nova. I would not lose Caelum, too.

As I searched for a way to stop the ceremony without drawing attention, I couldn't shake the thought of him, the comfort he brought, the way his presence had come to mean more than I'd ever anticipated.

Drakonis sat motionless, her presence casting a dark shadow over the ceremony as though the air thickened around her. I kept myself out of sight, my heart thumping as her cold stare scanned the crowd, unforgiving. Though her searches for me had grown less frequent, I knew she wouldn't hesitate to crush any hint of defiance.

This was her moment. She thrived in the ritual—every detail, every breath choreographed to remind us of her control. Over the last three centuries, she had ruled with iron precision. This reign left no room for rebellion, no room for tenderness. Like so many before, this ceremony was nothing more than a show of dominance. Tradition, power, and control—these were the pillars of Drakonis' rule. She would not be swayed by compassion, not for me, and certainly not for Caelum.

I couldn't afford a single mistake. I had to let the ceremony play out, even as the desperation gnawed at me. Thoughts of Caelum clung to me. I wasn't ready to let go of him, not yet. Any move I made would have to be calculated—timed perfectly, or I would lose more than just the chance to save our species. I would lose him, too.

Rhea's gaze shifted, and for a brief second, our eyes met. The tension between us was unbearable, a shared knowledge of the doom that loomed over Nova. Though her expression remained unreadable, I knew that Rhea was feeling the same helplessness and gnawing dread. We were both bound by the same unbreakable chains.

The final crescendo of the drums filled the chamber, drowning out the frantic beating of my heart. The Primavex dancers stopped, forming a perfect circle around the Elders. A different choreography, perhaps, but a predictable ending.

The crowd roared with approval, cheers echoing off the vaulted ceiling. I stepped into Nova's line of sight, forcing myself to watch in support, finding it odd that this ceremony was stretching out the killings for some twisted spectacle.

The previous one had been swift—over before anyone realised it had begun. It was clear that Drakonis was raising the stakes for entertainment purposes.

I fixed my gaze on Nova as she gracefully approached the Nxyaran assigned to her. My chest tightened, and my throat was dry as I battled the overwhelming urge to shout, to rush in and stop her. But I was trapped, just as she was. The air was electric, the crowd holding its breath for the moment of sacrifice.

"Nova..." I whispered, barely audible even to myself.

Helpless, I could only watch as she raised her blade. The tension in the air was suffocating. The Elder stood tall, willingly offering her throat to Nova, who hesitated for the first time in our lives, her hand frozen mid-motion. No words were exchanged between them, but the body language spoke volumes. Then I recognised her. The Elder offering herself to Nova had mentored us both through the centuries as we strove towards joining the Primevex class.

My breath hitched at the realisation of the cruel twist of fate. My mind raced as memories flooded back of long nights spent in conversation, the Elder's wisdom guiding and encouraging us to see our potential when no one else did. Nova's eyes flickered with doubt, uncertainty clouding her resolve. Seconds felt like hours as the inner conflict played out across her features.

A knot of dread tightened in my stomach as the horrifying truth became clear. Drakonis was using Nova as bait, orchestrating the sacrifice of a friend to push her beyond breaking point, manipulating her with cruel precision. Drakonis didn't care about Nova's hesitation. She planned on it, hoping it would compel me to expose myself. The Elder was the key, a calculated emotional trigger, knowing I wouldn't stand by as one friend's life rested in the hands of another.

This entire renewal ceremony was devised for...

me!

It was a twisted game, one I hadn't foreseen but should have. My thoughts spun wildly, calculating every possible outcome. If I stepped in now, I'd reveal myself and unravel everything we had fought to protect. But if I stayed silent, Nova would be forced to go through with the unwarranted execution of a loved one, and the weight of that guilt would destroy her. I only had seconds to choose.

Nova's knuckles whitened as she forced herself to breathe, her chest rising and falling unevenly, eyes narrowing as she tried to push through her internal turmoil. The crowd watched, a sea of silence waiting for the first cut, the first life to be taken.

Unlike the previous renewal ceremony, where the sacrifices happened simultaneously, this performance required Nova to go first. Once she had made the first sacrifice, the others would follow suit. The Elder dancers, all of them, would die.

My body tensed as muscles threatened to move, but I couldn't expose myself. I couldn't give Drakonis the satisfaction.

I could almost feel the Elder's pulse quicken as Nova's warrior hand raised the blade to rest on the Nxyaran's throat.

"I'm sorry," I whispered, a single tear falling as

I watched the light fade from my friend's eyes, her resolve hardening. She was a heartbeat away from spilling blood.

"This stops now!" A sharp, authoritative voice sliced through the tension, reverberating across the arena.

The crowd fell silent, every eye straining to identify the source as the entire ritual ground to a standstill.

Nova's dagger dipped, confusion and disbelief flickered across her face. Her eyes frantically searched for the unseen speaker. The other Primevexes followed suit.

Rising from her seat, Drakonis scanned the crowd for the fool who dared to defy her. My gaze locked onto Rhea. Her expression was more fascinated than confused, and a glimmer of hope seemed to spark within her. But I knew that voice and what came with it.

Something far worse was about to unfold.

FIFTEEN

He stood in the centre as if he had every right to be there, though I knew he didn't. My breath caught as Caelum's striking, blue eyes seemed to pierce through me, unravelling every defence I had painstakingly built. The way the dark tunic hugged his muscular frame stirred something in me that I wasn't prepared to admit. I hated how drawn I was to him. There was power in his presence, a magnetic pull that I couldn't resist. It agitated me. His tousled hair framed his rugged face. Subtle scars enhanced his allure.

He wasn't supposed to be here, and yet, deep down, part of me was glad he was. Every line of his body screamed danger, yet there was calm in his presence. How could someone in such danger be so serene?

Moving towards Nova with confident and deliberate steps, Caelum gently removed the blade from her hand with one quick motion. I watched as the weapon slipped from her grip like it no longer had any meaning, and for a moment, the scene's absurdity almost made me laugh.

Barely reaching the shoulder of the shortest Nxyaran, Caelum felt oddly out of place. His stocky, muscular build contrasted sharply with the lean, agile forms of the Nxyarans surrounding him. Making him seem undeniably captivating.

"You won't need this," he said softly to Nova, his voice reassuringly like the fight was already over.

Nova looked at him in utter disbelief. I thought she would attack for a moment, but she didn't move. Her gaze flickered to me, her eyes filled with betrayal. Nova had trusted me. Trusted us. And now, with Caelum standing before her, the new species I said was not ready; cracks were beginning to form.

I should've prepared her better, I thought, guilt twisting in my stomach. But it was too late now. The damage was done.

"Zarya Elyssan!" Drakonis' voice roared throughout the crowd like a crack of thunder.

Everything inside me stopped as my attention snapped to the High Council. My eyes locked with Rhea's. Her expression was unreadable, but her message was clear as she shook her head slowly to avoid detection.

Don't do it. Don't reveal yourself.

Her warning was sharp, a thread of reason pulling me back from the brink. I exhaled, trying to steady myself, though every fibre of my being wanted to rise up to confront Drakonis. To save Nova and Caelum. I forced myself to stay hidden. Rhea was right. This wasn't the time. Drakonis obviously couldn't see me, and if I revealed myself now, the situation would spiral out of control.

"The name is Caelum, actually," Caelum said casually.

Oh great. I bit down on the inside of my cheek, stifling the groan building in my throat. Addressing Drakonis directly, let alone informally, was a mistake that would have severe ramifications. Drakonis won't let this slide. Not for a second. There was no turning back.

The crowd shifted, their fear unmistakable yet intertwined with a bizarre curiosity as they tried to get a good view of the creature amongst them.

"Arrest that thing!" Drakonis' voice cut through the murmurs like a knife, her eyes narrowing.

A collective gasp rippled through the crowd. Caught between their loyalty to Drakonis and the unsettling aura surrounding Caelum, the guards looked at each other, unsure and nervous. Frozen in indecision, their eyes darted between the High Council and the being standing centre stage.

"No," Caelum countered, his voice steady and commanding. "You will stay put."

It was astonishing how he held sway over them, commanding respect even in their confusion. Caught off-guard by the power in his words, the guards slowly lowered their weapons. My heart lept. Could he truly have this kind of authority? Were we witnessing the birth of something new?

Weighing my options, I formulated a plan. I could intervene, but would that help or hinder?

Drakonis' face twisted in fury, her jaw clenched, and her posture radiated aggression. I took a deep breath, wrestling with the urge to step into the open. If I didn't act soon, all those present would suffer.

"Caelum," I quietly wished, "please stop talking."

"You host this ceremony fully aware of the geno-cide you perpetuate," Caelum's gaze lingered on Drakonis for what felt like an eternity before turning to address the crowd.

"Each renewal ceremony is a strike against the very essence of your history. The Elder form you revere is just one of the many forms Nxyarans take over millennia. You've never seen the other forms because you're killing your Elders off before they can evolve!"

Gasps echoed through the crowd, and murmurs swelled into a cacophony of disbelief. Faces turned pale, eyes wide with realisation as the magnitude of Caelum's words sank in. Whispers of doubt and allegiance mingled in the air as some struggled with loyalty to their beliefs and others teetered on the brink of betrayal.

"Lies!" Drakonis spat, but her voice trembled slightly. "You're just a—"

"I'm not here to discuss what I am," Caelum interjected, raising his voice just enough to drown her out. "I'm here to show you the truth you've been denied. The Elders are not just figures of your past; they are an essential part of your future."

Returning his attention to Drakonis, he continued, "You kill them for what? For fear? Control? You've built a society on the bones of your ancestors, and you dedicate yourself to silencing the truth!"

The crowd shifted again, some stepping back, others inching forward, caught in the wave of uncertainty and curiosity. I could feel the indecision in the air. This was the moment we had wanted. The moment where truth could ignite a spark of rebellion against the oppressive darkness of Drakonis' reign.

Caelum's eyes burned with fierce determination, and I marvelled at his bravery. He wasn't just fighting for himself; he stood for all Nxyara. For a future where truth triumphed over tyranny.

A flutter of admiration coursed through me, dangerously intertwined with something more profound. I longed to urge the crowd to heed his words, yet I remained rooted in place, caught between desire and caution. One wrong move could shift the balance, and the thought of jeopardising everything held me back.

"You may not have seen the Elders in their future forms, but they are still out there—watching, waiting," Caelum moved within the inner circle formed by the crowd, his voice lowering slightly to draw them in. "What if they could guide you? What if you allowed them to exist alongside you instead of exterminating them?"

The murmurs grew louder, and I caught glimpses of doubt etched on the faces of those who had once believed so fervently in Drakonis' propaganda. The seeds of dissent were being sown.

Drakonis's chilling laughter rang out, sharp and devoid of warmth or compassion.

"You think words will change anything?" she gestured dismissively. "If truth is what you seek, let's see how much you value it when your life is at stake."

"The first to kill him will have their heart's desire fulfilled. Power, riches, whatever they wish!" she announced to the guards, keeping her eyes on Caelum.

Shock spread through the crowd, and the guards exchanged uncertain glances. The dark temptation pricked at their loyalty and morality. A chill crept down my spine as I glanced at Caelum, who remained defiantly still, exposed and defenceless, his composure relaxed in the face of impending danger, infuriating Drakonis further.

The tension hung like a taut string, waiting to snap. I could see the hesitation etched on the guard's faces. Suddenly, one lunged forward, succumbing to the desperation. Weapon raised, her eyes fixed on Caelum with fierce determination.

"No!" I screamed, adrenaline surging through my veins as I pushed past the crowd, diving in front of Caelum just as the guard swung her weapon. The force of her movement sent me crashing into the ground, but I didn't care. I felt the whoosh of air as the blade sliced past us, my body shielding Caelum from the impending strike.

"Zarya!" Caelum exclaimed, shock and alarm

flooding his voice.

I quickly regained my footing, standing tall between him and the guard, who halted, uncertainty flickering across her face as she processed my sudden appearance. The crowd had fallen silent, and I could feel Drakonis's seething gaze boring into me.

"Zarya Elyssan!" Drakonis cooed, her voice low and threatening. "So nice of you to join us."

"Caelum is not your enemy. He's not here to harm anyone!" I shot back, unsure if I was trying to convince Drakonis, the crowd or myself.

The guard's weapon lowered, the tension in her muscles easing just enough to signal uncertainty.

Caelum stood behind me, the warmth of his presence a comforting reminder that I wasn't alone in this fight. I could feel his strength radiating toward me. As I stole a glance back, I caught an intensity in his eyes. A silent promise that we were in this together. The unspoken connection between us sent a rush of courage through me, igniting a fierce determination to face whatever came next together.

"Choose your side carefully," I urged the guard, my gaze steady on her. "This isn't just about us. We'll all suffer the consequences."

Drakonis looked down at us in the arena below, surveying us like a queen observing her subjects, her eyes flashing.

"Enough of this!" She sounded almost bored as her snarl twisted into a wiry, deceptive smile. "Surely we can negotiate."

The guards began to lower their weapons one by one. The tension shifted from imminent violence to something more uncertain yet hopeful. Relief flooded me, but I knew we weren't out of the woods yet.

Fury burned behind Drakonis's eyes like molten steel. She was not to be trifled with, and I could sense her cunning beneath her calm exterior. But for now, we had bought ourselves a moment to breathe, rethink, and hope.

As I closed my eyes briefly and envisioned the chaos that Caelum had naïvely stirred. The Nxyarans around us were unsettled, and Drakonis was up to something. Caelum had started something monumental, but it would spiral into chaos if we couldn't negotiate our way out, and countless lives would be lost in the wake of Drakonis's wrath.

"Leave!" Drakonis's voice cut through my thoughts like ice, her composure returning as she dismissed the performers. "You are discharged!"

The Primevex and Elder dancers looked at each other as they began to disperse. I caught Nova's eye, and time stood still between us. Her expression mirrored my internal turmoil as if she could sense the impending disaster, too. I wanted to reach out to her, to tell her to be careful, to warn her of what might come next, but the words caught in my throat.

She turned away, leading the others with a trail of bewildered Elders following behind. I wondered if they were even aware of their future evolution. The Hexaryan and Octaryan that lay dormant within them.

Drakonis composed herself, looking over the crowd who hovered at the arena's edges. Caelum and I stood at the centre, caught in a tense but oddly relaxed standoff with the guards, the air thick with anticipation.

The High Council stirred, reflecting doubt as they weighed the unfolding events whilst Rune remained statuesque, its presence a steadfast reminder of the protective barrier surrounding the small group.

It struck me that Drakonis remained unnaturally still and realised that she couldn't, wouldn't risk stepping out of Rune's reach.

Good. You stay there, I thought, a wave of determination rising within me. If Drakonis remained in place, we could hold our ground. The tension between us might simmer, but we would be safe for now.

"We're not here to fight," I called out, my voice clear and firm to all who would listen. "We're here to protect Nxyara. Drakonis wants to manipulate fear and control our future, but we can choose differently."

"You're a fool!" Drakonis laughed.

Rune remained motionless, a silent guardian, and I felt a surge of hope. If we could hold our ground just a little longer, perhaps we could turn the tide of this conflict. We needed a way for them to see that Drakonis was the threat. Maybe then, they would help us.

"Your bodyguard is impressive," Caelum's voice cut through the charged air, drawing everyone's attention back to him. His tone was casual yet teasing. "It must be hard to rule over a species without trust."

My heart lurched in my chest as I elbowed him hard in the ribs, a sharp jab meant to convey urgency.

"Shut up, now!" I hissed through clenched teeth, hoping to draw him back from the edge of recklessness.

He winced slightly but held his ground, confusion flashing across his face. The crowd's murmurs quieted as they processed his words, and I could feel the tension shift again, this time directed at Drakonis.

"Is it not true?" Caelum pressed, his gaze unwavering as it met Drakonis's furious glare. "You stand there, cloaked in a protective shield, but without your pet, you would not be able to demand obedience."

Drakonis's eyes narrowed as the crowd's attention teetered between the weight of Caelum's words and the power of Drakonis's wrath.

"Enough, Caelum!" I urged, my voice low but insistent. "This isn't helping!"

"Look around you," he ignored me, gesturing with an open hand, "You rule Nxyara with fear and mistrust in an attempt to maintain control through intimidation."

The crowd murmured as if in agreement. Drakonis visibly struggled to maintain her composure as the threat of potential conflict returned.

"Do you think your empty words can sway them?" she spat, venom dripping from her voice. "They know what happens to those who defy me."

"You mentioned negotiations," I stepped in front

of Caelum, pushing him back as my eyes pleaded for him to understand the gravity of our situation. He clearly didn't.

The faces of the High Council, the guards, and even some in the crowd looked contemplative, while others held tightly to their fear, unsure where to turn. I could feel Drakonis's fury boiling over as she pinned her eyes on me. Still, the flicker of doubt crossing her features suggested that she also acknowledged the changing tides.

"A challenge," she hissed.

I glanced at Rhea. Her help wouldn't go astray at this moment but she remained in place, her expression unreadable. A wave of uncertainty washed over me. What side was she on?

I followed her line of sight to the entrance where Caelum had come in, and there, partially hidden in the shadows, were Theo, Astra, and Lyra. Their faces were etched with concern and shared guilt, offering me an apologetic shrug. It was apparent they had been powerless to stop Caelum.

Best they stayed where they were. Heaven forbid Drakonis discovered Theo, or Nyx and Nox for that matter. The last thing I wanted was to divert Drakonis's ire toward my closest allies.

I was trapped between the looming presence of

Drakonis and the oddly serene figure of Caelum, waving casually to the curious Nxyarans in the crowd, an unassuming smile gracing his face. How could he be so relaxed in such a volatile situation? Was he enjoying this?

His nonchalance frustrated me. This wasn't a game; lives were hanging in the balance. Yet he was playing celebrities, exuding a captivating confidence that drew the audience in like a moth to a flame. His presence was magnetic, making my heart race and my thoughts scatter. Part of me admired his calmness, even as another part desperately screamed for him to acknowledge the gravity of our situation.

"Infants are known for their amateur tactics," Drakonis sneered, her voice dripping with disdain as she directed her comment at Caelum. "True battles are won with experience."

A ripple of laughter echoed through the crowd as I felt my heart sink, knowing that she was trying to dismantle Caelum's confidence, to make him feel small in the face of her overwhelming power.

Before I could respond, Drakonis pivoted to face me, her expression shifting into something more sinister.

"A gladiatorial contest," she proposed. "If your thing can beat Nxyara's best warrior in combat, you may walk away."

She paused, letting her words hang like a guillotine's blade.

"But should it lose, it will die, and your execution will make a fitting replacement for the Elders' deaths that never occurred here today."

The crowd gasped, the murmur of disbelief washing over me as my stomach twisted in knots. I turned to look at Caelum, standing beside me. Was he bracing himself? I could tell by the resolve in his posture, the way he squared his shoulders and the fierce determination lighting up his eyes. He was ready to accept!

Maybe we overdid the self-confidence a little, I thought.

"Stop it!" I whispered fiercely, ensuring only he could hear. "This isn't a game. You can't even beat me on the mat; you wouldn't last seconds against a Nxyaran warrior who has triumphed in real battles!"

"And if I back down now, what will that say about our future?" he countered. "Weren't you the one who taught me we can't let fear dictate our choices?"

"Wonderful, now you pay attention!" I snapped, frustration bubbling over. "If one of us has to fight, it will be me."

"Fine," Caelum sighed, his tone reluctant. But as he looked at me, there was an intensity in his gaze that sent a flutter through my chest.

"Just be careful, Zarya." His words held an undercurrent of concern that made my heart race. The arena and its audience disappeared momentarily, leaving only the connection between us. I nodded, determination flooding my veins. It was time to negotiate.

"I will take his place," I announced, my voice firm as I stepped forward.

The crowd murmured as Drakonis raised an eyebrow, clearly amused. "This ought to be entertaining."

"But if I win," I continued, my voice steady, "not only do we both walk away, but we walk away free of you, the High Council, and the rebel branding that holds us captive."

Drakonis considered my request, a smirk creeping across her lips. "And if you lose, your thing will be executed in your stead."

"Only on the condition that Rune cannot intervene in any way," I counter-proposed. "The fight must be clean. Warrior against warrior."

"I suppose you consider yourself the other warrior," Drakonis laughed, making a rich, mocking sound, and the audience joined in. "Very well. I accept your terms."

The arena was a whirlwind of whispers and gasps as the excitement of the challenge took hold. My heart raced as the reality of my choice settled in.

"You're sure about this?" Caelum asked, concern etching across his features. He took a step closer, his hand brushing against my arm, sending a jolt of warmth through me as our eyes locked.

Caelum's gaze on me felt like a steady warmth that helped ground my swirling thoughts. With a determined flick of my wrist, I unfastened my delicate cape and let it fall to the ground, the elegance it offered now replaced by a more pressing need for readiness.

"I have to be," I replied.

I hadn't anticipated needing my steel-grey corset for battle. The silver accents shimmered like a warning in the light. For the first time, I fully appreciated the intricate patterns of armour-like scales adorning my arms, expertly crafted by the Twins. Their foresight to integrate armour features into my attire provided a reassuring layer of protection. I had come here expecting little more than a display of strategy, not a fight for survival.

As I adjusted my stance, I could sense the energy

in the arena, and with it, the thrill of battle began to stir inside me. I was no longer Zarya the Rebel; I was a warrior ready to fight for the future of Nxyara.

SIXTEEN

At first, it was subtle, like the world was breathing beneath my feet. My knees buckled for a moment as, without warning, the ground began to shift. A deep, guttural rumble echoed through the arena. The trembling intensified, sending cracks spiralling outwards from the centre.

A sharp, oppressive stillness replaced the thunderous cheers that had filled the air moments ago. The kind that makes the hair on the back of your neck stand on end. All eyes were fixed on the shifting earth, and I could feel fear rippling through the arena like static.

Swallowing hard, I forced myself to stay calm. This was no time to lose focus. Whatever was happening, I needed to be ready.

I locked my knees, bracing against the erratic movements of the ground. Every instinct screamed at me to move, to find stability, but I knew moving meant losing control; if I lost control now, the fight would be over before it began. I wasn't about to let that happen.

Another violent tremor surged beneath my boots, stronger this time. Dust and small rocks scattered across the arena floor as the cracks grew wider, splitting the ground open like surgical wounds. I tightened my core, bending slightly at the waist to keep my centre of gravity low, my heart pounding in time with the earth's quakes. Sweat trickled down the back of my neck, and I clenched my jaw, willing myself to stay upright.

I could hear the audience holding their breath. Fear gripped them like a storm about to break, their uncertainty feeding into the heavy silence. No one knew what was coming. Not them. Not me.

Another shift. This one was sharper, almost like something beneath the arena was trying to claw its way to the surface. I had to fight the urge to step back, to retreat to safer ground. There was no safer ground.

Stay focused, I scolded myself, fingers tightening around the hilt of my blade. My breath came in shallow, steady beats, and my muscles tensed.

A low hum vibrated through my boots as a hidden mechanism churned somewhere underground.

Then, the earth beneath my feet dropped for one terrifying second, and the arena floor seemed to cave inward as a massive slab of earth sank into the darkness below. My heart leapt into my throat as a platform began to rise with a grinding noise that echoed through the air as if the earth's bones were being wrenched apart.

Dirt cascaded into the cracks like falling sand, and the ground rumbled, almost as if it was reluctant to let go of whatever it had buried deep beneath the surface. The platform continued to ascend, revealing a heavily armoured figure standing motionless.

My eyes locked on the individual as more of her was revealed. I could tell by the height and build that she was one of us. A Nxyaran warrior. But something was different.

I was startled as the crowd erupted. Hundreds of thousands of voices, screaming, chanting, their fear and anxiety replaced by raw anticipation. The energy in the arena surged. The rhythmic stomping of feet and the ringing clash of weapons on metal rang out, as the crowd became frenzied. This was what they had been waiting for. Not just a fight but a spectacle.

I stayed focused on the warrior facing away from

me. The back of her armour gleamed in the dim light, and her still, controlled stance spoke of deadly precision.

A cold knot formed in my stomach. This wasn't an accident. This was all planned. Drakonis loved her theatrics. The tremors, the sinking earth, and the platform were all part of the performance. She thrived on every opportunity to show her power and control.

I could feel the heat rising in my chest, anger swelling beneath my ribs. I ground my teeth and planted my feet, the ground still shifting beneath me. My grip on the hilt of my blade tightened as I narrowed my eyes. If this was one of Drakonis' tricks, I would play along on my terms. No theatrics. No games.

"Turn around," I muttered, heart pounding against my chest.

The warrior didn't move.

The crowd's energy crackled in the air, surging with every passing second. I could feel their eyes on me, waiting, watching. They wanted blood. They wanted a show. And Drakonis was giving it to them.

My pulse quickened. I refused to back down. Not with all of Nxyara watching. Not with Drakonis pulling the strings from the shadows.

"Turn around," I said again, louder this time.

In her own time, the warrior turned slowly and deliberately, her every movement dragging the moment out. Black leather straps and buckles crisscrossed her arms and legs, securing her sleek, cobalt-blue scale armour. Her form gleamed under Nyxarya's twin suns, each metal plate perfectly overlapping like scales while the reinforced bracers and knee-high boots added to her formidable presence. A belt cinched tightly at her waist held curved daggers that shimmered ominously. My pulse pounded in my ears as I waited, poised, blade ready. Instead, she raised her arms triumphantly. The crowd went wild again, their cheers crashing against the arena walls like thunder.

A dark, featureless helmet hid her face, yet something about how she moved tugged at my memory. Her posture, the subtle weight shifts, and the way she commanded the space around her all felt... familiar.

My eyes narrowed as I studied her, trying to place the nagging sensation gnawing at the back of my mind. Whoever this was, I had faced them before. Or at least trained with someone like them. But that wasn't possible. All of those warriors had been accounted for. Every one of them is loyal to me... or dead.

I shifted my stance, blade raised in anticipation. I had no time to wonder about ghosts from the past. I needed to be ready if this was one of Drakonis' new creations or some puppet from the shadows.

The warrior tilted her head slightly as if sizing me up. My grip on my weapon tightened. This standoff couldn't last much longer.

Then the ground trembled again, but it wasn't beneath my feet this time.

The earth began to ripple from behind the warrior, and the crowd's cheers became an excited, nervous frenzy. Dust rose in thick clouds as something massive began to stir behind her.

A colossal serpent emerged from the cracks in the ground, its pale scales glistening as it slithered upward with terrifying grace. Larger than any beast I'd ever seen, its body twisted as it rose higher and higher, towering over the warrior and the arena. Massive wings unfurled from its sides, feathery and sleek, spreading wide as if preparing to strike.

The crowd's excitement turned into a frantic roar, and I felt my blood run cold.

The serpent's eyes gleamed like burning coals, locking onto me with a predatory hunger. Its wings beat once, creating a gust of wind that nearly knocked me back, and its mouth opened in a slow, deliberate hiss, revealing dagger-like fangs.

I took a step back, adjusting my stance, heart racing. The serpent coiled behind the warrior, its massive body curling around the platform like a living shadow, its wings half-raised, ready to strike. As I felt its heat, a single name tore through my mind with chilling clarity.

Solvyr.

The pieces fell into place. The familiar movements, precision, and fluid grace.

The warrior was... Nova.

I stared in disbelief, my mind reeling. Nova, the one Caelum just saved. Nova, who had stood beside me over centuries in loyalty. Now here, fighting in Drakonis' name.

"Nova!" I shouted, my voice cracking with equal parts shock and rage.

But there was no response. No flicker of recognition. No breaking of the mask. She stood tall, Solvyr coiled behind her in agitation.

Nova raised her hand, and with a single, effortless motion, Solvyr stood down. Her massive body was relaxed but watchful, her glowing eyes never leaving me. Still simmering with hunger, she obeyed her command without hesitation, folding her wings slowly as she settled.

The crowd fell into a stunned hush. Every eye was on us. The tension in the air was suffocating. And then, with deliberate calm, Nova reached up and removed her helmet, her face twisted with something dark and sinister.

Her lips curled into a cold, calculating smile dripping with cruel amusement that made my stomach lurch. This wasn't the Nova I knew. The Nxyaran standing before me, standing against me, was a shadow of the friend I trusted with my life.

She tossed the helmet aside, the sound of it clattering against the stone echoing in the stillness. Her eyes gleamed with malice.

"This," she began, her voice smooth and sharp, cutting through the silence like a blade, "is where you die, Zarya Elyssan."

The words hung in the air, heavy and final. She said them with such certainty and calm that I almost believed. Almost.

I felt the ground beneath my feet steady, the tremors gone, the arena eerily still. But inside me, the battle was already raging. My heart thundered in my chest, and my muscles tensed, ready for the inevitable. The betrayal and the shock of seeing her standing before me as an enemy all crashed down on me at once, threatening to consume me.

I couldn't afford to lose focus. Not with Solvyr lurking just behind her, the crowd watching my every move, and Drakonis observing from the balcony with the rest of the High Council, revelling in her twisted spectacle. I had to think fast.

My mind raced as I tried to make sense of how my friend from just moments ago was standing with weapon raised, intent on killing me. It didn't make sense.

"Nova..." My voice wavered slightly, but I forced myself to stay firm. "You owe me an explanation."

"You left me to die," she spat, her voice trembling with barely restrained fury. "When your plan to approach the High Council failed, I was fatally stabbed, and you just disappeared. Drakonis saved me. She gave me a second chance when no one else would. I owe her my life."

The words stung. I shook my head, trying to grasp what she was saying. "No, it was Solvyr who saved you. You told me that yourself."

At the mention of the serpent's name, Solvyr let out a low, agitated growl, her massive form shifting restlessly.

Nova's lips twisted into a bitter smile. "And who do you think brought Solvyr to me?" her voice cutting through the arena like a blade. "Drakonis. It was Drakonis who sent Solvyr to find me. Without her, I would have been another casualty of your rebellion."

I blinked, taken aback. Why did Drakonis have Solvyr? But I couldn't allow myself to get distracted by things of the past.

"Nova, you can't trust her," I stepped forward. "Drakonis uses and manipulates to get her way. She's doing the same to you. Can't you see that?"

Nova's eyes flared with anger, and her grip tightened on her weapon. She took a step closer, her voice dropping into a deadly whisper.

"You think I can't see manipulation? That I don't know when I'm being used? You were the one who kept secrets, Zarya. You lied to me."

Her hand gestured sharply toward Caelum.

"You kept him from me." Her voice cracked with fury, and suddenly, I understood why she had pushed with so many questions, knowing I had made an oath not to answer. This was all part of Draknosis' revenge.

"You kept me in the dark, lied to my face when I asked you questions, all while you played god!"

My heart sank. She already knew about our progress as I deflected all her questions about the new species. Despite agreeing to be kept out of the loop along with Rhea, she had taken it as the ultimate betrayal.

"Nova, I—"

"You had no right!" she shouted. "Creating something so dangerous, so unnatural, and passing it off as Nxyara's saviour. You are not Nxyara's saviour! Nor is your creature!"

Solvyr let out a rumbling hiss as if she could feel Nova's fury fueling her own. Her massive form rippled, her wings twitched, and her tail scraped the arena floor.

I raised my hands in a desperate attempt to calm the situation. However, my heart was racing as her accusations crashed down on me.

"Nova, please, listen to me. You know what Drakonis is capable of-"

"You didn't trust me," she cut me off, her voice laced with venom. "You didn't trust me, Zarya."

The hurt in her voice was undeniable. Pain laced into every word.

Solvyr's massive head dipped lower as if waiting for Nova's signal to strike.

The air between us was charged with anger, betrayal, and the battle to come. I could feel the ground beneath my feet tremble again as Solvyr's agitation shook the very arena.

Nova's chest heaved as she glared at me, her eyes ablaze with fury.

"This isn't about Drakonis," she said, her voice lowering to a growl. "This is about you. You, Zarya. You were supposed to be my friend. My leader. And you left me to rot."

Her blade lifted, ready to bring an end to whatever bond we had left.

I tightened my grip on my own weapon, heart pounding. This was it. There was no turning back now.

Nova's long blade glinted under the dim light. My heart pounded in my chest, but my body stayed still. I could feel every nerve screaming at me to move, to fight. I knew there was no way out of this. Not with Solvyr coiled and ready, not with Nova so close. Her eyes burned with betrayal and resolve, a lethal combination.

As she stepped in front of me, she raised her weapon, the edge of her blade pressing against my throat. The cold metal bit into my skin, and I swallowed, fighting to stay calm.

"You chose your creature over me in life," she hissed calmly in my ear, "and now you can join him in death."

The blade pressed harder, the slightest movement threatening to end everything. My muscles tensed as I prepared for my end. I thought about Caelum, the others, and how I had failed to save Nova from Drakonis' grasp. I deserved this.

Nova's hand twitched, and I saw her body tense, ready to push the blade forward and take my life. Suddenly, her eyes widened, and her entire body went rigid, the blade trembling slightly but still hovering against my skin. She looked... stunned.

I exhaled shakily, my instincts taking over as I took half a step back, trying to gain even the smallest advantage. But instead of moving away from her blade, I bumped into something solid yet strangely soft. My heart skipped a beat, confusion flooding my senses. There shouldn't have been anything behind me.

Nova's eyes flicked upward, her expression shifting from anger to something like fear.

Slowly, almost as if drawn by some unseen force, I looked up too.

Towering above us was Aetheris, her colossal form casting a massive shadow over the arena. Her fur shimmered in the low light. Her wings were outstretched, enormous and powerful. Large, intelligent eyes gleamed with a quiet fury as they locked on both of us.

Aetheris' size matched Solvyr, who let out a low, uneasy hiss from across the arena. For all of Drakonis' theatrics and manipulations, there was something ancient, about Aetheris that made even the colossal serpent pause.

Nova's blade hovered at my throat, and for the first time since this confrontation began, uncertainty flickered in her gaze.

"Aetheris..." I breathed gratefully, my voice barely a whisper.

The giant creature above us remained still, her gaze shifting from Nova to me. There was a protectiveness in her eyes, a silent understanding as if she had been watching, waiting for the moment to intervene.

For a moment, all was still.

Nova turned her gaze back to me, her expression torn. The anger was still there, simmering just beneath the surface, but now there was something else—doubt.

"This isn't over, Zarya," she whispered with conviction.

Aetheris let out a deafening roar that reverberated through the arena. The sound was primal and powerful, sending a shiver down my spine and causing Nova to step back, instinctively recoiling from the immense presence of the creature.

Solvyr, coiled tightly, remained poised, ready for the signal to attack, muscles rippling beneath her scales, an embodiment of fierce loyalty and aggression.

The crowd erupted into a frenzy, cheers and shouts filling the air as anticipation crackled like electricity. In that moment of chaos, I took a deep breath, composing myself amid the madness. Maybe, just maybe, there was hope after all.

I glanced at Caelum, who stood well-guarded behind the barrier of warriors, his eyes filled with concern. I could sense he was prepared, holding out for the right moment, and that insight kindled a spark of inner strength within me.

With a shared understanding, Nova and I turned to face Drakonis, looking up at her as she surveyed the arena with a smirk. She raised her arms, and the arena fell into an almost eerie silence, the crowd's noise fading into a tense hush.

"Welcome, warriors!" she called out, her voice smooth and authoritative, echoing across the arena.

"Today, we witness the ultimate test of strength and strategy. You will fight for glory, loyalty, and the future of Nxyara! Let there be no mercy!"

The crowd erupted into a cacophony of cheers and shouts, urging us on as she continued.

"But first, the rules: no outside interference, and the battle will only end when one fighter dies. Zayra, if you live, you and your creature will no longer be rebels, free from the High Council. But if you die, your creature does, too."

Her gaze lingered on Nova and me, a hint of amusement dancing in her eyes. With a sweeping motion, she signalled for the battle to commence.

Suddenly, the arena came to life with excitement. A wave of energy pulsed through the ground as the spectators erupted into a frenzy, their voices blending into a deafening roar. I could feel the adrenaline surging through my veins with anticipation.

Nova squared her shoulders, her gaze locking onto mine with a blood-chilling intensity. I could see her resolve hardening, the betrayal and anger merging into something fierce and unyielding. A moment hung in the air between us, thick with tension.

"Let's finish this," she said.

SEVENTEEN

Nova moved first, faster than I expected. Her blade sliced through the air, aimed directly at my chest. I barely had time to react, twisting my body just enough to dodge the lethal strike. The cold wind of her weapon passed inches from my skin, and my heart raced, adrenaline flooding my veins.

Before I could counter, Solvyr launched into the air. Her wings spread wide like sails as she soared toward Aetheris. The clash of titans had begun.

Aetheris rose to meet her with equal force, massive wings beating against the air as she lifted herself effortlessly off the ground. Her roar tore through the arena, reverberating against the walls as she prepared to defend herself from Solvyr's onslaught. The sheer size of the two creatures battling above us was awe-inspiring—and terrifying.

The sky above became a storm of scales, fur, and feathers as Aetheris and Solvyr collided mid-air.

Their massive forms twisted and struck. The impact sent tremors through the arena, dust and debris falling from the cracks in the ancient stone walls. For a brief moment, I lost my balance, staggering backward.

Nova was advancing, her eyes locked onto mine with a deadly focus. If I wasn't careful, I wouldn't just die by Nova's hand—I'd be crushed by the beasts above us. Aetheris and Solvyr's colossal battle was just as dangerous as anything Nova could throw at me. Every time their bodies slammed into each other, waves of chaos rippled across the arena. This wasn't just a fight. It was a war of giants, and everyone was caught in the middle.

Nova struck again, her blade coming down in a deadly arc, and I barely managed to evade with my own weapon. The impact sent a shockwave through my arms, and I grit my teeth, focusing on the battle. I couldn't afford to be distracted—not by the creatures above, the screams of the crowd, or the ever-growing fear gnawing at the edges of my mind.

Nova's movements were sharp and precise, each strike more aggressive than the last. She was unconcerned by the titans battling around her, her anger fueling every blow. I dodged and blocked, but she pushed me further into a corner. She'd wear me down if I didn't find a way to turn the tide soon.

As I parried another strike, I risked a glance at the sky. Aetheris and Solvyr were still locked in combat, their enormous forms circling each other, claws flashing, teeth bared. Aetheris snapped at Solvyr's neck, but the serpent twisted away just in time, her tail whipping dangerously close to the crowd. The force of it sent a gust of wind rushing past me, pulling at my balance once again.

Nova's blade came at me in a blur and rolled to the side just as the ground where I stood cracked under the weight of Aetheris' massive tail. I scrambled to my feet, my heart pounding as I realised the full gravity of my situation. I had to find a way to fight back, to end this, before the arena became a mass grave.

Nova's blade flashed toward me once again, a lethal streak of silver aimed at my chest. I twisted, the edge grazing my armour as I staggered backward. The ground trembled again, yet Nova remained unphased. She trusted Solvyr completely.

Aetheris' enormous wings cut through the air as she flew higher, only to vanish in a blink, her massive form disappearing completely. Solvyr reared back, her body coiled mid-air, searching, her forked tongue flicking as she tried to detect her opponents' presence.

Suddenly, Aetheris reappeared behind her, claws extended, slashing at Solvyr's back. The impact was brutal, and the serpent screeched in pain. Still, she quickly recovered, twisting her body to avoid another strike, tail slamming into the ground just a few feet from where Nova and I stood. The floor split beneath the force, sending debris flying in every direction. Nova didn't falter.

I ducked under a wild swing of her blade, breathing hard as I darted sideways, trying to find some space, some moment to regain my footing. But there was no reprieve. I could see the betrayal she felt in her eyes. The pain that Drakonis had twisted into hatred. She had become a weapon, and that realisation only steeled my resolve.

Aetheris gave a vicious snarl and suddenly froze mid-strike. Time. Solvyr had used her unique power to stop time for a fleeting moment. It barely lasted a minute, but it was enough for her to reposition herself before launching forward in a deadly strike as time resumed.

Aetheris resized in the blink of an eye to avoid the serpent's fangs. She was a blur of movement, disappearing and reappearing as she outmaneuvered Solvyr, her fury equalling her opponent's aggression. A spectacle of power and ferocity, each of them wielded their abilities with deadly precision.

The crowd shouted and cheered, taking sides as they watched the beasts tear into each other. Some called for Solvyr's victory, while others screamed for Aetheris to prevail. I blocked the chants out of my head, their voices mingling with the sounds of the battle.

My breath was ragged, my muscles screaming for relief. My only plan was to keep defending until I wore Nova out. I was not going to kill my best friend. However, hoping this would end due to sheer exhaustion from all parties was a fantasy.

A gust of wind from above nearly knocked me off my feet as Aetheris and Solvyr collided again. Solvyr's tail thrashed into the stadium, shattering the walls and sending clouds of rubble spiralling as the crowd cried out in terror. I ducked instinctively, glancing toward the stands where Caelum watched helplessly, his face pale with fear. He was well-guarded, surrounded by warriors who wouldn't let him intervene. But his eyes never left me, and for a moment, our eyes locked.

I couldn't fail him. I couldn't fail Nxyara.

Nova's blade came at me again, but this time, I was ready. I sidestepped, using the chaos of the arena to my advantage, and swung my own weapon toward her, aiming low. She blocked it, her eyes flashing with adrenaline. It was evident that she was holding back to match my skill level. However, that didn't mean she was being nice. The sly smile on her face made it clear that she was playing with me as a predator playing with its prey. She wanted me dead.

My muscles screamed in protest as I barely dodged another strike, Nova's movements so fast and fluid that I could hardly anticipate them. Each clash of our weapons sent shocks up my arms, and it took everything I had to keep up.

"Is this it, Zarya?" Nova taunted, her voice laced with a chilling amusement. She stepped lightly, almost dancing as she moved around me, her blade twirling effortlessly in her hand. "This is the rebel they're all whispering about? You're not even fighting back."

Her words stung, but I knew better than to respond. She wanted me rattled, distracted, and vulnerable. It wasn't hard for her to pull the strings. We used to be best friends, but now I was just her target.

I spared a glance upward as Aetheris and Solvyr's monstrous forms clashed again, the sky filled with their roars. Aetheris darted through the air, her wings beating powerfully, but I could see she was holding back. Her most dangerous ability, those needle-like quills that could impale her enemies, remained dormant. She couldn't risk releasing them with the crowd surrounding us and me within range. It was as if she was fighting with one hand tied behind her back. And Solvyr knew it.

The serpent moved with a brutal grace. For all her skill and size, Aetheris was at a disadvantage. I was running out of time.

I had to hold Nova off long enough for Aetheris to defeat Solvyr. That was my new survival plan. But as I watched Aetheris struggle, the sinking realisation hit me—she might not be able to win this. Not with her full strength locked away for fear of hurting innocents.

Nova's laughter snapped me back to the immediate danger. She lunged. I deflected the strike, but she quickly exploited the opening, leaving me off-balance. Her elbow struck my side with a sharp thud, and I stumbled, gasping for breath.

"There it is," Nova sneered. "You've got so much fight in you now. Where was that when you left me to die? How unfair, don't you think?"

Unfair.

The word echoed in my mind, bitter and raw. This was all so unfair. We were supposed to stand together, to fight for Nxyara's future, and now here we were, locked in a battle to the death. Nova had been my friend. Solvyr and Aetheris had once flown together through the skies, part of us. And now there was only anger and hate. How had everything turned so dark?

Another strike came, and I felt the sting of the blade's edge as it sliced my cheek. Blood ran down my skin, but I didn't have time to wipe it away. Nova's strikes were more playful than serious, as if she hadn't even begun to show her skills. She was toying with me, and that was what terrified me most.

If she wanted to, she could have killed me already. But she was enjoying this. She wanted to make me suffer before finishing me off.

"I don't understand…" I managed between laboured breaths, dodging another wild swing. "How did it come to this? I thought we were on the same side."

Nova laughed again, cold and sharp.

"We haven't been on the same side since you ran away and hid yourself in the dungeons. You chose your path, and I chose mine. This is how it ends."

She swung at me again, and I barely blocked it, feeling the strain in my arms as her strength pushed me back. I was running out of room to manoeuvre, the arena floor rumbling beneath me as Aetheris and Solvyr's battle raged above.

The crowd was a frenzy of noise, taking sides, cheering, roaring. They wanted blood, and it didn't matter whose.

I glanced again at Aetheris, my silent plea lingering in the air. She was all I had left now. If she could just find a way to defeat Solvyr, maybe I could survive this. But as Solvyr let out another vicious hiss, I knew Aetheris was losing ground. Nova knew it, too.

Stay sharp, Zarya! I scolded myself. I needed to stop thinking about a past I couldn't change. I could survive this moment if I kept my head straight.

I couldn't keep dodging Nova forever, and her armour showed no apparent weakness. Each plate looked like it had been meticulously crafted for protection and flexibility. Not a single gap, not a single flaw. There was no weakness. Unless...

"Nxyara's best warrior needs to be fully armoured to take on an untrained rebel?" I scoffed, my voice loud enough for the crowd to hear. "Looks like I was right all along. You've gone soft."

I saw the flash of anger in her eyes. I could sense the shift in her posture as the taunt hit her ego. She was too proud, driven by her need to be the best. Sneering, her grip tightening on her blade as she advanced toward me with more intent.

"You've always been a mouthy little brat," Nova spat, her voice cutting through the roar of the crowd. "Let's see how long that tongue lasts when I slice it off."

I braced myself as she raised her blade to strike. A deafening roar shattered the tension. Nova backed off, mirroring my surprise and confusion. The sound reverberated through my bones, leaving my ears ringing and my heart pounding. The ground quaked beneath our feet, and the arena walls trembled like they would collapse.

Thud!

Solvyr's massive head landed between us with a force that nearly knocked us both off balance. The serpent's eyes gleamed with a malevolent hunger. Her nostrils flared as she let out one final exhale, sending a blast of hot breath over us.

We stood on opposite sides of the head, our eyes darting between it and the rest of her massive body on the far side of the arena. For a moment, neither of us moved. The great serpent was dead, and I wasn't sure whether to feel relieved or utterly terrified.

It was over.

It was Nova's laugh that broke the silence. Not a sinister laugh from before. This time, it was lighter, almost mocking.

Reaching up, she unclasped her armour with deliberate ease. One by one, the plates fell away, clanging to the ground until she stood before me, stripped of her protection but radiating confidence. Smiling at me as if she held a secret.

"You thought that was it?" she teased, stepping back from Solvyr's enormous head. "Oh, Zarya. We've barely begun."

Fear froze my veins as we watched thin, glistening tendrils snake out of Solvyr's head, forever reaching towards her body, which was reaching back. As they met, they curled around each other like vines, latching on, pulling the pieces together in a grotesque regeneration display.

Solvyr could heal.

The tendrils pulsed with energy as they fused the massive beast's head back to her neck. What should have been a fatal blow was reversed as if it had never happened. The severed flesh knitted together with horrifying speed, and Solvyr's eyes flickered back to life, glowing with the same terrifying intensity as before.

Panic surged through me. How was Aetheris supposed to fight something that could return from the dead?

Nova stood there, watching me with that smile, her arms now free from the weight of her armour. She seemed lighter, quicker, and more dangerous.

"Did you really think this was going to be that easy?" she asked, her voice filled with amusement. "You know nothing of what we're truly capable of."

Drakonis' laugh echoed through the arena, reverberating off the stone walls like a death knell. It was deep and menacing, reminding me of the real enemy. I had forgotten about Drakonis's presence since Nova appeared, and I used the interruption to gather my focus.

The crowd erupted, a frantic wave of excitement sweeping through them, their cheers and jeers blending into one loud roar. They wanted to be entertained, and Drakonis gave them precisely that.

Nova's smile widened as she stepped forward, her bare arms flexing as she shifted into an attack stance. Without her armour, she looked even more dangerous. Her eyes locked onto mine, glinting with a hunger for victory. The earlier playful taunts were gone; now she was all business, ready for round two, and I had a sinking feeling this round would be my last.

The arena trembled as Solvyr's colossal body slithered back into motion, fully healed, its power undiminished. Aetheris roared in response, wings unfurling, but I could sense the strain even from across the battlefield. As much as I wanted to believe she could defeat Solvyr, I knew the odds were stacked against us.

With a growing sense of dread, I realised this was hopeless. With Solvyr's ability to heal, not just herself but Nova, too, they were invincible. Now I understood why Nova was Nxyara's greatest warrior.

I glanced at Caelum, my heart aching. He will die because of me. He wasn't even given a choice.

Nova's voice cut through my thoughts.

"What's the matter, Zarya?" she taunted, stepping closer. "Starting to see how this ends?"

I swallowed hard, my throat dry. My grip on my weapon tightened, though I wasn't sure if it was for courage or fear. I couldn't let her see me falter or let her know how close I was to breaking. But deep down, I knew. And as I looked at Aetheris, standing tall and proud, I wondered if I had made the right choice in bringing her into this.

EIGHTEEN

The battle recommenced with ferocity. Drakonis's laughter was somewhere above us, her delight in the chaos reverberating like a sickening pulse through the arena. Aetheris and Solvyr clashed overhead, a titanic struggle of wings, claws and coils. Aetheris fought bravely, her mighty wings batting against Solvyr's massive body, trying to keep the serpent at bay. But I could see the blood staining her sleek black fur, the laboured beat of her wings. She was hurt, worse than I had realised. Yet, she refused to abandon me.

Nova swung her blade, striking my shoulder. Pain flared, hot and sharp, but I gritted my teeth, refusing to cry out. I hit back, narrowly missing my mark.

"Is that all you've got?" she sneered, eyes glinting with amusement.

She was faster without her armour, stronger, and

each strike from her blade felt more deliberate. I was outmatched, and she knew it.

Solvyr's tail whipped around Aetheris's body, slamming her to the ground beside us with a force that knocked us both over. As I rose to my feet, Nova pressed her advantage, kicking out my legs from beneath me and pinning me to the bloodstained dirt. Her knee dug into my chest, knocking the wind from my lungs. I gasped, struggling, but she was too strong, her weight pressing me down as I fought to stay conscious.

Above us, Solvyr had Aetheris pinned, her fangs bared and ready to strike. Aetheris was injured, her wing dragging along the ground, yet her eyes met mine—steady, unwavering. She wasn't giving up. She never would. But I could see it in her movements. She couldn't last much longer.

"No," I whispered, trying to push Nova off, but she only laughed, her breath warm against my ear as she leaned in.

"Look at you, Zarya," she purred, her voice dripping with condescension. "Once so proud, so full of fire. Now, nothing more than a rebel about to die in the dirt."

She raised her blade, the cold steel gleaming in the arena's light, the crowd's frenzied cheers reaching a fever pitch.

"And just like your precious Aetheris," she added, her lips curving into a cruel smile, "you'll die for nothing."

Her blade came down.

Time seemed to stretch as I lay pinned beneath Nova, the cold steel of her blade hovering inches from my throat. The weight of inevitability pressed down on me as heavily as Nova's knee, a sickening sense of finality filling the air.

I felt the heat of her body above me and the mocking glint in her eyes as she savoured my helplessness. This was it. I was about to die, and there was nothing I could do to stop it.

I couldn't even bring myself to fight anymore. I simply turned my head, drawn to Aetheris in the chaos of the arena. I knew this would be the last time I saw her in all her glory, and the thought filled me with sorrow. My heart ached at the knowledge that my choices had led us to this moment.

She was locked in a deadly dance with Solvyr, both beasts soaring through the air, their colossal forms casting ominous shadows. Aetheris's sleek black fur shimmered with the blood of her injuries. Still, her bright, intelligent eyes locked on Solvyr as they circled each other.

The crowd's roar swelled around me, a cacophony of excitement and anticipation as they witnessed the titanic struggle unfold. Nova seemed to be waiting for the audience to turn their attention back to her. After all, what is a victory without a crowd to witness it?

In a breathtaking display of agility, Aetheris spun in mid-flight. Her sleek body twisted upside down, defying the laws of nature as she reoriented herself in the air. In that instant, she shrank, her form compressing until only one massive claw remained, sharp and deadly. My breathing faltered momentarily as Aetheris soared under Solvyr, that singular claw slicing through the serpent with lethal intent. Gutting her from head to tail in a single, fluid motion, a stunning display of precision and power. A rush of red from Solvyr's body rained down on the crowd as she let out a cry filled with pain and shock, revealing the betrayal she must have felt in her final moments.

Solvyr's massive form faltered, wings collapsing as both halves plummeted. The impact caused alarms from parked spacecraft to sound warnings as her organs spilled out, a grotesque explosion of blood and flesh that painted the arena in a grim tableau of death. Tendrils desperately tried to reach out to each other, but the disembowelment had rendered them disabled. The sight was horrific and awe-inspiring all at once, and for a moment, there was an absolute, eerie silence.

Aetheris, now medium-sized and composed, landed gracefully beside the carnage, her posture regal despite the chaos surrounding her. She gave a satisfied huff, her nostrils flaring as she surveyed her handiwork. Confident Solvyr was dead, she began to clean her fur with the nonchalance of a cat grooming itself after a hunt. It was as if the battle had been nothing more than a minor inconvenience, and in that moment, I felt a swell of pride and relief wash over me.

The crowd was in shock. Some vomited as they peeled pieces of Solvyr off their bodies, taking a moment to process what had just happened.

I turned my gaze to Nova, still poised above me, blade hovering millimetres from my heart. Her focus was so intense, so consumed by her desire to end me, that she didn't notice the downfall of Solvyr until the silence that enveloped the arena was shattered with the echoes of the crowd's frenzied cheers.

A sickly glow of confusion washed over Nova's face.

"No," she whispered. It was a plea, a prayer that some miracle might undo the devastation.

She began to tremble as if the essence of Solvyr's power was leaving her body, unravelling like threads of a tapestry being ripped apart. Still pinned beneath her, I watched in horror as her form began to dissolve, flesh and bone turning into a sickening amalgam of organs, blood, and chaos.

My closest friend was collapsing into a mass of mush and bone on top of me as if she had never been a warrior at all. The blade that had once threatened my life clattered to the ground, forgotten and irrelevant. Her screams were drowned out by the roaring crowd, their cheers morphing into shrieks of disbelief and horror. There was nothing I could do.

The grotesque transformation filled the air with the metallic scent of blood. Nova's face contorted in agony, her eyes wide with the shock of her own mortality. I couldn't tear my gaze away, caught in a surreal and nightmarish moment. As the remnants of Nova slumped onto me, hot and visceral, soaking into my skin, I realised that I was no longer Zarya, the Rebel. I was Zarya, Nxyara's greatest warrior.

Glimpses from our past came rushing back as I

lay there, sobbing. The laughter, the camaraderie we once shared, the plans and dreams. It was all over. I had fought for my life, and yet the reality of this victory felt hollow, tainted by the loss of someone I had once cared for.

From the corners of my vision, I could see Aetheris feasting on Solvyr's remains. She was alive, and so was I, but the cost weighed heavily on my soul.

Time felt suspended as if the world had paused to absorb the weight of what had transpired. I lay there, heart racing, smothered in remnants of Nova. The aftermath felt surreal, a haunting spectre of triumph overshadowed by loss.

Like a dam bursting, a vast celebratory cry erupted from the crowd. Cheers and roars cascaded through the air, and a wave of exhilaration swept over the stunned arena. Some chanted my name, others called for the next fight as the thrill of survival washed over them.

Turning my head, I caught a glimpse of Caelum breaking free from his guards with blazing determination. He sprinted towards me, eyes wide with relief and something deeper. Kneeling beside me, he gently lifted my head, cradling me in his arms, pulling me close as if to shield me from the horror.

"It's over," he whispered, his voice trembling with emotion, and in that moment, I felt the world around us fade away.

"We've won."

All I could focus on was the thrum of his heartbeat against my ear, steady and reassuring. I felt a sense of safety in his embrace. It felt as though nothing else mattered; we were cocooned in a moment that belonged solely to us. I leaned back slightly, searching his eyes, and I saw a mix of joy, concern, and an unspoken bond that ran deeper than words.

"Are you okay?" he asked, his voice soft, picking pieces of Nova off as he searched my body for severe injuries.

I took a breath, allowing the moment to linger, feeling our connection strengthen.

"I will be," I assured him, forcing a smile even as my heart ached for what we had lost.

His expression softened as he brushed a thumb along my cheek, a tender gesture that sent a shiver of warmth through me.

"I was so worried. When I saw you... I didn't know what would happen."

"I told you that you wouldn't last two seconds," I whispered, my heart swelling with gratitude.

The crowd's noise faded into the background,

and all I could hear was the sound of our breathing, perfectly in sync. Lost in our shared moment, I couldn't help but think about how better Nxyara would be, how better our lives would be.

Caelum stood and held out his hand. To my surprise, I rose quickly, easily and unassisted. Confused, I looked at Caelum for an explanation.

"Theo says you're welcome." Caelum smiled, clearly having reached out for assistance with his telekinesis. "But she says from here on in, you are on your own."

"Tell her I said thanks for the assist," I smiled gratefully, allowing myself to feel the joy of our victory.

Caelum's hand slipped into mine, his short, stubby fingers intertwining effortlessly with my long Nxyaran digits as if they had always belonged together. The warmth of his touch ignited a spark of hope within me.

Raising our joined hands in triumph, the crowd ignited one last time.

NINETEEN

Victory always has its price. I felt a sharp tug in my side as blood soaked through my uniform, seeping into the crevices of the fabric, yet I stood firm, refusing to crumble in front of everyone. Not now.

The cheers began to fade, and my vision blurred at the edges, but I held onto Caelum's arm, his grip firm and steady.

"Let's get you back," he whispered, concern etched across his face. His dark eyes softened, but the urgency in his voice was unmistakable.

Theo appeared at my other side, her expression unreadable, as always. She didn't say a word, simply nodding to Caelum as they conversed silently, shifting their weight to carry me.

"Zarya..." Nyx and Nox were restless shadows on Theo's broad shoulders, their voices low and quick. I couldn't understand a word, but I didn't need to.

They were worried. Every step felt heavier, my body protesting as adrenaline began to wear off.

"I'm fine," I lied, but I knew none of them believed it.

"Don't be stubborn." Theo shot me a glance, her usually stoic face betraying a flicker of frustration.

I opened my mouth to argue but bit back the words. It wasn't the time for pride. Not now. The resistance needed me whole, and deep down, I knew they were right.

With every step toward the lab, a growing ache made it harder to keep my eyes open. The blood loss was worse than I thought. My breaths grew shallow, and my grip on Caelum tightened, my knuckles white.

"Almost there," Caelum's voice cut through the fog in my mind.

The lab loomed ahead, its sterile walls promising relief. The doors slid open with a soft hiss, and Caelum and Theo guided me to one of the medical tables. The bright lights overhead made my head spin, but I kept conscious. I wasn't ready to let go. Not yet.

Theo was already prepping the medical equipment, her hands moving with practised precision. She didn't waste time on words; she never did. The

Twins flitted about the room, grabbing supplies faster than I could track. Caelum hovered nearby, his eyes never leaving mine.

"Stay with me, Zarya," Theo muttered as she cleaned the wound, the sting snapping me back into the present.

I winced but didn't make a sound. I'd been through worse. Much worse.

"You'll be alright," Caelum took a step closer, his gaze flicking between Theo and me. "This is nothing compared to what you've done out there."

I managed a weak smile, though it was more for his sake than mine, as the Twins buzzed in unison over my head, their hands working swiftly. For a moment, I thought about how strange this must seem to Caelum. He woke up to a world in chaos, tethered to a cause he barely understood, yet here he was, helping like he'd been a part of this from the beginning. When in Nxyaran years, he was an infant.

Theo worked in silence, her brow furrowed as she stitched me up. I clenched my fists, the pain searing but welcome. It reminded me I was still alive, still fighting.

"Rest," Theo said, her voice a low command.

"Rest can wait," I muttered, trying to push myself

up, but Caelum's hand on my shoulder stopped me. His strength was gentle but unyielding.

"You've done enough," he said quietly. "Let us take it from here."

I wanted to argue, but the exhaustion was pulling at me, threatening to drag me under. I closed my eyes, just for a moment, letting the lab sounds wash over me. The hum of machines, the soft voices of the Twins, and Theo's steady breathing as she finished tending to my wounds. I allowed myself to breathe for the first time in what felt like an eternity.

As I drifted on the edge of consciousness, I noticed the unmistakable blur of Aetheris, cornered on a smaller table by none other than Nyx and Nox. Despite her usually stoic demeanour, Aetheris looked exasperated as the Twins fussed around her like frantic medics.

"Nyx, hold her still!" Nox's voice was high-pitched and filled with urgency, though it was nothing more than incomprehensible chatter to me. Only Theo and Caelum could understand the Twins, and from the way Caelum smirked, I could tell he was following every word.

"She's not even injured," I muttered, but my voice was too weak to carry far. Caelum heard me, though, and his grin widened.

"They're convinced she's in critical condition," he said, chuckling softly. "Apparently, she's showing all the signs."

I stifled a laugh, my ribs protesting the movement. "All the signs of what? Boredom?"

Theo focused on my stitches, but her lips twitched in mild amusement. "To them, it's serious."

Aetheris huffed in response, trying to wiggle free, but Nyx was determined, holding her down with surprising strength for his size. Nox zipped back and forth, retrieving tiny supplies. Bandages, a glitter-filled syringe, and what looked like a miniature stethoscope. They moved so urgently that you'd think they were in the middle of an emergency surgery.

"They're playing hospital again," Astra remarked, a flicker of humour in her eyes. "I'd recommend letting them finish before Aetheris decides to rebel."

I raised an eyebrow. "She's already rebelling."

"Quiet!" Caelum said, his voice mockingly stern as he adjusted a loose strand of my hair, watching the chaos unfold nearby. "Nyx says she's on the verge of a breakthrough."

I glanced at the scene just in time to see Nox squirt a puff of glittery dust from the syringe onto Aetheris's fur. The poor creature blinked in confusion before sneezing, sending a cloud of pink glitter flying everywhere. Aetheris shot the Twins a murderous look, but they were too engrossed in their 'operation' to notice.

"What was that supposed to do?" I asked, glancing at Caelum, who looked like he was trying not to laugh.

"That," he said, translating between chuckles, "was their version of an anaesthetic. Glitter, apparently, works wonders in their medical practice."

"I'm sure it does," I shook my head, fighting to hold back my laughter.

Undeterred by Aetheris's growing frustration, Nyx and Nox proceeded with the rest of their "treatment," wrapping a tiny bandage around her paw with the seriousness of actual surgeons. They chattered in their language, rapid-fire and excited, as if Aetheris's life depended on it.

"She's stable now," Caelum translated with a grin. "But they'll need to keep her under observation for... the next hour, at least."

Aetheris looked utterly defeated and gave an indignant growl. However, it was clear she wasn't going anywhere under Nyx's watchful eye. Nox nodded approvingly, tucking a miniature blanket around her as if that would somehow aid her recovery.

"She's going to hate them for this," I whispered, trying to keep the laughter from breaking through. Every chuckle rained pain through my side, but it was worth it.

"She already does," Lyra glanced at the Twins as Theo finished her last stitch, wiping her hands clean. "But they take their work very seriously. Interrupting them would only make things worse."

Caelum crossed his arms, still clearly amused. "They think they're doing a favour. Nyx says, 'If we don't help, who will?'"

"Tell them she's in excellent hands," I said, trying to keep my tone steady.

Theo let out a rare, low chuckle. "They say they're the best doctors in the room and suggest that I should take notes."

Satisfied with their work, Nyx and Nox finally backed off and gave Aetheris a pat on the head before flitting back toward us, their medical supplies still in hand.

"She's a fighter," Caelum said with mock seriousness, glancing at the glitter-covered, exhausted Aetheris.

"A fighter," I agreed, wiping a tear from my eye as I lay back, pain momentarily forgotten.

The moment Theo finished with my wounds, I sat up, my breath still laboured but steady enough to speak. The laughter that briefly lit the mood had faded and was replaced by a cold tension.

" You were told not to get involved," my voice was low and dangerous as I glared at Caelum.

His eyes flicked up to mine, and for a brief moment, he didn't say anything. Then, slowly, he straightened, no longer the easygoing figure who had been watching Nyx and Nox with amusement just moments ago. Now, he was the one responsible for something much graver.

"You know why I did," he replied calmly, though his voice had an edge.

"Nova was my sister," I spat, my hands trembling with barely controlled rage. "And Solvyr-"

"Solvyr is gone," he interrupted, his voice hardening. "And Nova betrayed you. Betrayed all of us."

A deep, searing anger bubbled up in my chest, burning hotter than the physical pain I'd endured. My fists clenched at my sides as I glared at him.

"You don't get to make that call. You don't get to decide who lives and who dies."

He stepped toward me, trying to maintain his

composure, but I could see the frustration behind his calm façade.

"I didn't decide anything. She did, Zarya. The moment she allied herself with Drakonis, she sealed her fate."

I stood, ignoring the sharp protest of my muscles.

"You think that justifies what you did? You were told to stay out of it. We agreed. No interference. We weren't ready! I wasn't ready!"

Caelum's jaw tightened. He met my gaze, unflinching.

"You weren't ready because you didn't want to accept the truth. You saw the signs, you knew she couldn't be trusted—"

"She was my sister," I shouted, my voice cracking, "and I would have handled it. I would have decided when to act."

Theo stood to the side, silent, though I could see the tension in her posture as she observed the exchange. Even the Twins, still tidying up the medical instruments, seemed to sense the change in atmosphere and quietly focused on their work.

"You couldn't have handled it," Caelum shot back, the frustration finally spilling into his voice. "You were too close to her. You would have hesitated, and she would have destroyed everything we've worked for."

I shook my head, the rage and grief mixing into a whirlwind of emotions I could barely keep straight.

"Sacrificing Nxyarans was not part of the plan."

"The plan?" Caelum repeated bitterly. "The plan was to introduce a new species, and we've done that. We succeeded. Nxyara, all of us, are free from the High Council and Drakonis. You should be focused on that, not mourning a traitor."

"She was more than that." My voice trembled with fury. "She was a part of me. You can't just—"

He cut me off again, his voice steely. "What would you have had me do? Let her finish what Drakonis started? Execute another innocent Elder because of some misguided sense of loyalty?"

"Now we have a future to protect," he looked around at everyone in the room, as they nodded in agreement. "We've done what no one thought was possible. We've created something new, something stronger. That's what matters now."

I couldn't bear to hear him speak so coldly, as if all the loss and betrayal were another calculated step. My heart ached, torn between the knowledge that he was right and the overwhelming grief of losing Nova and Solvyr.

"Is it that simple for you?" I whispered, my voice

shaking.

"You think it was all worth it because we achieved our goal?"

"I think that sometimes the price of freedom is too high," Caelum's expression softened slightly. "But we can't change the past. What we can do is move forward. Together, we have all started something that will change Nxyara forever. We've given them hope, and we've given them a future."

For a moment, the lab was silent, the air heavy with the weight of everything that had happened. I stared at him, my heart torn between the desire to scream at him and the knowledge that he was right in some twisted way.

Nova was gone. Solvyr was gone. And nothing I said would change that.

"Get out," I whispered, barely holding back the tears that threatened to spill.

Caelum hesitated, his face unreadable. But then, with a single nod, he turned to leave me shattered in the cold, sterile light of the lab. I could feel the rage burning in my chest, the words boiling up, desperate to escape. I didn't want this. I never wanted this, not like this.

I took a shaky breath, trying to calm the storm inside me, but it was useless. The image of Nova's disintegrating face and Solvyr's final moments flashed before my eyes, overwhelming the triumph I should have felt at our so-called victory. The High Council was gone, Drakonis was finished, and Nxyara was free, but at what cost?

"That's it then?" I shouted at him. "That's how you wanted to introduce a new species? First, you couldn't keep your smart mouth shut, and then you started a fight, resulting in death? The death of Nxyara's best warrior? Tell me, exactly what message were you trying to send, Caelum?"

He stopped mid-stride, his hand on the doorframe. Turning slowly, his brows furrowing in confusion, clearly not understanding the words I was throwing at him.

"You stand here, all righteous, like you've saved the world. But what have you really done?" The anger pouring out now, unstoppable. "You've shown people a new species. One that is disrespectful and needs a Nxyaran to fight its battles. That you're nothing more than a—" The word caught in my throat, sharp and bitter, but it pushed its way out. "—korkak."

Caelum blinked, clearly not understanding, his brow creasing further in confusion. His lips parted as if to speak, but the words didn't come. He looked toward Theo, and I saw the silent question between them. He didn't understand. Of course, he didn't.

She called you a coward. Theo, ever the silent observer, translated and Caelum's eyes flicked between Theo and me, widening slightly in realisation. His posture stiffened, and I could see the change wash over him. A sudden shift from confusion to something darker. He looked at me, his eyes narrowing.

"A coward?" he echoed, his voice quiet but charged with something that made my skin prickle. "Is that what you think of me?"

"Yes," My blood pounded in my ears, but I forced myself to hold my ground. "You didn't listen to me when I told you to stop. Then you stood by and watched everything we built fall apart because you were inept for the challenge you accepted. You took the easy way out."

Caelum's voice simmered with barely contained anger. "You think this was easy for me?"

"You betrayed everything we stood for," I shot back, my voice rising. "You didn't trust me. You didn't trust any of us."

"And what would you have done, Zarya?" he snapped, his calm façade finally cracking. "Let Drakonis win? You weren't about to make the hard choices."

"I don't want to make choices like that!" I yelled, my throat burning.

Caelum's jaw clenched. "We built a world free from Drakonis. That's what matters."

"Korkak," I hissed, the fire in my eyes matching his.

The word hung in the air between us, sharp and accusing. Caelum's face darkened, his eyes hardening like stone. For a moment, neither of us spoke, the silence thick with everything left unsaid.

"Throwing that word around isn't going to change what happened." Theo finally stepped in.

I shot a glance at her, my breathing still ragged.

"Just saying," Theo shrugged, keeping her eyes on my wounds, her hands moving deftly as she finished applying the last bandages.

Astra and Lyra flitted between their stations, barely glancing at us as if pretending not to notice the storm brewing beside them.

Caelum's chest rose and fell steadily, a flicker of frustration behind his eyes. He wasn't going to apologise. I knew that. He thought he was justified. Maybe in his mind, he was. But it didn't matter. What he had done changed everything.

As Theo tied off the last bandage, she finally spoke as if discussing something as mundane as a broken tool. "You need to rest, Zarya. Your body can't handle any more stress right now."

I shot her a glare, but she didn't flinch. Smart.

"Did anyone see what happened to Drakonis?" Lyra spoke up, always the voice of logic.

The question cut through the charged air like a knife. Everyone's eyes shifted. Even Caelum, who had been ready to continue our argument, paused. The gravity of the question sank in.

Drakonis.

In the chaos, with everything that had happened, I had almost forgotten her. A shiver ran down my spine as I thought back to the battle. I hadn't seen Drakonis in the aftermath. Our greatest threat, the mastermind behind so much suffering, somehow, her fate had slipped through the cracks.

"If Drakonis is still alive..." Lyra began, her voice trailing off as the implications hung.

The room grew colder as the realisation settled over us. We had fought so hard and lost so much, yet the greatest threat might still lurk, waiting for her chance to strike again.

Theo crossed her arms, deep in thought. "If Drakonis still lives, then this fight isn't over."

The thought that Drakonis was still out there made us all feel fragile. Like one wrong move could send everything crashing down again.

"Did anyone see her?" Lyra pressed, glancing around the room as if someone might hold the key to this mystery.

No one answered. No one knew.

"She was the first to get on the royal vortex pod." Rhea's voice immediately grabbed everyone's attention as she entered, her face flushed but determined. She moved with a calm purpose that sent a ripple of relief through the room, her gaze steady on me as she explained.

"While we were dealing with the High Council and their guards, Drakonis slipped away. She left the High Council and the VIPs to fend for themselves. She just took a royal vortex pod and escaped."

I felt fear solidify, hard and cold in my chest.

Rhea must have seen the terror creeping into my expression because she stepped closer, her presence suddenly grounding. Her hand rested on my shoulder.

"Zarya," she said softly, her voice calm and reassuring. "She's on the run. She's not staying to fight. She's running."

I blinked, trying to let her words sink in. Rhea's grip on my shoulder tightened, a gentle but firm reminder that I wasn't alone.

"Drakonis is scared. If she weren't, she would've stayed. She's fleeing, Zarya. You need to remember that."

Her words were meant to calm me, and they did, to some extent. But Drakonis didn't run because she was scared. She ran because she was calculating, always thinking five steps ahead. She left the others behind because they were expendable to her, not because she feared us. She was regrouping, escaping to plan her next move, which terrified me more than anything.

I nodded, though the knot of fear still twisted inside me. "But we can't let our guard down," I muttered, almost to myself. "If she's running, that means she's preparing. She'll come back."

Caelum, who had been silent since Rhea entered, finally spoke up. "Then we make sure she doesn't get the chance. We find her first."

His words, though spoken with confidence, only made the situation heavier. We had won the battle, but now we face a war. Drakonis was still out there, a shadow in the dark, waiting to strike when we least expected it.

"We'll find her," Rhea said firmly, and in her eyes, I saw a promise.

I just hoped it wasn't too late.

We had no idea where Drakonis would go or what her next move would be. Yet as we sat around the table, enjoying our meal, the room brightened as we recounted the absurdly daring moments of the Renewal Ceremony and ensuing battle. Even I found myself smiling, albeit faintly. It was hard not to, with the way the Nyx and Nox threw themselves into their retelling of the battle, hands gesturing wildly.

I was in better spirits, but Nova's betrayal, her death, and the devastation she left behind still clung to me. I could still see her face melting. Those last moments were etched in my memory like a scar.

Unexpectedly, a flash of that terrible moment gripped me. Nova, disintegrating before my eyes. Her body collapsing, the heat of her life force burning through the air. The look of confusion and terror in her eyes as she realised what was happening. The screams. The awful, gut-wrenching screams that had echoed in my ears even after her voice had been silenced. I blinked hard, trying to push it away and stay present in this moment. But the feeling of helplessness, the ache of losing her in such a brutal, unforgiving way, remained.

"Zarya?" Rhea's voice broke through the fog in my mind, bringing me back to the room. I hadn't even realised I'd drifted.

I shook my head, forcing a deep breath as I turned to her. The tension that had built up inside me, the anger, the grief, still gnawed at my core. I couldn't hold it in any longer.

"A little help from you wouldn't have gone astray, Rhea," I said, my tone sharper than intended.

Rhea, sitting across from me, met my gaze without flinching. She wasn't surprised by my outburst; she was steady and calm, as always.

"I know," her eyes soft. "Losing Nova like that... it wasn't supposed to happen. None of this was supposed to happen.

Rhea's voice was calm as she explained, "No one could leave the balcony. Rune had secured all the entrances with a force field, ensuring we were all protected."

I blinked, processing her words slowly. My gaze shifted to the others in the room. Theo seemed deep in thought, her fingers tapping lightly against her arm. At the same time, Astra and Lyra quietly observed the conversation with interest. It was Caelum who broke the silence.

"That makes sense," he said casually, sitting on the windowsill now, one leg draped over the side, the other tucked beneath him. His posture was so relaxed as if he were discussing something as mundane as the weather. "That's a clever move, keeping them trapped in one place. Rune might not speak, but it knows how to take charge when needed."

His casual demeanour grated on my nerves slightly. Still, I couldn't help but feel a tiny flicker of appreciation for Rune's foresight. That level of precision and planning was pretty impressive for a snail.

Rhea gave a sharp nod.

"It's proven repeatedly that it knows how to handle a situation. So many underestimate it, but it knows exactly what it is doing. Sometimes, I would argue that Drakonis is Rune's pet, not vice versa."

"Zarya, don't blame yourself for what happened with Nova. We all made the choices we could with the information we had. Drakonis played us all in the end."

I looked at her, nodding slowly but not feeling entirely convinced.

"We'll get Drakonis," Caelum met my eyes, his expression soft and confident. "The war isn't over. We have the tools, and we have the knowledge. We just need time to regroup."

I turned away from them all, frustration bubbling up inside me, threatening to spill over. I wasn't sure if I was angry with myself, with Drakonis, or with the whole damn situation.

"The battle..." I said, my voice strained. "It only distracted everyone. We got caught up in the spectacle and fight and forgot about the bigger picture. Caelum, the concept of a new species that opens our minds to new possibilities, is why we started this whole thing in the first place. It got lost in the thrill of the battle. And now, it's all for nothing. We've failed."

The words tasted bitter on my tongue, but I couldn't stop them from escaping. There it was. Everything I'd been feeling. The whole plan had been to evolve Nxyara and find a way to preserve our future without resorting to genocide. Instead, we'd replaced genocide with battle, a distraction. There was nothing to show for it but death and unanswered questions.

I felt the weight of every life that had been lost, every sacrifice made, and the crushing sense of failure that followed. What was the point?

Caelum, to my surprise, didn't argue. He only looked at me for a moment, then turned toward the window, his brow furrowed in thought.

"You may want to come and see this," he said, his tone oddly serious.

I wasn't sure what he was getting at, but the urgency in his voice made my legs move before my mind had fully caught up. The others followed suit, all of us crowding near the window.

And there it was.

An endless sea of Nxyarans gathered around our lab, their forms filling the horizon. They were waiting and watching. There were hundreds, thousands, maybe more. Standing there in the spacious areas surrounding the lab, the sight of them almost seemed unreal.

I was speechless. This wasn't a small group of rebels or supporters who had gotten wind of our plans. This was something far bigger. Something we hadn't anticipated.

Caelum's voice broke the silence, the slightest trace of amusement in his words. "Guess our lab isn't so secret now."

It wasn't just that they had found us. It was that they were here. All of them were waiting for something. Waiting for us. Their collective gaze was heavy with expectation. This wasn't just a gathering of curious onlookers; this was the beginning of something more profound. A movement. A change.

I swallowed, my throat dry, and turned away from the window. "They want something," I murmured to myself.

"Direction," Theo replied.

It was true. They were here because of what we'd started. The new species, the future, the chance to rewrite everything. They weren't here to tear it all down. They were here because they believed, just as we did, that this was the next step for Nxyara.

I closed my eyes, steadied myself, and returned to the window. There was no going back now. We couldn't undo the spark we'd ignited. The best we could do was keep moving forward.

"Get ready," I said, my voice firm, though my heart still raced.

"Whatever happens next, we face it together. And we do it right."

They nodded in unison, their faces set with resolve. Even Nyx, Nox and Aetheris seemed to understand the gravity of the situation. We weren't fighting for survival anymore. We were fighting for a future.

A future that was still unseen, a future no one could predict, but one that would be shaped by those brave enough to embrace possibility. This was

about the future generations of Nxyara and the freedom to become everything we were meant to be.
Change was coming and we had to be ready.

The fight for Nyxara's destiny is only just beginning.

As the dust settles and the future of Nyxara hangs in the balance, Zarya and her allies must confront the consequences of their choices. New threats loom on the horizon, and old enemies are not as defeated as they appear.

With the emergence of a new species, alliances will be tested, and sacrifices will be made. The battle for a future worth living is far from over—and what comes next may change everything.

To be continued...

www.ingramcontent.com/pod-product-compliance
Lightning Source LLC
Chambersburg PA
CBHW030509120726
47904CB00005B/1398